JENYA KEEFE

THE UNCANNY AVIATOR

RIPTIDE
PUBLISHING

Riptide Publishing
PO Box 1537
Burnsville, NC 28714
www.riptidepublishing.com

The Uncanny Aviator

Cover art: L.C. Chase, lcchase.com
Editor: Veronica Vega
Layout: L.C. Chase, lcchase.com

ISBN: 978-1-62649-998-0

First edition
June, 2024

Also available in ebook:
ISBN: 978-1-62649-997-3

JENYA KEEFE

THE UNCANNY AVIATOR

RIPTIDE
PUBLISHING

For M again.

TABLE OF CONTENTS

PROLOGUE

Cay knew it was a dream but could not escape from it. Lehoia Pass: It was thirst and heat and fear. The sound of tattered flags clapping in the constant wind; the black shadows and burning sun; the orange rocks streaked with red; the smell of blood. He felt again the terror and grief and rage, sickening in their intensity. Worst of all, the awful sense of responsibility, and the loneliness of knowing no one would help him with what he had to do.

The dream—the memory—progressed as it always did until a soft, deep voice murmured his name, and he woke in darkness, with Adrio stroking his hair from his sweating face. He turned his head and tucked his cheek against Adrio's neck, breathing deep with relief.

It's over. That's all over now.

In his dreams, Muntegri was always winter-gray, snow-heavy clouds rolling across the sky. And Lehoia Pass was a brilliant, pitiless summer. And now, awake, he remembered that Lucenequa was his home. Lucenequa, where the air was soft and sweet against the skin. A land of frequent warm rains, good soil for gardens, and gentle misty skies, pale blue like cloth faded into softness from washing.

He had endured—survived—many sudden changes in his life. His home city of Turla in Muntegri had erupted in violent revolution. He'd fled the city, hidden in a southbound wagon. His parents died in blood; his sister, skinny as a weed and so sick with fear and grief she could or would not speak, had been his responsibility. He had endured sorrow and fear and a scathing rage, and survived. And then he found a home in Lucenequa, in the golden city of Valette, in the arms of a husband who loved him.

"What do you dream about?" whispered Adrio.

"Hm?" Denial came automatically to his lips. "I don't think I was."

"You were making noises."

"Really? I don't remember."

A kiss on his shoulder. "Was it the riots in Turla?"

"Perhaps." Cay snuggled deeper into the bed. "I really don't remember. Let's go back to sleep."

"Cay." Adrio's voice was grave. "Please. You know there's nothing I wouldn't do to ease you, if only you would tell me."

"Don't be so anxious, love." Cay found Adrio's hands and squeezed them in the darkness. "I think it is you who are distressed tonight. Perhaps you're having nightmares, not me." He brought one of Adrio's hands to his lips and brushed kisses onto his fingertips. "Why don't you tell me what I can do to ease you?"

CHAPTER ONE

Six months later

Adrio looked splendid.

He appeared in Cay's vanity mirror, where Cay sat fussing with his curly black hair. "Are you ready?" he demanded. Though Adrio was beautiful in a midnight blue suit, his eyes were cold and his face bore the signs of impatience.

"Nearly."

"Well, don't delay."

"No, my lord." Cay rose, checked the mirror to make sure he had not creased his trousers. His outfit matched Adrio's in color, but his was embellished with embroidered peonies and silver laces. Adrio's was tailored in the style of riding clothes, its simplicity emphasizing his height and rangy frame. He held out his arms. "Am I suitable for the Harvest Ball?" he asked with a nervous twirl. "I'd like to be a credit to you."

"Of course, you always will be," replied Adrio. His words were reassuring, but his expression was bored. "But we must not be late."

"No, I'm ready. Oh, except earrings." Cay hurried to his jewelry box and searched for his sapphire drops. He found one and heard Adrio sigh as he poked around for the other. "Sorry! One quick moment, I know it's just here—"

"Wear these," said Adrio.

He was holding out a small velvet jewelry box.

A gift?

Adrio had not given Cay a gift in a while. Indeed, this was the longest conversation they'd had in a week.

Hesitantly, Cay reached for the box and opened it. A pair of new earrings lay on a bed of silk: five-petaled blossoms carved from the lustrous pink nacre of a Lucenequan clam. They would not match his suit the way the sapphires would have; instead, they would stand out, bright against his hair. Cay's tradesman's mind instantly assessed their value: not cheap.

"They're lovely. Thank you." He took an earring from the box and then paused, wondering if a cutting remark would accompany the gift.

But Adrio only said, "You may wear the sapphires if you prefer them."

Cay's face warmed. "I love the sapphires, as you know." They had been Adrio's betrothal-gift to him, and they still held echoes of his former joy. "But these are too beautiful not to wear." He slipped the wires through his lobes and combed his hair back from his face with his fingers. Meeting Adrio's eyes, he smiled. "How do they look?"

Adrio sighed with impatience. But he said, "Handsome."

Delight bloomed in Cay's heart.

Adrio turned away. "And now we must go. The prince will notice if we are late."

Though they did not speak as they walked down the stairs, donned their cloaks and gloves, and got into the carriage, Cay was probably beaming like a lovestruck idiot. Their marriage was not happy. Cay gave Adrio all his sweetness, his best manners, and his gentlest voice, but he could not pretend it was happy. But now his husband had given him a lovely gift and a compliment. They were on their way to the most glittering ball of the year in this most glittering city of Valette. As a child he dreamed of such events, and now he was here, on the arm of a husband who had given him a gift.

"They are roseapple blossoms," Adrio said, gazing out the window as the carriage approached the Sunlit Palace. "In case anyone asks."

"And what do roseapple blossoms represent?"

"Marriage," said Adrio. Perhaps he saw something out on the street he disliked, for his eyebrows drew together in a frown. "You're as beautiful as a roseapple tree on a hill."

"Thank you," breathed Cay.

Cay was still smiling when the prince's majordomo announced their arrival in the ballroom of the Sunlit Palace: "Adrio, Heir of the Bai of Lodola, and Lord Cay of Lodola!"

They entered the ballroom arm-in-arm, and the wealthiest, most powerful people in Lucenequa bowed and clapped. Cay, a foreign-born commoner who had come to Lucenequa as a penniless refugee from war-torn Muntegri, stood tall and smiled, knowing no one but Adrio could perceive how tightly he clung to his husband's arm. Soft music played, and hanging gold-glass lamps cast warm and shifting shadows, making everyone look beautiful and joyous. Adrio seemed joyous too; his eyes crinkled with pleasure, and his dimples showed as he led Cay toward the dais where the prince was greeting his guests. He slanted a glance toward Cay. "Pretty, isn't it?"

He had entirely transformed from the cool and silent Adrio Cay lived with into a cheerful and friendly one. But they were in public now, and Adrio, Cay had discovered, was an exceptional actor. An audience always improved their relationship immensely.

As they made their bows to the prince, Cay allowed himself to believe, just a little, that Adrio was not acting tonight. Perhaps tonight he really was as happy and as proud to be seen with Cay as he seemed.

"What next?" Adrio asked after they completed their courtesy to their host. "A drink or a dance? Or shall we go find something to eat?"

Breathlessly, Cay said, "A drink and then a dance?"

"Excellent choice, Husband." Adrio caught the eye of a passing servant and signaled for two glasses.

Cay was a little surprised to see the servant's purple-plum hair. She was Chende; she had the characteristic dark eyes and small frame too. He might have asked Adrio about it—Was the palace hiring Chende staff now?—but then Adrio tossed back his drink and invited him onto the dance floor with a smile, and he forgot.

They danced several dances together: the dignified, old-fashioned Lucenequan dances Adrio had had to teach Cay before their wedding. Then, by mutual agreement, they bowed to one another and turned to seek other entertainments. In fine spirits, Cay set about making himself charming, giving his deepest and most respectful bows to the most conservative and crustiest old nobles.

Cay did not belong here. Lucenequan society, these very people, had been scandalized when he'd snagged the Heir of Lodola, one of the oldest, richest, and most respectable holdings in the kingdom. Though most of them were at least polite, and some were genuinely warm, Cay could not forget that these people had once gossiped cruelly about him. Perhaps they were willing to forget that they had once believed he had tricked, seduced, or somehow trapped Adrio into marriage. Cay was not likely to forget it anytime soon.

But tonight, still intoxicated by Adrio's warmth and gift, it didn't bother Cay. He chatted with those with open minds and tried not to dimple mischievously at those who would never open theirs. He was here now, whether they liked it or not. And his happiness must have shown on his face as he moved from group to group, for several members of the cream of Valette society smiled with him.

"Lady Faldi," he said to a middle-aged bai. "How exquisite your necklace is. Those are garnets among the diamonds, are they not?"

She nodded, not encouragingly, but he continued to admire. "Lovely. And as I am from Muntegri, I assure you, I know good garnets. But—" He ventured to tease: "I hope you are not engaged in smuggling, my lady."

Her nose went up. "These have been in my family since long before the embargo, Lord Cay."

"That necklace? But that necklace is at the very forefront of fashion."

Lady Faldi thawed a bit. Cay was stylish, and his approval of a necklace or a gown was coin worth having. "Do really you think so?" she said, touching the necklace. "I did have the stones reset."

"It is gorgeous. I think everyone who sees you will plan to reset their own old rocks to match it." They were joined by another noblewoman, and Cay turned to her. "And how does your daughter, Lady Russi? I haven't seen her tonight."

"She is home, awaiting harvest," replied Lady Russi.

"A winter crop?" asked Lady Faldi.

"With the gods' blessing, yes."

They continued to speak of Lady Russi's daughter's harvest while Cay stood by with an expression of alert interest.

If these women were Muntegrise, Cay would ask after Lady Russi's daughter's health and comfort and wish her an easy pregnancy. But they were Lucenequan, and interrupting Starlight Conversation with plain speech was seen as a bit crude—the kind of thing a proper Lucenequan did not do. If he'd had a Lucenequan education, he would know how to invoke some poem or play to wittily hope Lady Russi's daughter's fields weren't full of weeds or vermin, or some other such image. But he was not fluent in Starlight Conversation, and the possibility of accidentally using a vulgar or insulting metaphor kept his mouth shut until he escaped.

Cay flitted from group to group, smiling, dancing, watching, and listening to the chatter. A few Chende were among the servants who circulated unobtrusively through the crowd, bearing trays of food and drink. Adrio had once mentioned something about the new queen wanting to change Lucenequan policy toward the Chende, but he'd steered the conversation away from the topic. Cay reminded himself again to ask his husband about it when they got home and devoted himself to the party.

"Did you see Lord Ultato's lace collar?" one young lady whispered to another.

"He is quite a peacock in winter. Taste this dessert, my love, it is like cottonwood fluff."

"Oh, it is! How delightful."

The music changed to something light and tripping, and a young man interrupted Cay's eavesdropping. "Dance with me, Lord Cay?"

"I do not think I know this one."

"Ah, this is the cottonwood song! Come, I'll show you!"

The cottonwood song involved a good deal of jumping and whirling. Cottonwood did seem to be all the rage: he heard someone's hairstyle described as "in cottonwood mode," and a man wondered audibly whether the cottonwood fluff dessert was specially ordered by the prince.

Several dignified older men had their heads together, complaining about jackals. "They've always been in the city, but this season the jackals are overrunning the countryside too."

"Are they breeding? Or are they coming down from the mountains?"

"Oh, these are new ones, I think. Escaped from Muntegri somehow, poor devils."

The first gentleman snorted with contempt. "'Poor devils,' you say? Careful those purple-headed jackals don't rob you blind while you're feeling sorry for them."

"Ah, they do no harm, so long as they keep away from polite folk."

Along with all the cottonwood and jackal chatter, he heard plenty of references to weeds in a well-tended garden and mushrooms clinging to the side of a mighty oak. He smiled and pretended not to understand who *those* comments were aimed at.

It was a useful reminder: these people were not his friends. Despite his beautiful suit and the jewels from his beloved husband in his ears, he did not belong. If they were nice to him, it was because they wanted access to Adrio—his money, his taste, his influence. They were getting used to him, but they did not know him. And wouldn't have let him in the front door if they did.

It was getting late when he was approached by one person here whom he did consider a true friend. Lord Ondrei Rege, Bai of Noresposto, came sailing through the crowd, dispersing his hangers-on with a cheerful "Later! Now I must speak to Lord

Cay!" Ondrei was resplendent in butter-colored satin and a collar of yellow diamonds around his throat, and he reached for Cay's hands and clasped them. "Having a good time, darling?"

"I am."

"You are a cypress among willows."

"Thank you. You look very handsome as well."

Ondrei laughed. "Still no patience with our Starlight Conversation, I see! It would be proper for you to say, 'And you are a lark among blackbirds.'"

"I fear to give offense, my lord. For all I know, a lark is a symbol of lies and deceit."

"No, the lark is an excellent bird. You might avoid calling people whip-poor-wills."

"I will remember."

"Now let me see your doublet."

Cay spun.

"Ah, the laces up the back. Did you design it?"

"I did. Do you like it?"

"Very fine. The cinched waist wouldn't do for me, though!" Ondrei laughed, patting his belly fondly.

Adrio had two inseparable friends: Fonsca Calareto and Bai Ondrei of Noresposto. Ondrei, who might be the richest person in Lucenequa besides his cousin, the queen herself, was a large, good-natured young man with silky fair hair and a silly, ingratiating personality. He loved food and fashion, horses and clothes. He had a thousand friends and no interest in lovers, and seemed to possess a deep aversion to any serious topic of conversation. He might not be the most brilliant of men, but he was unfailingly kind, and he had warmly accepted Cay. It was Ondrei who had stood beside them at their wedding, and for their honeymoon he had loaned them one of his many country homes, Wind House, in the Elurez foothills.

"Will you dance, Lord Cay?"

"I think I would prefer to sit and talk for a little while, if it suits you?"

"It suits me to the ground." Ondrei led them to a little private grouping of chairs, well away from the orchestra, where they might chat. "Let me guess: you want me to translate some Starlight Conversation for you."

"If you please, my lord. People have been talking about cottonwood fluff all night, and I haven't the least notion of what that is or what it means."

"Big trees. They grow in the river bottoms and make this cottony puffy stuff. Every spring it fills the air and blows on the wind."

"Oh. A symbol of lightness?"

"Something very pretty flying on the breeze."

"But why should the prince have ordered a cottonwood-themed dessert?"

Ondrei snorted. "The prince leaves such details to the kitchen staff, I assure you. Drink a glass with me?"

"With pleasure."

Ondrei signaled a waiter, and when they each had wine in hand, Cay asked, "And have the Chende done something particularly upsetting? Everyone is talking about jackals."

"Ah, the Chende! You know the queen has reversed her father's policy on the Chende; she says all are welcome in an enlightened society. But conservatives don't like any change, you know."

No one knew much about the Chende: wild and lawless clans who made the passes through the Elurez Mountains impassible, as much a barrier to travel between Lucenequa and Muntegri as the mountains themselves. There were a few Chende in both kingdoms, as well—peddlers, tinkers, itinerant laborers, identifiable by the purple streaks in their hair. They were tolerated with contempt in Lucenequa; loathed and persecuted in Muntegri.

"Is that all? People seemed to be complaining that there are more of them."

Ondrei tipped his head thoughtfully. "I've heard some say Chende newcomers have been appearing in the countryside, gaunt and full of lice, trying to find work. They say they've escaped the Muntegrise prison camps and come here as refugees."

"Surely not. Even if they could escape the prisons, how would they have gotten here? The Grup roadblock certainly lets no Chende through."

"No, of course not. Some think their brother Chende in the mountains must have let them through."

"I don't think so," said Cay, seriously. "I've heard the mountain clans hate the city Chende and kill them on sight. Like wolves killing dogs."

"Yes, you are not fond of the Chende, are you?" Ondrei smiled at him. "Well, don't let it trouble you. However it is they come here, they do no harm."

Cay bit his cheek, hoping to change the tone of the conversation. He teased, "The only way they could get over the mountains would be to fly. I know! That must be why cottonwood is such a rage right now. The Chende float over the mountains, light as cottonwood fluff on the breeze."

"Cottonwood fluff!" Ondrei laughed heartily. "Chende flapping their arms and flying right over the heads of the poor Muntegrise manning the roadblock! What a joke!"

They laughed together.

"One more thing," asked Cay. "If you have time."

"All the time in the world for you."

"Thank you. Can you tell me why roseapples mean marriage?"

"Oh, roseapple trees. That's an old one. Where to begin?" He scratched his head, where his fair hair was just beginning to thin at the temples. "It was the great Cinna in *The Romance of the Leaves*. He compared a spouse to a roseapple tree in a garden, where, sheltered from the winds by the garden walls, it will continue to grow and bear fruit for decades. And then Trantor—or was it Telleri? No, Trantor, I'm sure of it—also wrote about a roseapple tree growing old against a garden wall, which was of course, a reference to Cinna, and by which he meant a good marriage, growing more beautiful over time."

"How lovely," said Cay, flushing a little.

"Yes, rather," agreed Ondrei. "And then Trantor—or was it Telleri? No, Trantor—went on to scold those who would plant a roseapple tree on a hill, where its beauty would be seen by everyone. 'Keep it close in the garden, where few will see it, and the scent of its flowers will grow sweeter with the years. But do not plant it on a hill, for the winds will twist and blight it, and its limbs become those of a hangman's tree.' Good, eh?"

"You're as beautiful as a roseapple tree on a hill."

"Very nice," Cay agreed, through lips gone stiff. He looked out over the crowd of Lucenequans, dancing and laughing. He did not see his husband.

"Those old poets knew their stuff. I say, are you well?"

"I—"

"Did someone say it to you, about the tree on the hill?" demanded Ondrei, with unexpected quickness. "Only tell me who, Lord Cay, and I'll see to it they keep their tongue in their mouth from now on."

"No, no, it was nothing like that," protested Cay, feebly.

But from one moment to the next, the fun had drained out of the party. Now it seemed too loud, too crowded and hot, too false and dishonest and secretly cruel.

"Lord Ondrei, you know, it's gotten quite late. I might head home."

Ondrei nodded. "I'll fetch Adrio for you, shall I?"

"No, don't bother him. It's only two miles home, I can—"

"Absolutely not," said Ondrei firmly. "He'll want to take you home. And it would reflect on his honor if you left without him, wouldn't it? No, no. You sit and finish your wine, and I'll go get your husband to escort you. Won't be a tick."

Damn Adrio, and damn his honor with him, thought Cay, watching Ondrei walk away through the glittering crowd. But he bit his lip and sat, seething, staring unseeingly at the dancing couples, waiting for his husband.

Its limbs those of a hangman's tree.

"Cay Olau? May I join you?"

A man slipped into the seat just vacated by Ondrei. He appeared to be fifteen years or so older than Cay and burly, with the short-cropped hair of a soldier and the fair skin of a Muntegrise. His accent revealed that he was from Turla, the capital city of Muntegri; it sounded exactly like Cay's own. On his lapel he wore a red and yellow hexagonal badge.

Inwardly, Cay recoiled. He hadn't encountered a Grup member in years, and the sight was unexpected and bitterly unwelcome. It was a matter of reflex, almost, to not let his loathing show but instead to curve his lips at the man, to tilt his chin and blink up at him from beneath his lashes. "Oh, but you are mistaken, sir. Since my marriage, I am Lord Cay Santauro or Lord Cay of Lodola. It's no longer appropriate to call me Olau."

"Ah," said the Grup man. "Forgive me, my lord. I meant no offense. But I wanted you to know that I recognize your family name." He met Cay's eyes with the straightforward frankness prized by the Muntegrise. "There was once an Olau Pottery on the Fifth Circle, I believe?"

If he intended to shame Cay with his tradesman's birth, it would not work; Cay was adept at parrying such thrusts. He smiled. "That's right! And you are from the Fourth Circle, unless I am much mistaken."

Turla was a city with its back to a looming cliff and its face to a deep river chasm, encircled by centuries-old walls to repel invaders from the north. The need for those defenses was gone, and the city's population grew, but the walls, the cliff, and the crevasse remained. Unable to spread outward, Turla burrowed down into stone and rose toward the sky. Over the centuries, it came to have distinct levels, each guarded by its own walls and gates: the palaces of the uppermost First Circle for royalty and the highest nobility, down to the desperate slums of the Sixth.

The man bowed. "You are correct, my lord. I am Hob Fierar, Lord Envoy to Lucenequa."

Cay raised his eyebrows at him. "I didn't know the Lord Chancellor of Muntegri had sent an envoy." *I didn't know we were letting Grup snakes cross the border.*

"I am but newly arrived," agreed Hob Fierar pleasantly. "Lucenequa's new queen wishes to reverse some of the previous monarch's harsh policies and perhaps repair the relationship between Muntegri and Lucenequa."

Six and a half years ago, the Grup, a loose coalition drawn from the ranks of the army, the palace guards, and those who supported them, had slaughtered Muntegri's ancient royal family, from the oldest dowager to a six-year-old prince. The King of Lucenequa had declared Muntegri to be a pariah and severed all diplomatic ties, but he had died last year.

"It certainly will be a mountainous task," agreed Cay.

The envoy chuckled. "You have adopted the indirect speech of your adopted home," he observed. "Say rather the plain truth: it will be nigh-impossible due to the hasty actions of Muntegrise and the obstinate resentment of Lucenequans. But one must make a start somewhere."

Cay nodded, maintaining his friendly expression. The Grup warlord who now called himself the Lord Chancellor of Muntegri had cemented his authority by killing most members of the ancient nobility, anyone else who seemed to oppose him, and not a few hapless bystanders. People had been cut down in the streets and in their homes; others brought ceremoniously to the gallows erected on Level One, designed to hang five people at a time, all day, every day. Cay had escaped the atrocities; his parents had not.

"But that is why I have sought you out, my lord," Fierar went on.

"Me?"

"You are still a child of Muntegri, I believe," said Fierar.

"In spite of my accent, I am now a citizen of Lucenequa. My marriage made it so."

"You have risen to admirable heights here. But I'm certain these people—" the envoy waved a vague hand in the direction of the ballroom "—do not accept you as one of their own."

Cay did not acknowledge this. "Oh no, they are very kind."

"They are deceitful, full of pretty words and sideways looks." Fierar nodded with an air of regret. "And the Muntegrise are too blunt, too quick to action. The fault lies with both sides. Certainly, some of the aftermath of the Revolution was unfortunate. But I am sure you still love your homeland and want to help her prosper."

Cay had no interest in assisting the Grup. "I'm not sure how I could help."

"Neither am I. Not at this moment. I still have the dust of the Muntegri Road on my feet! But I hope to find friends here who can bring me news and insight into the doings of Lucenequan society."

At last, he gets to the point. "Thank you," he said as though he missed it. "I am happy to make new friends as well, no matter where I am." Smiling, he stood. "But I am tired and must find my husband now. I wish you the best of luck, my Lord Envoy."

"I thank you for your good wishes, Lord Cay," said Hob Fierar, who remained seated. "Perhaps we'll meet again soon."

Not if I can help it, thought Cay, bowing.

He made his way along the periphery of the ballroom, entirely fed up with this ball and intending to leave whether he found Adrio or not.

But he did encounter Adrio, who said, "Ready to go so soon?"

"If you don't mind."

"I don't mind. I've already made my excuses to the prince and called the carriage around."

The thought of sitting with Adrio in the close carriage made Cay's skin itch. "Might we walk? It's not far, and the night was fine when we arrived."

"Of course."

Adrio dispatched the carriage, and they walked out of the arched portico into the streets of Valette. The autumn night was indeed fine, starlit, and cool, and they walked shoulder to shoulder, not touching, in silence.

How Cay had once loved walking with Adrio. In the springtime, they had walked all over this ancient city together, showing each other their favorite places—the sunny plazas at the summit of the hill, the wide thoroughfares, the busy market squares. Beyond the broad avenues near the palace, the medieval character of the city revealed itself: a cobweb tangle of steep, narrow alleys spread out toward the old walls and docks. It was a city of fountains and canals, sunlit courtyards and walled gardens, fragrant with lemon and rose. There were shrines at the street corners, trees and birds and stars carved into the golden limestone walls. The oldest streets were still paved with the rounded stones that had long ago sloshed and rolled in the ballast holds of Lucenequan ships. Once Cay had twisted his ankle on a cobblestone and Adrio had carried him home on his back.

They didn't speak now as they walked in the cool autumn darkness toward their home. His mind whirled with anger and hurt, and he could not think of a thing to say.

"You seemed to be having a good time," Adrio commented after a while. "Flying from flower to flower."

"Shouldn't I?" snapped Cay.

For the last several months, Cay had gotten into the habit of responding to Adrio's veiled insults with sweetness. He smiled and flattered him, much as he had just done to the Muntegrise envoy. He'd hoped if he were kind enough, gracious enough, Adrio would rediscover whatever had attracted him to Cay in the first place. Tonight his patience for that pretense had thinned to nothing.

Ahead shone the lights in the windows of Adrio's townhouse, called Rossoulia for its cinnabar-painted door. Rossoulia was Cay's home, now: six narrow stories of blond limestone, studded with high windows to let in the light, linked by a spiral stair of white marble. A small walled yard in back let onto stables for Adrio's beloved horses. Rossoulia was his home for the rest of his life.

At the little shrine on the corner of their street, Cay paused and pulled the roseapple-blossom earrings out of his lobes and dropped them with a *clink* into the alms box. Walking past Adrio toward the red door, he said, "I find I prefer the sapphires."

Adrio silently fell into step beside him. Cay sensed his surprise.

"I met the envoy from Muntegri tonight," Cay said. His voice was unsteady. "A Grup man. He asked me if I truly was a

Lucenequan now. I said yes. But I must admit I cannot imagine any Muntegrise spending all that money just to tell someone they are no longer loved. Really! Only a Lucenequan would make such an extravagant gesture."

After a moment, Adrio said, "Did I make the gesture because I'm Lucenequan?"

"Excellent point, my lord. I so rarely have the slightest idea why you do anything."

A servant opened the door for them, and without a word, they made their way up toward their rooms, their shoes tapping on the marble stairs.

Cay's suite was on the third story, Adrio's on the fourth, up a flight of stairs Cay no longer ever climbed.

He opened the door to his suite and then paused, looking at his husband. "Who wrote about the poor roseapple tree on the hill: Was it Trantor? Or Telluri? Or the great Cinna? Everyone condemns it for its twisted limbs, but what of the careless man who planted it there, doomed to wither with no protection?" Drunk with anger, he threw his habitual caution to the winds. "Do you know what I think is funny, Husband? All the people who think I seduced or tricked you into marriage, all the people who call me a vine, or a weed, or a mushroom—they all pity *you*. They don't know the real fool in this marriage is me."

He slammed the door behind him.

Cay dismissed his servant. His heart was pounding; he was furious and shocked at himself for speaking so savagely to Adrio. He paced, cracking his knuckles, and then, too agitated to remain in this room, threw his window open and climbed up the wall, past Adrio's ajar window, to the roof.

The night was clear and the stars dim through the hazy Lucenequan night. The roof was home to a large half-tailed stray cat, who perched on a cornice and warily glared at him. Cay stood on the roof and looked out across the spires and monuments and glowing lights of his adopted city. There, with no one to see him but the cat, he remembered.

"We should get married."

It was their first time alone together in Cay's little flat. He shared this single room above a restaurant with his sister, Kell, who had gone to spend the night with their cousins. The room was loud with the sounds of the customers below until well into the night, and no amount of cleaning could remove the smell of fried fish and beer. But Adrio had brought a bundle of firewood as a courting gift, and so the room was warm despite the cold rain rattling on the window. They were pressed together in Cay's narrow bed, naked in the fire's golden light. Both of them eager for love. But Adrio, the tease, was in no hurry.

"You're a maniac," said Cay. "Kiss me."

Laughing, Adrio pinned him, wrists and legs, and pressed a noisy smooch on his nose. "I want you to be my husband."

"That is a ridiculous idea."

"It's the best idea I've ever had."

"Adrio." Cay frowned up at him. "I am Muntegrise. My father was a potter."

"I don't care. And don't tell me you do, either, because I won't believe you."

"Well, the rest of the world would care," said Cay.

"It would be my honor to protect you from the world."

"And who would protect you? Can you imagine the gossip of all those fancy folk? Adrio, someday to be twelfth Bai of Lodola, married to a tailor's boy? They would flay you alive."

"I've known those fancy folk my entire life. They are not so fearsome."

Cay snorted. "Only so long as you don't upset the way things are done. Stop." Cay tested Adrio's grip on his wrists. He could not break free, so instead, he pressed upward and parted his lips and smiled when Adrio's gaze dropped to his mouth.

"Stop talking and kiss me."

Adrio obeyed, and his mouth was warm and sweet and possessive. Cay's toes curled, and when Adrio released his wrists in favor of stroking his body, palming his ass, Cay wound his arms around Adrio's neck and kissed him deeper.

It wasn't their first assignation—they'd enjoyed some hurried encounters in carriages—but this was different. Now they had privacy and comfort and time. Adrio kissed him like he was praying, and explored him with reverent questions—do you like this? Have you ever tried this? He was slow, patient, and devastatingly thorough, and it felt like worship. Adrio cradled Cay's head and stared into his eyes like he was the only other man in the world. He whispered Cay's name over and over like a prayer.

Cay didn't want to think about love, or marriage, or any of the things he couldn't have. He would have this, now, and return it; this sweetness, so good it almost brought tears to his eyes. It was no less sweet because someday it would end; he would have it, all of it, while it lasted.

Later, when the fire was reduced to embers and the restaurant below was quiet at last, Adrio bathed the evidence of pleasure off their bodies and cuddled with Cay beneath his coarse blanket.

"I want you to marry me," he whispered.

"Adrio . . ." groaned Cay with exasperation.

"No, but . . . I've done nothing to deserve the noble status that seems such a barrier to you. My mother, and her uncle, and his father, and all the bais of Lodola before her, all they do is maintain the estate and collect the revenues. I was chosen to be the next bai, and I shall do the same. I hope I shall treat my tenants fairly. And that's all. For that, something I haven't even done yet, I've wealth beyond what any man could spend in a lifetime, a high place in society, and the respect of people who have never met me and never will. What is it for? Surely the only possible point is this: so long as I behave with honor and do my duty, I have the wealth and power to do as I wish. And I wish to marry Cay Olau."

"You're arrogant," said Cay shakily. "Heir of Lodola, you can't bend the world to your liking."

Adrio stroked his cheek with the backs of his fingers, gazing at Cay's face. "I can walk upon a fresh snow and make the first tracks. What could be easier?"

"You are lying to yourself."

"Am I?" Adrio kissed him and said, "If you tell me you don't love me, I'll be silent. But if you do, you will be lying."

"Sometimes love isn't enough."

"Is it just?" Adrio's voice went low and throaty with passion. "You believe you cannot marry the man you love because of society's rules—is that just? What is the honorable response to injustice—conceding to it or challenging it?"

"So arrogant," whispered Cay.

"Yes. But you love me, Cay Olau. When you look at me, your eyes are stars. When you look at me, you tremble with love." Adrio's face was so close Cay could feel the brush of lips against his skin. "Marry me. Marry me tomorrow, Cay. I don't care what the world thinks. You love me, and I shall be the twelfth Bai of Lodola, and I. Love. You."

They'd married in the early spring, when the fields of Lucenequa were soaked with snowmelt and the mountains were still white. They'd honeymooned at Wind House, the beautiful ancient tower house in the foothills, loaned to them by Ondrei. There he'd picked purple flowers as they pushed their star-shaped heads up from the softening snow, and been scolded:

"What, were you outside in your shirt in this cold night air?"

"It's not so cold. It's beautiful."

"You're beautiful. Your cheeks are like cherries. Ah, but your feet are frozen! Were you not wearing shoes?"

"I stayed on the cleared path."

"Foolishness. Were you so confident that I'd warm your toes for you?"

"A week ago I would not have been. But now you've married me, and my cold toes are your responsibility."

Then they'd come to their red-doored house in Valette, to Rossoulia, where they had ignored scandal and made a home, and Cay had never been happier.

And then, in late spring, Adrio had gone on a trip to attend to his properties and returned a week later: sun-browned, tired, and ominously silent.

He'd stopped talking to Cay. He'd stopped touching him, spending time with him, or sleeping with him. With no explanation, Adrio had ordered the servants to move all Cay's things out of Adrio's bedroom. He'd always had a suite on the third floor but slept in his husband's bed. Until this.

"But why?"

"It's fitting that you should enjoy the privacy of your own suite. Indeed, it has been shabby of me not to see to your comfort sooner. Are you not glad?"

"Adrio. You see that I am not glad."

"I have seen ugly birds that sing sweetly, and pretty birds that impale grasshoppers on thorns."

"I— Adrio, I don't understand you. I just want to be close to you."

"And you are. You honor me by sharing my home, my title, and my fortune. And I honor you by granting you sole dominion over your own bed."

Cay had pleaded for an explanation to no avail. He'd tried seduction, tears, begging. When nothing seemed to break through, he'd lapsed into sweetness, giving Adrio his most pleasing side, his warmest words, and his most hopeful glances.

Now, on the roof of his lonely, beautiful home, staring at the stars, Cay paged through his memories of Adrio's love and wondered.

Had Adrio somehow learned Cay's secrets?

A hangman's tree?

No. Impossible. Only Cay's sister knew, and she would tell no one.

But then, why had Adrio stopped loving him? What had shattered Adrio's faith? How could he win Adrio's love back if he didn't know why it had gone away?

He was just a tree on a hill, vulnerable to the harsh winds, unprotected, still showing his prettiest flowers but rotting inside from grief and longing.

Tears spilled down his face, and his breath shuddered in his chest. Cay buried his face in his arms and cried.

CHAPTER TWO

The morning after the Harvest Ball, Cay carefully applied cosmetics to conceal the signs of weeping and exhaustion under his eyes.

As he came down the stairs, he heard his husband's voice in the dining room. His heartbeat accelerated as though in the presence of an enemy. He paused on the landing, clenched his fists, and breathed deeply, waiting for calm.

Adrio was saying, "Of course I've read about physical natural philosophy. I've seen demonstrations of experiments—the magnifying lenses and so forth. But do you really think you can study it for a lifetime?"

"For a hundred lifetimes."

The second voice belonged to Cay's sister, Kell. Adrio paid her tuition to the University of Valette—something they would never have been able to afford without him. Cay stood on the stairs and listened to the sounds of the two people he loved most in the world eating breakfast. The clink of a cup in a saucer, the rustle of cloth. And then Kell went on, "The study of the natural forces, things like friction, inertia, and magnetism—it's how the world works. Professor Curio says the study of natural forces will someday explain everything in the world."

"Everything?" repeated Adrio, a smile in his voice.

"Don't laugh," said Kell. "You see it as a game, something your fine friends do for entertainment at parties. 'Let us gather round and look through lenses at the wriggly things in the cheese!' But between the studies of mathematics and natural forces, someday we will know enough to explain the stars, the oceans, and everything. How the world began, and how it will end."

"How terrifying," Cay said, coming into the dining room.

He avoided looking at Adrio and came around the table to where Kell, her brown hair messily braided, was plowing her way through a full breakfast of eggs, ham, and praji. He kissed the top of her head. "Good morning, you little rodent-faced brat. What are you doing here?"

"I had a fluxions exam this morning, and then I was hungry."

"Fluxions at the crack of dawn?" gasped Cay. "Have you been to a physician?"

"It's almost eleven o'clock, and you know perfectly well what fluxions are."

As a child, Kell had been sunny-natured, curious, and brilliant. After their exile from Muntegri, she'd retreated into numb silence. That had been the worst time: they'd stayed with cousins who didn't particularly want them, and she'd felt unwelcome as well as grieving and haunted by memories. She'd crept around silent and hollow-eyed, barely able to groom herself or speak. He remembered cutting mats out of her hair. He was heartened now to see her eating and smiling, with light in her eyes as she spoke of her studies at the university.

Cay was glad she and Adrio loved each other. Adrio was not university-educated, but he, too, had a curious mind, and he read books on all sorts of topics. They often talked about intellectual pursuits. And Kell, habitually wary and quiet with people she didn't know, was lively and chatty with Adrio. It was one reason Cay hadn't told her his marriage was so strained. Adrio was her brother too. He never wanted her to feel she had to choose between them.

He sat beside Kell and poured a cup of tea, and she handed him a praji.

"Remind me about fluxions?"

"Maths."

"Oh."

She smiled at him. "Imagine if Mother could have gone to university! She'd have been so happy."

Cay returned the smile, his lips pressed together against a wince. Kell wasn't to know he usually avoided this topic with Adrio. "She would certainly have done all the maths," he agreed.

"Your mother enjoyed studying mathematics?" said Adrio.

Cay turned to Adrio for the first time since he'd shouted last night. He seemed untroubled as he lounged in his chair, graceful and lazy as a big cat. His hair was loosely tied back at his nape, his long-fingered hands wrapped around a teacup. He glanced slyly at Cay out of the corner of his eye and then turned his attention fully on Kell.

He was too smart to be so handsome, too beloved to be so unkind.

Kell said, "Oh, she was brilliant. She could add up father's accounts just by running her finger down the columns."

"So could you," said Cay. "You were doing mathematical puzzles when you were ten."

"Mother made those puzzles for me. She figured them out first." Kell smiled at Adrio. "I especially miss her in my mathematics classes. She would have loved them."

Cay surreptitiously began to crack his knuckles under the table.

"Did your father like maths too?"

"No, he and Cay didn't really join in the maths."

"So Cay takes after his father?"

Kell fell silent and cast Cay an apologetic glance.

Cay shrugged one shoulder at her. "Adrio and I once went to one of those parties with the philosophical experiments," he said. "It was awful, actually. They cut a dog so we could see its blood through the magnifying lenses."

"What did you see in the blood?" asked Kell, picking up the changed subject.

"I couldn't bear to look," Cay confessed.

"Why don't you ever talk about your parents, Cay?" Adrio asked, pleasantly.

"Adrio did, though," returned Cay, in the same bright tone. "What did you see in the blood, Adrio?"

Adrio gazed at him from beneath drooping lids. Cay glared back. Kell's eyes flickered between them.

After a moment, Kell said, "He was a good father, but he was busy. He had a shop to run, and orders to fill. He didn't spend as much time with us as our mother did. I got to see water from a rain cistern once through lenses and saw lots of little animalcules moving around in there. Did the dog's blood have moving things in it?"

Adrio relented and smiled at her. "I don't know if they were animalcules, but you could see little spots. Our hearts were hyacinth petals for the dog, though. We bought her and gave her to a friend down in Lodola."

"Oh, good. It sounds like she deserved a better home."

Cay had fallen in love with the dog and asked Adrio to rescue her. It had been their first public outing after Adrio had moved Cay to his own suite, and Cay had been so furious and miserable he'd barely been able to speak to his husband, except for begging for mercy for the dog. He'd also wanted to keep her but had been afraid to ask for so much. The memory was humiliating.

He said, "Can you stay this afternoon, Kell? I've hardly seen you since the term started."

"I really can't." She mopped her plate with a praji and finished her tea. "I have to go study my Principles."

"Whatever Principles are, I'm certain you already know them backward and forward."

"I do, but there's a debate this afternoon on the Principle of Levity, and I can't miss it."

"What is the Principle of Levity?" asked Adrio.

"The opposite of the Principle of Gravity," said Kell, grinning at him. "Professor Curio says the nature of some objects pulls them toward the center of the earth, which is gravity, and the nature of other objects pulls them toward the heavens, which is levity. Things like smoke and steam."

"And cottonwood seeds," said Cay.

"I guess so. Do they fly?"

"Apparently. Everyone at the ball last night was wearing fluffy white cottonwood motifs." He returned her smile. "A fashionable illustration of the Principle of Levity."

Adrio said, "Cay, we are talking about the laws that make the world, not fashion."

His tone was mild. Kell must have thought Adrio's teasing was kind, for she laughed.

"Are they real?" asked Adrio. "These Principles?"

Kell shrugged. "It's a theory. Have you seen smoke-balloons demonstrated? They fill a cloth bag with smoke from a fire, and it goes up. Why does smoke go up, but the unburned wood goes down?"

"I've never thought to wonder," admitted Adrio.

"The Principles are an explanation for observed phenomena. But Professor Redond from Harodj says that's all nonsense. She says both heat and cold are invisible liquids which go up or down as they are governed by the Principle of Pressure. And others believe the world is made of particles, and energy is created by collisions of the particles, which explains both falling and floating."

"Which do you believe?"

"I'm not sure. That's why I have to go to the debate." She picked up her bag and headed for the door. "Thank you for breakfast."

"Wait. Kell, take the rest of the praji to snack on." Cay glanced at Adrio for permission, and he nodded.

"I'll have Lirano bag them up."

"Oh, wonderful. I'll be the envy of my dormitory," said Kell.

"Sister Kell, next time you come, bring me a book on the Principle of Levity," Adrio suggested.

"I will bring you ten. Thank you, Adrio."

When she was gone, Cay and Adrio were alone in the breakfast room. Cay sat in silence, unable to think of a single thing to say.

"I learned so much about your parents today," said Adrio.

"Why do you care?" demanded Cay.

"Naturally, I am interested in my husband's family."

"Oh, naturally," snapped Cay.

"I've asked you about them before. You never wanted to say."

"They're dead." Cay's voice was still harsh from last night's tears. "What else?"

Adrio hesitated for a moment and then, in the same reasonable tone, went on, "You told me Kell didn't like to talk about them because of her grief. But today, she brought them up, unprompted. Could it be you didn't tell the truth?"

"You don't give a damn about me, so why are you pumping my sister for information about our parents?"

Adrio snorted softly. "*You've* stopped being a daisy in a field," he said.

"Aren't you relieved?"

"Yes."

Adrio stood. Cay did not rise respectfully, as he would have just yesterday. Instead, he remained insolently in his chair, sipping tea.

"I'm going to the palace today," Adrio said.

"Of course."

"I'll be in meetings with my solicitor all day."

"Fine."

"Don't expect me back for supper."

"I rarely do," said Cay.

Adrio nodded, lips tight. "Until later, then," he said before striding out of the room.

It would be a long marriage if neither of them was going to pretend to care.

Not long after the dog's blood party, Cay had attempted to befriend the stray cat.

The gray tom's territory extended across the roofs of several houses in this neighborhood. Cay had seen him leaping the narrow gap between houses; he'd once glimpsed him in the alley below. He'd lost half his tail in some mishap, but this disability did not prevent him from hunting mice and starlings. He noisily coughed up their bones and washed their blood off his face on the ledge outside Cay's window. At night the cat howled, again and again, and the eerie hollow sound seemed to resonate with Cay's loneliness and misery.

Desperate for company, Cay had begun leaving his window open, a dish of his leftover dinner on the sill. Eventually, the cat began coming to eat. Then on cold or rainy nights, he would venture inside, a warning glare keeping Cay at bay while he explored. Cay called him Mandru, an old Muntegrise word for a vain man. Mandru still did not permit Cay to touch him, but now he regularly made himself at home in Cay's suite, giving Cay someone to talk to.

Mandru wasn't exactly a secret—the servants were surely aware of him—but Cay didn't know if Adrio was.

After Kell and Adrio left, Cay was alone in the house but for the servants and Mandru, who had assumed the loaf-of-bread shape on Cay's bed. Cay lay curled on the bed, head on his folded arms, far enough from the cat to escape danger. "Do you think I should leave? Does he *want* me to leave?"

Mandru blinked at him.

"If I abandoned him, he could divorce me after a year. The scandal would be bad—it was bad enough when he married me. If I jilted him, it would be much worse. He would be *dishonored*."

Mandru had no opinion.

"If he wanted me to go, he wouldn't keep displaying me at parties like a new hat. Would he? He wouldn't be paying Kell's tuition. All he'd have to do is cut her off." Cay rolled onto his back, combing his hands through his hair. "If he wanted me to go, he could *tell me to go*."

His sudden movement, or the frustration in his voice, must have alarmed Mandru, who slid off the bed and disappeared under it. Cay glared at the ceiling.

"I could go whether he wants it or not," he whispered. It hurt to say; hurt like an abscessed tooth to even think about leaving Adrio forever. And pulling Kell from the university. And, gods, starting over again, penniless and alone *again*, in yet another new city . . .

He was exhausted just thinking about it.

He didn't want to go. He wanted the life he'd had, with Adrio, only a few months ago. How could he repair his broken marriage, make his home a home again, instead?

A tap on the door. Cay sat up, aware that his curly hair stood on end, and called, "Come."

It was Lirano, the housemaster. "A visitor is here."

"My lord is out."

"He says he wishes to speak to you, Lord Cay."

"Really? Who is it?"

"He says he is the envoy from Muntegri, my lord."

"Oh!" Cay raised his eyebrows. How rude had he been to the man? He honestly couldn't remember. He'd been so furious with Adrio last night he'd been in no mood to entertain his fellow Muntegrise. "Thank you, Lirano. I'll see him in the parlor."

"Shall I bring tea, Lord Cay?"

"Yes. Good idea."

He combed his hair, washed his hands, and arrived in the parlor just as the tea did. "Good afternoon, Master Fierar," he said to the man who stood waiting there.

"Lord Cay," said the Muntegrise man, bowing.

Last night, the man had worn a semblance of Lucenequan formal clothing. Today, in plain Muntegrise leathers, he looked like the Fourth Circle man he was: fit and muscular, with a direct gaze and a square stance. In the years before the coup, it had been the style for those politically aligned with the Grup to affect a military style, whether they had ever held a weapon. On Hob Fierar it looked as natural and as earned as the calluses on his hands and the scar on his chin.

"I am honored by your visit," said Cay, waving a hand toward a chair. "I am afraid my lord is away, but I hope you will join me for a light meal?"

"Thank you," said Fierar, perching on the edge of the chair. "I consider myself lucky to find you at home. I wished to offer my apologies, for I believe I offended you at the ball last night."

"Oh, no," said Cay. "Please don't give it another thought. These pastries are our chef's best approximation of Muntegrise praji. Will you try one? You'll find they're not quite right, but they are not bad."

They ate and chatted lightly. Fierar described the house he had been granted here in Valette by the queen—how it was small but gracious, and how the queen had been so attentive to him. He seemed to think a process of reconciliation was possible, and Cay nodded, pretending to believe it too. He recommended a few places in Valette Fierar might like to go, including a shop that could make him clothes for court. "Therescu and Sons Fine Tailoring. I got a job doing piecework for them when I was eighteen, with the snow of Muntegri still wet on my shoulders."

Fierar asked cautiously, "Does your husband know you worked at a shop?"

"I doubt there's a soul in Lucenequa who doesn't know it. I mended the breeches and petticoats of many nobles and made deliveries. I'm afraid they all remember me well."

"Nobles often take no note of tradesmen and servants, I believe," observed Fierar. "They might not have recognized you?"

"You would think so," agreed Cay drily, "but recognize me they certainly did."

The wealthy folk of Valette hadn't just been shocked that Adrio had married a tailor's assistant. They'd been shocked he'd married the tailor's assistant several of them had attempted—and failed—to seduce. Cay had refused disrespectful propositions and formal offers of patronage, which one might think would give him a reputation for spotless virtue. On the contrary, his relationship with Adrio only confirmed, in some minds, that he'd been angling for a noble marriage all along.

He'd first encountered Adrio while delivering new linens to the Valette palace of Ondrei Rege, Bai of Noresposto, on a chill afternoon in winter. Naturally, he'd headed for the back entrance, as was appropriate for a servant, but he'd been unable to reach it because three young men had occupied the walled yard behind the big house. It was cleared of snow, and the men were sparring with practice swords, two against one. Cay had paused to watch, impressed with the speed and

grace of the man who held off his two attackers. It was a whirling melee, almost too swift to follow, punctuated by grunts and gasps and the clacking of the wooden swords. All three men were sweating in the cold air. Cay could not have passed them if he'd tried, so he waited and watched.

The man who was assailed by his friends was alight with joy. Handsome too, with fine high bones, curved lips, and dark liquid eyes beneath slanted brows. He was mesmerizing in motion: bold and fluid and concentrated. He was overmatched, but he held them off with wild whirling delight. It was a pleasure to watch. At some point, his tawny hair loosed itself from its clasp at his nape, and he tossed his head to get it out of his eyes. Apparently, this gave one of his attackers the opportunity to dart in and mightily thwack him in the abdomen with his practice sword.

He dropped his weapons, coughing, and the fight immediately came to an end; the two attackers were suddenly solicitous about their opponent's health.

"All right, Adrio?"

"Yes, and damn you for hitting so hard," he wheezed, straightening with apparent effort. He laughed, pushing damp hair back out of his face, his chest and throat shining with sweat. Cay, lurking near a wall with a bundle of linens in his arms, subconsciously smiled as well.

That was when their eyes met.

Adrio immediately straightened, the laughter falling from his face. He suddenly looked like a nobleman in an ancient painting, his head high and haughty, the lines of his face remote and fine. His shoulders seemed strong enough to carry the armor of centuries past.

Cay recalled himself.

"Pardon, masters," he said politely, bowing low. "I am seeking the kitchen entrance, but I am in no hurry."

"No trouble," said the burliest of the men. "Have you a delivery there?"

"Yes, sir, from Therescu and Sons, for the Lord of Noresposto."

"Very good," said the burly man, gesturing for him to pass. "My housekeeper is expecting you."

Cay skirted the three men. He rapped on the kitchen door and delivered the linens to the servant within and returned through the *yard, bowing again. The handsome man's dark eyes followed him as he left.*

"It was a bit of a scandal when we married," said Cay, with considerable understatement. "But it's blown over now."

Fierar sipped tea, his face lively with interest. "His reputation survived the blow, I take it."

"Of course."

"Of course. Adrio Santauro, Heir of Lodola, is known to be a man of unimpeachable character. And though you are a commoner, there is no smudge on your name. I suppose the scandal could have been much worse if . . ."

He paused and sipped tea. Cay sat still, belatedly wary.

After a moment, he prompted, "If?"

"Well. Every soul in Lucenequa may know you were a tailor, but they don't know the rest of it, do they? I rather imagine Lord Adrio doesn't, either."

Cay widened his eyes. "I have no idea what you mean, sir."

"I think my meaning is clear," said Hob Fierar, "but I'm happy to explain further. I have comrades who patrolled the Muntegri Road through the mountains the year of the coup. Some of them remember you well. They remember what you did in Lehoia Pass that summer. Wouldn't it be a scandal if those details were known? A scandal so great even Lord Adrio's fine reputation might not survive."

Cay sat frozen, staring at the man, who resumed eating. After a moment, he said, "How openly you work against the queen who invited you here."

"I am openly visiting my countryman. No one need know more about my work, unless you tell them. Which, for the sake of Lord Adrio, I think you will not."

"Lord Adrio knows everything about me."

Fierar sipped tea. "I don't believe you. He would be regarded as a very great fool, or possibly a traitor, did he know. And he might be . . . annoyed . . . at having been tricked." He put down his plate and brushed crumbs delicately off his fingers. "But please do not be alarmed, Lord Cay. As I said last night, I, and Muntegri, want your friendship."

Since Fierar was not fooled by Cay's innocent mask, he dropped it. "The Grup, you mean. It is not synonymous with Muntegri."

"It is now, or will be."

"Exactly what do you want?"

"Oh, nothing much. I know your husband is often at the palace. Any bit of information about what is happening there might be useful. How much money is allocated to the army, for instance, and for what. Movements of troops, movements of supplies, training . . ."

Cay's cup rattled in its saucer. He put it down and folded his hands in his lap. Silence stretched between them for the space of five heartbeats. Then he managed to say, "I don't think my husband knows anything about any of that."

Fierar smiled. "Do you know where the Heir of Lodola is today? He is at an inn, in a private room with several others, one of whom is the daughter of the Minister of the Army."

"Lucca of Olega?"

"Correct. Among others. What on earth could they be discussing?"

"Truly, sir, I have no idea."

Fierar shrugged. "I expect you know a great more than you pretend. And what you don't know, you have the means to learn." He stood. "Your husband has a reputation for being a man of upright character. An honest man. Spend a moment, please, imagining his response if he knew you are not. And, of course, such information would affect your sister, as well, would it not?"

"Sir," said Cay, hating the pleading note in his voice, "my sister was a child when we left Muntegri."

"Thirteen," agreed Fierar. It was appalling how much he knew. "You should find out what your husband is up to. For Muntegri's benefit, but also for your own. And your sister's."

"Adrio and I don't talk about such things."

"Show an interest. Men love to talk about their business to attentive young spouses."

Cay tried to imagine seducing Adrio into giving him information and closed his eyes with horror. "Master Fierar," he said hoarsely, "I assure you, it is simply not possible—"

"Oh," added Fierar as an afterthought, "and any information that might pertain to the Chende escapees."

"The what?"

"The man or woman who is stealing Chende prisoners out of Muntegri and bringing them over the mountains to Lucenequa."

"Sir, the Chende travel where they will. No law forbids them from coming to Lucenequa or staying here. They are no concern of the Grup."

"The queen wishes to reestablish relations with her neighbor Muntegri. The diplomatic process can hardly go forward if one of her subjects is committing acts of trespass, espionage, and sabotage across the Muntegrise border. No. I want to know who it is and how he does it. The prisons are guarded. The Road is guarded. The passes are full of vicious, cutthroat Chende clans, little better than animals. And yet, somehow, prisoners are escaping into Lucenequa. Who and how, Lord Cay. I want names. Be sweet to your husband tonight and give me names tomorrow."

Cay clenched his fists hard enough to dig his nails into his palms.

It was unthinkable. Help the Grup? Betray whoever was assisting the Chende refugees? Spy on his husband? Unthinkable.

Through a mouth gone dry, he said, "Actually, I think I might have heard an interesting rumor."

The sneer of triumph on Fierar's face was unmistakable. "Go on."

"It wasn't from Adrio. Adrio knows nothing of such things, I assure you. But at the Harvest Ball last night, someone said something. Someone said the Chende fly over the mountains. They don't take the Road or the high passes. They fly."

Fierar narrowed his eyes at Cay. "Do not toy with me, Lord Cay."

"I'm not." He groped for inspiration. "They said the Chende have smoke-balloons. Smoke-balloons, you know, employ the Principle of Levity."

"What in damnation is the Principle of Levity?"

"The opposite of the Principle of Gravity," Cay replied helpfully.

Fierar scowled. "How are the balloons not seen? Surely they would be plain against the sky."

Why hadn't he thought of that? Cay groped for an answer. "Perhaps, as well as Levity, there is another Principle affecting . . ." He trailed off uncertainly. "Visibility."

Fierar looked furious.

Cay stammered, "Sir, I am no scholar. I haven't made any study of—of Principles. This is just what I heard last night."

"Who told you this?"

"I—"

"Name them, Lord Cay."

"I overheard it in the crowd. I don't know who said it."

Fierar's eyes narrowed. "I was watching you," he said. "I arrived before you did, and I saw the way you talked to everyone. But never for more than a moment or two. Except for two: you spent time with your husband, and you spent time with Ondrei Rege, the Bai of Noresposto. Which of them told you about the flying machines?"

Oh, gods. Implicating Ondrei would almost be as bad as implicating Adrio. "No, no, it is not—"

Fierar waved a dismissive hand. "Enough. Listen. If Lucenequa has this technology—flying machines, invisible to the eye—Muntegri would be most interested. Find out. Find out more."

"I don't—"

"I don't care. Go to your informant and find out. I want to know about the invisible smoke-balloons. How do they work? Where are they made? Is Lucenequa planning an invasion over the mountains?"

Cay gulped. "What? No! I don't know. Surely not."

"Find out who does know, Lord Cay, and fuck them or suck them until they tell you everything." Fierar stood. "Thank you for the tea."

Adrio didn't come home until late.

The house was dark, except for the candles in the library where Cay waited for him. He had sent the servants to bed: "I will wait up for my lord and take care of him when he comes in."

So he waited, listening for Adrio's footsteps.

He had very nearly been sick when Fierar left. He had paced in a panic, cracked his knuckles until they ached, and, in a moment of true madness, had tried to hug Mandru. His left arm bore deep scratches.

Only one solution came to him. He must throw himself upon his husband's mercy.

"You're as beautiful as a roseapple tree on a hill." Cay kept remembering those words, given along with an expensive gift. As if to say, *You look beautiful, but I know at the core you are twisted.*

Why would a man do such a thing to his husband? Did it give him pleasure knowing Cay would think the words were a compliment when really they were an insult? Or was he confident Cay would interpret the words and understand Adrio's scorn? Was Adrio toying with Cay or trying to drive him away? Or did he have some other motive?

Gods. Adrio had once loved him. Through the winter and into the spring. Adrio had loved him enough to face the laughter and contempt of Lucenequan society, to say, *I am the Heir of Lodola, and this is the one I want. I know of his common blood and foreign birth. I will have him, not as my lover but as my husband.*

If Hob Fierar had tried to blackmail him when there was still snow on the ground, Cay would have laughed at him, dared him to try, so confident had he been in Adrio's love.

But Adrio's love had melted away in the spring. He might no longer be willing to face the public uproar that would follow the revelation of Cay's past. He already despised Cay, but he maintained the public façade of a respectable marriage and paid for Kell to attend the university. Fierar could strip those things away with a word.

Cay needed help. He didn't want to betray Lucenequa. He didn't want to help the Grup. He certainly didn't want to hinder whoever was rescuing Chende from the Muntegrise work camps.

So he must turn to Adrio. Here in the library, he looked around at his husband's books: books ranging in topic from natural philosophy and history, to law and social justice, to swashbuckling tales of adventure. He would keep this Adrio firmly in his mind— the Adrio who admired those who defied society in the name of honor. The Adrio who had defied society himself because he loved Cay.

He would tell *that* Adrio all. And they would talk about it, and even though they were no longer happy, together they would work to find a way to defeat this common threat. Perhaps together they could feed Fierar lies or stories or half-truths to benefit Lucenequa. Adrio would know what would be best.

Cay heard the scuff of boots upon the front stairs. He jumped up and hurried to the door, opening it to Adrio.

"Well, good evening," said Adrio softly, coming in. Cay shut the door behind him and helped him off with his cloak. "You're up late."

"I told Lirano to go to bed."

"How considerate."

Cay took his gloves and hat and hung them tidily in the wardrobe, just as Lirano would have done had he been awake. Cay had never been a house servant, but sometimes he felt closer to the staff than Adrio's peers. He closed the wardrobe door and turned to his husband, who stood studying him.

"Did you want something, Cay?"

Cay attempted a smile. "Are you hungry?"

"No, I had supper."

"Would you like a glass of wine?"

"I suppose so." Adrio strolled into the library, where a decanter of fortified wine stood on a sideboard, and poured a glass. "Will you have one?"

His stomach roiled at the thought of alcohol. "No, thank you."

"Very well." Adrio took his glass and sat in an armchair, crossing one leg elegantly over the other.

Cay hesitated, holding his own hands in his nervousness. Adrio sipped his wine.

After a moment, Adrio said, "Is this about your visitor this afternoon? Hob Fierar, from Muntegri?" He eyed Cay narrowly. "He is an attractive man, and no doubt one with whom you have much in common. He stayed for over an hour, I believe. Quite long enough for a rendezvous."

Cay gazed at him, speechless with outrage.

Adrio sipped his wine, letting the silence stretch between them.

Finally, Cay managed to say, "If you know he was here, you also know I fed him tea and sent him on his way. There was no *rendezvous*."

Adrio's eyebrows lifted ironically, as if something about Cay's distress amused him or annoyed him.

Cay seethed. He needed Adrio's help, he reminded himself. In as calm a tone as he could manage, he said, "I'm sorry. It's difficult for me to begin because you're angry with me." He perched on the edge of a chair, clasping his hands. "Even though you surely don't think I've betrayed our marriage with the envoy from Muntegri, here in this library with the servants about. So I am not sure why you're so angry. I hoped we could talk."

"How brightly the moon shines tonight," said Adrio, "when this morning it was dim and pale."

Cay flushed. The moon was a symbol of inconstancy: bright until it waned, dark until it waxed. Sometimes it rode through the daytime sky, sometimes it confined itself to the night. It was unreliable, the moon. Changeful. Manipulative.

He tried to speak but couldn't. Couldn't even meet Adrio's eyes.

"Do go on," said Adrio, with a hint of impatience. "Upon my honor, all I own is yours to claim. You have only to name what you want."

He couldn't. He simply could not confide his worst secrets to Adrio, not when Adrio spoke to him that way. He turned away, whispering, "Never mind," and got up to leave the room.

"No?" said Adrio, behind him. His voice lowered. "Cay. Are you well? Did the man offer you any threat or insult?"

"No," he said over his shoulder as he headed for the stairs. "It was a passing fancy, and I have rethought it. Just like the moon, wouldn't you agree?"

CHAPTER THREE

C ay spent the night seething with anger between restless
dreams, remembering over and over his last conversation
with Adrio. Especially when Adrio had said, condescendingly,
Hob Fierar was an *attractive man*.

Damn him.

Adrio was the most captivating bed partner of Cay's life.
They'd spent hours naked together, experimenting, teasing,
discovering all the ways they could gratify each other. Their
estrangement had not just broken Cay's heart; it had included a
sudden and complete suspension of all such pleasures. Frustration
was not Cay's greatest hurt, but it was certainly a perpetual and
bothersome one.

He had to assume Adrio was not bothered by lonely celibacy.
He went away, sometimes for an afternoon, sometimes for weeks
at a time. He was a vigorous and enthusiastic lover who probably
felt no compunction about seeking satisfaction elsewhere.

Cay did. He was married and still hoped to be until death.
If Cay was not to spend every night for the rest of his life in
an empty bed, either Adrio would have to thaw—which seemed
increasingly unlikely—or Cay would have to find a lover. Which
he found difficult to imagine.

He could not claim it had never occurred to him, but he
certainly had not considered it with Hob Fierar. The charge stung
like a wasp, and so did the necessary speculation: Did Adrio's
rude accusation stem from a guilty conscience?

Cay supposed he should count himself lucky. If Adrio had a lover, at least he was discreet. At least he was not bringing anyone *here*. But as he rose in the morning, sullen and headachy, to find Adrio had left the house before breakfast, it seemed cold consolation.

"Should I leave?" he had asked Mandru. Was Adrio trying to goad him into running away? The scandal would be ruinous for him. He had weathered the disgrace of marrying Cay; he might not weather the disgrace of being discarded by him. He might be rejected by Valette society, and his folly would be remembered for years. If it was bad enough, his mother, the Bai of Lodola, might choose a different heir.

And he would *still* be in danger from the Grup envoy. And Cay would be alone.

No. Cay would fix it somehow. He'd been in worse straits before, with fewer tools in his hands, and managed it. He could do it again.

Restlessly, he paced his bedroom and tried to force his tired brain to formulate a plan to get him out of this predicament.

He did not intend to tell Hob Fierar the truth about anything. With all its faults, Lucenequa was his home now. He loved Muntegri with an aching nostalgia, but Muntegri had fallen to the Grup and was lost. The queen might want to forge a relationship with the new Muntegri, but she was a fool. Cay knew exactly how evil the Grup was. It would have no assistance from him.

And then there was the matter of the escaping Chende refugees. After the coup, the Grup had raked through the Sixth Circle, the only part of Turla where the Chende could live or work, rounded them up by the hundreds, murdered them in the streets or forced them into labor camps. Lucenequans tended to be pleased with themselves for being less brutish toward the Chende than the Muntegrise, but Lucenequa had been but little help. If someone was helping free Chende prisoners from the Grup and getting them over the mountains somehow, Cay would not betray them.

He drank tea and forced his tired brain to work through his plan. The first step would be to misdirect Hob Fierar. His ridiculous, impulsive lie about the smoke-balloons had been unexpectedly diverting.

Very well, he could divert even more.

He rang the bell, and when Lirano appeared, he said, "I am going to begin a new project. A gown for my sister. I'll need a stock of paper and ink."

"Do you not have enough of these already, Lord Cay?"

"I do, yes. But for this project, I want common paper. The gray pulpy stock, you know? And the purplish ink used by tradesmen?"

"I see." Lirano plainly did not see why Cay wanted cheap tools when he was well-supplied with reams of creamy white paper and inks in shades of raven black and midnight blue, all specially supplied to the Heir of Lodola by a stationer on Summit Street.

Cay smiled. "I know, it's silly of me. But when I started designing clothes, I could only afford the inexpensive ink and paper, and I rather miss it. One's free to experiment and make mistakes if one's using the purple ink and pulp paper, do you see?"

Lirano bowed. "Very well, Lord Cay. I'll see to it."

"Thank you."

He returned to his tea, thoughtfully.

The second part of his plan was to find out what Adrio was actually doing. Surely the real truth of the matter would lend his lies a solid foundation. It was important to be credible. Authentic.

But he also wanted to know for his own benefit. How was Adrio spending his days? With whom? Was he working? Was he indeed somehow involved in military planning? Or was he visiting a lover or series of lovers? Was he merely slaking his lust, or had he actually fallen in love with someone else?

Cay wrestled with the urge to follow Adrio. Was he indeed in secret meetings with important government ministers, as the envoy from Muntegri claimed? Or was he dallying with a lover, as Cay bitterly suspected?

Cay spent the morning in his suite, making preliminary sketches, and then carefully burning them. He attempted to lure

Mandru with crumbled bacon from breakfast. Still offended by Cay's attempt to hug him yesterday, Mandru remained on the roof of the house opposite and refused to come into Cay's room.

"I'm sorry," Cay called to him across the alley. "I was temporarily mad. It won't happen again."

Mandru gazed at him and then pointedly ignored him.

"I know," sighed Cay. "You wouldn't have let yourself get into a situation like this, I'm sure."

He emerged from his room at noon, when the servants were released from all duties for two hours. Usually, they congregated in the kitchen in the basement, eating together, but they were free to leave the house and go about other business if they chose. Cay slipped down the stairs and made sure that the servants were all gathered around the table.

He stealthily searched the house and did not find anyone else, so he slipped upstairs and let himself into Adrio's suite.

In layout, it was identical to Cay's: a bed chamber, a sitting room, and a dressing room, none of them large. Cay's suite was scrupulously tidy, his bed made, his clothes hung or folded into his chest. He had converted the dressing room into a sewing room, with a worktable under the window. His notebooks were stacked tidily on shelves, his pencils and inks tucked into their boxes, and fabric swatches folded in baskets under the table, sorted by color.

Adrio's rooms were far less orderly. The bed was unmade, clothes lay on the floor, and half-full cups of tea were on the tables. He had a shelf packed with books. History, mathematics, and great literature were downstairs in the library; these bedroom shelves held romantic adventure novels, an addiction of Adrio's since he was a child. Another pile of books teetered on the floor next to the bed.

Cay forced his thoughts away from the time he'd spent in Adrio's bed, warned himself not to think about the way the room smelled of Adrio's body, and turned his attention to the dressing room.

Like Cay, Adrio had altered his room into a kind of office lined with shelves, cabinets, and a big desk. These shelves were devoted to two types of bound ledger: blue and red. Listening for the servants' footsteps, Cay pulled down a blue ledger and flipped through.

Cay was neither a mathematic genius like his mother and sister nor a landowner like Adrio. But his father had made sure both his children were literate in what he called *the books*, and these ledgers formed a familiar pattern. The blue ledgers were the books for Lodola, Adrio's old and prosperous holding in the south. Adrio's widowed mother, the Bai of Lodola, still lived there, and Cay had visited once. He remembered rolling hills and lakes, sun-drenched orchards and vineyards, a big, ancient house, and the instant and implacable dislike of Lilia, the Bai of Lodola. (What a gorgon *she* was.)

Presumably Adrio had these ledgers as part of his training as the heir. Cay scanned the pages. Income: rents from tenants, farm goods, taxes, and tithes. Expenditures: salaries and pensions for employees, property improvements, expenses for food and wine, laundry, and so on. A loan, at three point five interest, appeared to be for some sort of drainage or irrigation project. It all seemed right and square to Cay, and so did the contents of the red ledgers for this household in Valette. Neither the blue nor the red ledgers were in Adrio's sprawling, slanted handwriting: the Valette ones were written by the housekeeper, Lirano. Presumably, Adrio's land steward wrote the Lodola ledgers. Cay was certain Adrio read them over, though. His habits might be a bit sloppy, but he had a sharp mind and a deep sense of responsibility.

It was all extremely unsurprising and unhelpful. Cay was gratified to find that the estate was financially healthy, and he did nosily dig until he found the order for the roseapple blossom earrings. Quite expensive, as he had thought, and commissioned in the early days of their marriage. Not originally intended as a cruel mockery, then; just turned to cruel purpose.

Pressing his lips together against hurt, Cay turned to rifling the desk, opening drawers and excavating pigeonholes. Pens, paper, a few scribbled notes and lists in Adrio's hand.

He discovered a heavy, polished wooden box containing a pair of shining ivory-inlaid dueling pistols and wrinkled his nose. He knew Adrio could shoot; once he had joined Adrio and his friend

Fonsca in target practice. He'd come away from the experience thinking guns were ugly, noisy, heavy, smelled bad, and kicked hard enough to hurt his wrists. He didn't like them. He closed the box with a *snap*.

He couldn't find anything about Adrio being involved in military or any other secret business. Hob Fierar would be unsatisfied.

"Find out."

He turned to a small cabinet beside the desk and discovered it would not open. A small brass padlock rattled against the wood when he tried its doors. He searched the desk for a key and couldn't find one. In the bedroom, he rummaged quickly through Adrio's things, keeping his eyes averted from the rumpled bed.

But he'd lost track of time. He heard footsteps tapping on the stairs, voices on the landing, and realized that the servants had returned. He frantically scanned the room for a way to escape or hide. He definitely did *not* want the servants to tell Adrio he'd been snooping around in here, so he dropped to the floor and rolled under the bed.

There he spent an agonizing twenty minutes, biting his arm against hysterical giggles, while Lirano and Roya (his own servants!) tidied Adrio's rooms. He stared at the pile of books beside the bed. Romantic adventure novels: *The Plum Chrysanthemum* and *A Sheaf of Swords*. Books about Chende religion and lore: *The Wind and the Mountains*; *Symbolism of the Chende Clans*. And, more surprisingly: *Castle in the Air: Being an Account of Air-Balloons*; *Report on the Death of Elvier Canto, Aeronaut*; *Discursions of the Nature of Air and Heat*.

"Say what you will about Lord Cay," muttered Roya, grunting a bit as she stooped to pick the books up off the floor, making Cay flinch, "he may be common-born, but he does keep his things tidy."

"Lord Cay's character is noble, even if his birth isn't," said Lirano.

"If you say so, I'm sure."

"I do say so," said Lirano. "His nature is honorable, which is why he makes no trouble for anyone."

"Except Lord Adrio," snickered Roya as they left the room.

Adrio courted Cay gently. He began with brief visits to Therescu and Sons, the tailor shop where Cay worked, bringing small, thoughtful gifts: oranges, or almonds, or a vial of rosemary-scented lotion for his hands. Cay liked him. He liked how deliberately chosen the gifts were: not so expensive as to make him feel beholden but a little more expensive than anything he'd have bought for himself.

He'd been approached by rich suitors before—suitors who assumed a tailor's apprentice would appreciate an offer to become a paid lover, suitors who were offended to learn they were wrong. The Heir of Lodola was by far the richest person who had ever displayed an interest in him. Cay knew it was unwise to encourage him, even the littlest bit, but he enjoyed the flattering attention and the gifts.

Once, in a rare misstep, Adrio brought his horse for Cay to meet. The animal was a tall, snake-necked red gelding named Sparrow. Though Adrio assured him Sparrow was a sweet-natured fellow, Cay refused to go near him. He'd been born and raised in a city of stairs, bridges, and narrow stone passages, so he knew nothing of horses. He disliked Sparrow's restless hooves and evil, flat-pupiled eyes. Adrio offered to teach him to ride. When Cay refused with horror, Sparrow never appeared again.

Then Adrio asked him to go on a dinner picnic after work. It was their first outing together. Adrio picked him up, not in his carriage, but in a dirty closed cart drawn by a small, non-intimidating pony. It was certainly not Lord Lodola's usual transport, and Cay had asked, "What on earth?" as he hoisted himself up into the cart's high seat.

"It's a surprise," Adrio said before clucking to the pony. The snow had melted—Valette's snow always melted in a few days, not like in Turla, where hard icy heaps would linger in shadowy corners well into spring. Frost glittered on the road, and the sunset painted the sky rosy pink.

"What is that smell?" Cay turned around in the seat and looked at the cart's closed box. Something was moving in there. "Is it pigs? Is this a pig-cart?"

"*Of course not,*" *said Adrio.* "*It's far too small.*"

He drove them to the lake, which was flat as a mirror in the gloaming. After removing the pony's bridle to let it graze, he opened the cart to reveal stacks of wooden crates. Four or five live ducks were packed into each crate, dirty and glassy-eyed from captivity. They had been quiet in the closed cart, but now, as Adrio carried the crates one-by-one to the lake shore, they began to murmur and flutter anxiously, sticking their heads through the bars and peering about.

"*Help me,*" *said Adrio.* "*Grab one.*"

"*No, thank you,*" *said Cay.* The crates were caked with guano and buzzing with flies, and besides, Adrio had removed his jacket and shirt and wore only his smallshirt despite the cold. His forearms were corded, and his biceps bulged while he hoisted the boxes. "*I'll just watch.*"

Once he had all ten crates lined up on the shore, Adrio stood up and stretched, arching his back. "*There,*" *he said.* "*Do you want to help me free them?*"

"*They'll get eaten by foxes,*" *said Cay.* "*They've never been free in their lives.*"

"*I know. I don't think they've even seen a lake before. Do you think captive ducks know how to swim?*" *He grinned, sparkling with delight, and held out a hand.* "*Come on!*"

Cay, entirely unable to resist his smile, jumped down and came through the frosty grass to help him open the crates. Forty-seven ducks, foolish with fear, emerged and clustered together on the bank, craning their bodies up to look out over the water. One brave soul ventured onto a rock and leaned over the water to dabble his bill, while the rest quacked, shook their feathers, and watched with apprehension.

Adrio gently pushed the brave one in. It shouted and clapped its wings on the water, splashing, then popped back up onto the rock, where it wagged its tail indignantly and shook droplets out of its dirty feathers.

Cay laughed. "*That is exactly what I would do if you pushed me into the water.*"

"*Do not tempt me, Master Olau.*"

"*I would murder you, Lord Lodola.*"

Adrio put his clothes back on, and he and Cay sat wrapped in blankets on the cart, eating their picnic and watching the ducks, *making bets on which one would swim first. Eventually, all forty-seven made their way onto the surface of the lake. They ruffled and bobbed in the water, ducking to bathe themselves, rearing up to flap their wings, all the while chattering among themselves. They looked ridiculous and happy.*

"This is a terrible idea," Cay said, popping hothouse grapes into his mouth. "What if they don't know how to find food? They'll be dead in a week."

"They would have been dead in a week anyway," said Adrio. "But now they're swimming. And we can feed them oats and the rest of the grapes. I brought extra."

Cay looked at him, so handsome in the twilight, as the inane babble of the ducks filled the air. "You're a romantic."

"Oh yes. I'm afraid so," said Adrio, and kissed him.

It was their first kiss. Adrio's hand on his cheek was cold, but his lips were warm.

After supper, Cay and Adrio went to a small gathering at the home of Fonsca Calareto, one of Adrio's bosom friends.

"Are you sure you still want me to come?" Cay had asked earlier.

"Of course." Adrio seemed mildly surprised by the question. "Why not?"

"Even now?"

"Nothing has changed. You are my husband and always will be; you must take your place in Lucenequan society."

Nothing has changed. From Cay's point of view, their pretense of a happy marriage had been ground to dust, leaving him wondering why he stayed. Tentatively, he suggested, "Would it be a scandal if I didn't?"

"That's hardly the point. People should wed whom they will without heeding small-minded gossip. Our marriage will make it easier for others to do the same."

"Ah." *Principle.* Of course. "Then I shall be ready in an hour, Husband, to display our happy marriage to the world."

Adrio responded only with a short nod.

They walked arm-in-arm the short distance to Fonsca Calareto's house. Fonsca was technically a commoner, and like Cay, he was subject to the occasional rude comment in Starlight Conversation: an alder in an oak forest, a lichen growing upon a castle wall, and so on. Unlike Cay, Fonsca had important connections as well as money. Noble society sought him out even as it condescended to him. Invitations to his little parties were highly prized.

This evening was informal. Fonsca would offer refreshments, a musical performance, and games. Probably he would offer no dancing, as he did not have a ballroom, and Cay secretly found music a bit boring unless he could dance to it. The food would be good, but the company would be chilly.

Cay dressed simply in black, his only jewelry was his wedding ring and small gold hoops in his ears. But his shirt was open at the throat, his waist emphasized by his wide black belt, and his face enhanced with a subtle touch of cosmetics. He needed no more finery to dazzle a room, and he knew it. Adrio's arm was solid and warm beneath his hand as they mounted the stairs toward Fonsca's door, but his profile was remote, and he was silent. Cay kept his chin up.

"Adrio." Fonsca gave Adrio a friendly shoulder slap. "Welcome! And Lord Cay."

Cay bowed. Unlike Ondrei, Fonsca had never been more than polite to Cay. Fonsca disapproved of him and made no secret of it. Cay had asked Adrio about it once, and Adrio had only smiled and said, "He thinks we married too hastily. Once he sees how happy we are together, he'll stop being such a fusspot."

Hah.

After the excellent supper and the boring music, the dice tables came out, and the conversation grew unexpectedly interesting. Lady Patra Jelola, a wealthy widow rumored to be Fonsca's current mistress, enthralled the gathering with the story of the mysterious man who was, at enormous risk to his own life, rescuing Chende prisoners from Muntegri and flying them over the mountains, right over the heads of the guards on the Road.

Cay choked on his wine.

Lady Patra told her story with gusto, appreciating the gasps and exclamations of her audience, and no one noticed Cay coughing into his handkerchief.

"My lady, is this true?"

"Amazing!"

"And so absolutely heroic," said Lady Patra, clasping her hands. She was an exquisite woman with the prized Lucenequan coloring, bronze skin and sun-streaked hair, and she glowed with excitement to be first to share this news. "Don't you think? They call him the Uncanny Aviator."

Someone asked, "But how does he fly?"

"In smoke-balloons," said Lady Patra. "Invisible ones. And the Muntegrise are absolutely seething, I can assure you."

Adrio was gazing at Lady Patra bright-eyed, his lips parted in a half-smile.

"Er," Cay ventured, "my lady, may I ask where you heard of this extraordinary person?"

"My source is quite credible," said Lady Patra, tossing her head. "I heard it from the Muntegrise envoy himself!"

"You spoke to the Muntegrise envoy?"

"Naturally not. But he was at the university questioning the scholars about whether it's possible. My sister's youngest boy is a student, and he heard all about it. He told her, and she told me."

"Certainly an unimpeachable source," Cay said.

Adrio shot Cay a glance: *shut up.* Cay raised his eyebrows at him.

"But surely it's not possible," said another young lady, Elia.

"Oh, I think it might be," said Adrio, startling Cay. "The Principle of Levity is a well-known scientific force. It causes things like smoke and steam to rise away from the earth. They fill a balloon with something imbued with the Principle of Levity, and up it goes."

Cay bit the inside of his cheek and averted his gaze.

An older gentleman exclaimed, "Quite right! I saw a demonstration of smoke-balloons some years ago. It was a big sack made of taffeta, I believe, and they heaped wet leaves upon a fire beneath it to make smoke. It rose up above the rooftops and drifted quite half a mile before it came down."

"Did it carry people?"

"Gods, no! Who would ride such a steed?"

"It would be a feat of astonishing courage," murmured Lady Patra.

Someone asked, "But how could they be made invisible?"

"Perhaps they are concealed, rather than invisible," said Fonsca. "If they fly only at night and are made from black silk or some other dark fabric, they might go unnoticed."

"Or perhaps they *are* invisible," said Adrio, genially. "Who knows what learned men might be capable of? If flight, why not invisibility? Lady Patra, did your nephew say how the professors responded to these questions?"

Lady Patra, regrettably, knew not. But the topic of the Uncanny Aviator and his bold deeds took up the rest of the evening. Cay said nothing more, but Adrio involved himself in the discussion, leading the group to wild speculation: perhaps the Aviator was rich, because black silk in such quantities would be expensive. Or perhaps the Aviator was a sailor or a pirate who understood the mysterious ways of the winds. Or perhaps the Aviator was a scholar from the university who understood science.

"But why should he do it?" wondered a gentleman. "Who would put his life at such risk for a few wretched Chende, who are now dirtying up the countryside and abusing our charity?"

"He must be a true nobleman," said Lady Elia, "who does it for the sheer love of adventure and danger."

The ladies liked this idea. They were even more delighted when Adrio said, "Is there any reason to believe the Aviator is not a lady? She snatches the unfortunate from the cruel Muntegrise because she is both fearless and kind—traits for which all Lucenequan noblewomen are famed."

The ladies laughed and preened. Cay caught Fonsca leveling a flat stare at Adrio. Cay glanced at his husband: Adrio was smiling with pure mischief, his eyes sparkling.

Adrio was still in a fine humor as they walked back home after the party. His delight at the ridiculous rumors of the Uncanny Aviator and his playful inflating of those rumors reminded Cay of the joyous Adrio he'd once known. How long it had been since he'd seen Adrio happy! He'd been so wrapped up in his blanket of misery he'd scarcely noticed Adrio's unhappiness.

He ventured, "An amusing evening."

"Hm."

"I shall enjoy telling Kell about the adventures of the Uncanny Aviator. I wonder if she knows Lady Patra's nephew?" Adrio did not reply, and Cay went on, "In all seriousness, though, I do keep hearing mention of these Chende refugees. I wonder how they evade the roadblocks without encountering the Chende tribes in the mountain passes. Have you heard anything?"

For several steps, Adrio said nothing. Then he said, "I am certainly not going to discuss such matters with you."

Greatly daring, Cay said, "Why not? I am not asking for any expression of affection from you, but may we not have a civil conversation about the events of the day?"

All good humor disappeared from Adrio's face, and he scowled ahead of him as he walked, his shoulders hunched. "You cannot convince me you give a damn about the fate of the Chende of Muntegri," growled Adrio.

"I do not believe we have ever spoken of the Chende of Muntegri in the whole of our acquaintance," Cay said a little stiffly.

"You don't speak of the Chende at all."

Cay did not reply.

Most Lucenequans did not particularly like the Chende. They decried Muntegri's brutality toward its Chende population, but that was because they didn't like the Muntegrise either, not because they were true champions of the Chende. Adrio was unusually curious and open-minded about people who were not like him. Perhaps during their courtship he had thought that Cay was too, but now he believed—Cay had allowed Adrio to believe—he despised the Chende as much as most Muntegrise did. The truth of the matter was more complicated than Cay knew how to explain. And it was probably too late for explanations anyway.

They walked in silence until they reached the red door of their house. "Well, Husband? Will you not complete my evening with a word from one of the great poets? I'm certain one of them would have an insult well-turned for just this occasion."

Adrio looked at him with an unreadable expression and said, "What sorrow, should the swan love the golden-headed duck."

CHAPTER FOUR

The next morning, after the breakfast things were cleared away, Cay brought his sketching supplies down to the dining room. He usually stayed in his room to draw, but (as he had explained to Lirano) heavy rain clouds had rolled in overnight, and his suite was a bit dark. Cay spread out his new rough paper and arranged his pens and pot of cheap purple ink on the dining room table, where the big windows let in as much light as possible, in spite of the gloom of the day.

No one could fail to see what he was doing: designing a new gown for Kell. Kell had no interest in a new gown, of course. But Cay enjoyed designing, and he rather liked his new idea for her. She was not tall, but a flowing skirt and a tailored waist would make her appear more so, and the high open collar would lengthen her neck. He thought a warm color would suit her hair, which, like their father's, was a medium brown. Amber, perhaps.

"I'm headed for Lodola tomorrow," said Adrio from the doorway.

"Oh?" Cay looked up from his drawing.

"Yes. I need to meet with my steward and see my mother. I'll be gone for about a week."

Valette in autumn was cool and rainy, but Lodola to the south would be warm still, with gentle salt-tasting breezes coming off the sea. And Hob Fierar and his threats could not reach him in Lodola. "May I come?"

"No," said Adrio. "You'll probably still be abed when I leave in the morning, so I'll bid you farewell now." Without waiting for an answer, he bowed and went up the stairs to his suite. After a moment, his voice reached Cay as he spoke to the servants.

It wasn't the first time Adrio had gone away for days or weeks at a time. But this time Cay would be alone with the threat of the Muntegrise envoy. Perhaps it was better so. But the loneliness of his life—a lifetime of wealth, luxury, celibacy, and his husband's disregard—seemed to stretch ahead of him.

"Lord Lodola is here," whispered Mara to Cay, passing behind his workbench at Therescu and Sons.

"Again?" Cay's tone was bored as he stitched tiny silver beads onto a velvet doublet. They had to be perfectly even.

"Yes, again." She giggled.

He tried to ignore the warm fizz of pleasure in his chest. "I'm busy."

"Get your ass up and go give the man a smile," she said. "Tollo wants to keep his business."

"There are things I will not do for Tollo." Cay carefully put his needle into its cushion and put the lid on the box of beads so they wouldn't spill.

Therescu and Sons was a high-end tailor shop. They sold custom-made clothing and accessories to a wealthy clientele. Tollo Therescu was one of the Sons. Mara was one of the tailors who designed and oversaw the creation of bespoke garments, and Cay was one of the small fleet of seamsters who brought their ideas to life with needle and scissors. Therescu also employed an armada of pieceworkers who did mending and sewing at home, which had been Cay's first job for Therescu. He had hopes of moving up to tailor someday.

"Well, if you must turn him down, send him to me," said Mara. "I'll take your place."

Cay bit down on the impulse to throttle her. His heart insisted that Adrio belonged only to him. But someone like Cay could only ever be temporary entertainment for the Heir of Lodola. Temporary entertainment was fine and highly enjoyable, but he'd be a fool to fall in love with the man. That could only lead to heartbreak.

He brushed thread fragments off his shirt and trousers, ran his hands through his hair, and wished he were wearing something more attractive. But that didn't matter. He went out through the curtain to the shop's public showroom.

It was busy on this winter afternoon. Not only was Lord Adrio there, as handsome a suitor as any impoverished seamster could dream of, but there was also a line of people picking up packages from Tollo at the counter, and a large man in the back alcove, standing on a small dais, being measured by another assistant, Cay's friend Illo.

Adrio spotted Cay and smiled, his dark eyes turning to crescents, and Cay's heartbeat fluttered. He seemed a bit out of place—too wealthy and well-dressed to visit a tailor's shop in person. His fashion sense was by no means ostentatious, but he (or his tailor) knew how to highlight his assets, preferring clean lines to draw attention to his height and leanness, his broad shoulders, his classic Lucenequan bronze skin and sun-streaked hair. Cay would very much have liked to run his fingers through that hair, smoothing it into place, tracing his fingers along Adrio's ears and the clean angle of his jawline.

Instead he said, "Good morning, my lord. How may I help you?"

"I don't want to interrupt your work," said Adrio. "But—with your master's permission—might I have a quick word?" He glanced around, noting they were being observed avidly. "Perhaps outside?"

Cay caught Tollo's nod. "Certainly, my lord. But only for a minute."

The street outside Therescu and Sons was little more than an alleyway in the busiest part of the shopping district of Valette, rendered narrower by piles of snow pushed to the sides and packed into dirty mounds of ice. Couriers ran to and fro, for this lane was a good shortcut from the center of town to the docks. The leatherworker across the way seemed to be doing a brisk business, and the bakery next door breathed the scent of hot bread into the air.

Cay crossed his arms against the chill, and concern wrinkled Adrio's brow. "You're cold," he said. "I didn't think." He immediately unclasped the brooch closure of his wool-lined cloak, which he made to put over Cay's shoulders. Cay stepped back.

"No, my lord. Thank you, my lord."

"No? Oh, I suppose not." Adrio smiled sheepishly and bundled the cloak under his arm rather than putting it back on.

"Now we are both cold, my lord."

"Like the sky to the lakes, and the lakes to the sky," said Adrio.

Cay blinked at him.

"Ah," said Adrio. "I was wondering if you might go for a drive with me this evening. When you are done with your work. The hills south of the city are beautiful in the snow, and I know of an inn by the lake where we might dine together. They are justly famed for their oysters, brought up fresh from the bay every day."

Cay looked down, letting his curls hide his face.

He'd been seeing a great deal of Adrio lately. They had walked the city together, talking and laughing. They'd held hands. Adrio had frequently ventured to kiss him, and Cay had been eager to accept those kisses and Adrio's caresses on his face, throat, and nape. He had begun to dream of Adrio at night, to miss him during the day.

And now this. This was clearly a step up in the possibility of intimacy. A long ride together in a dimly lit carriage, a meal for two at an inn, perhaps a private room upstairs . . . Adrio was planning for more than kisses.

Cay wanted him. He ached for him. If he was not careful, he would give his entire heart to this man. And so he must refuse.

"My lord."

"Yes?"

"I do not care for oysters. And I am an honest man."

"I believe they also serve lamb."

"An honest tailor, not a prostitute, my lord," Cay clarified. The smile fell from Adrio's face. "I am accustomed to earning my own money and buying my own dinner. My lord, I earn my money on my feet, not my knees."

Adrio was flushed. "I never thought—"

A commotion interrupted their conversation: a roar of outrage from inside the shop, a crash, a small scream. Cay turned in time to see the door fly open, and Illo staggered through, flinching away from the big man he'd been measuring, who, in his smallclothes, chased him into the snowy street with fists clenched.

"Illo!" Without a thought, Cay grabbed Illo by the hands and pushed him down the narrow alley, putting his body between his

fellow seamster and his attacker. He whirled to see Adrio blocking the man.

Cay squeezed Illo's trembling hand. "Did he hit you?"

Illo nodded.

"That incompetent idiot cut me!" roared the man, pointing past Adrio and Cay at Illo. He whirled to address Tollo in the doorway. "What kind of shambles of a shop is this, where a gentleman can be gashed by scissors while getting his clothes made?"

Tollo was apologizing and bowing. The man was demanding compensation and the immediate termination of Illo.

"An accident, Master Tollo!" cried Illo, whose mouth was already swollen from the customer's fist.

Illo had lived a highly irregular life before becoming a tailor: begging, thieving, and perhaps even worse. He wondered if Illo had cut the customer on purpose. Not that Cay minded. The man was a lout, and Illo needed this job.

The big man roared, "Unacceptable! He goes, or I will take my business to another tailor, and all of my friends will know Therescu and Sons is a butcher shop where you're likely to get stabbed."

"What a shame," said Adrio. His voice, while not loud, rang out through the street and could be heard by everyone from corner to corner. He stood tall, suddenly no longer Cay's diffident suitor but a man who bore eight hundred years of noble heritage lightly on his shoulders. "For if you do fire this employee, I will take my business elsewhere and tell my friends Therescu and Sons does not defend its workers from abuse."

A shocked silence fell, and everyone in the street turned to stare at Adrio, who added, "A shop that mistreats its employees will not do for me. Or my friends."

Cay gazed at him. He'd never in his life seen a rich man throw the weight of his privilege behind an ordinary worker in such a way. It seemed incredible.

"Mistreats its—" The big man's voice went high with outrage. "The brute cut me!"

Adrio lifted his head and stared down his nose at the man. "How loudly you cry at the prick of a pin. So a gull will cry, even as sailors throw fish guts into the sea."

This was apparently a shocking insult, for Cay heard a few gasps and Oooh's from the spectators. A laugh quickly stifled. The big man, barefoot and partly unclothed, went purple in the face and turned back into the shop.

He was blocked by Tollo. "If you have a problem with my employees, you will not lay hands upon them, but come to me, and I will discipline them appropriately. Please take your things and go." He looked at Illo, still standing with Cay, holding his hand. "Illo. I believe you have the beading on Lady Aspa's doublet to finish?"

It was Cay who was working on the beading, but Illo nodded and went into the shop, giving the big man wide berth. Tollo glanced at Cay, then turned to Adrio and said, "I assure you, my lord, I run a humane shop."

"I am glad to hear it, sir."

The two men bowed politely to one another, and then Tollo returned to the shop, and business resumed as usual now the spectacle was over.

Cay and Adrio faced one another in the street. Meeting his eyes, Cay was gripped by a wild euphoria. It was like flying, this swoop and flutter in his heart, and somehow it hurt too. Pain and astonishment and joy mixed, just at the sight of this man.

"Thank you," he said.

Adrio, his expression so haughty a moment ago, dropped his eyes and seemed almost bashful. "There's no honor to strike someone who dares not hit back. Nor for a rich man to assail a poorer man's income."

Cay nodded and did not tell him Illo quite likely cut the customer on purpose. Adrio might rethink his honorable stance.

"Well," Adrio said. He put his cloak back over his shoulders and fumbled with the clasp as though he was about to leave.

With a start, Cay remembered that, before the commotion, he had rejected Adrio.

Like an idiot.

"They serve lamb?" he blurted.

Adrio raised his eyes.

Cay dropped his chin a little and curved his lips. "You see, we do not have oysters in Turla, my lord, and I've never had one. They seem disagreeable. But I do like lamb."

A brilliant smile bloomed across Adrio's face. "You will have lamb, then," he said. "And if you choose, you might try an oyster from my plate and see if it suits. But only if you so choose."

"Thank you, Lord Lodola. That sounds lovely."

"So, what kind of lock is it?"

The night following Fonsca's music-party, Cay walked down to Therescu and Sons at closing time and invited all the staff to supper at the tavern around the corner. He bought his former colleagues a hearty meal of pigeon pie with fresh bread and as much wine as they could drink, and if they thought him a bit uppish, descending from his palace to treat them to tavern food, they were too hungry to say so. He kept Illo back after the rest of them had gone home, because Illo, at some point in his checkered past, had learned how to pick a lock.

"A regular lock?" guessed Cay.

Illo rolled his eyes. "Is it part of the cabinet, with the keyhole in the cabinet's door? Or is it a separate thing that hangs on the outside?"

"Oh," said Cay. "I see. It's hanging outside. There are metal loops attached to the wooden doors of the cabinet, and the lock is threaded through the loops to keep you from opening the doors."

"A padlock. Can you get at the metal loops? Or the hinges? Like to unscrew them?"

"No, all the hardware is inset into the doors of the cabinet. Nothing's on the outside except the metal loops, and the lock hangs from them."

"And is the keyhole on the bottom of the lock or the front?"

"The front. Here, I can draw it for you." He dipped his finger in wine and quickly drew the padlock on the polished wooden surface of the table: a curved shank set into an oval body, with a keyhole in the front. "This is bigger than the actual lock. It's quite small."

"Can you draw the keyhole?" Cay drew the keyhole: a circle with a rectangle extending beneath. "No notches or anything?"

"No."

"Can you see anything in the keyhole? Like a metal pin, right here?"

"No. It's just a hole."

"Easy-peasy," said Illo. "Small lock like that probably only has one ward. Bend a bit of metal wire like this—" he, too, drew in moisture on the table "—and then poke about in there. Feel through the wire, yes? You're trying to push the ward to one side. Once you find it, the whole thing will open up for you like a theater girl on market day."

Cay laughed. "It's easy? Really?"

"Sure." Illo drank his ale, studying Cay over the rim of his cup. "Clever fellow like you. I'm surprised you haven't learned lockpicking by now."

"I'm from a respectable family," said Cay. He frowned at the images now evaporating from the tabletop. "What if I can't do it? Will you come over some night and help me?"

"Maybe. Will you tell me why you're stealing from your rich husband's locked drawers?"

"No! I mean, I'm not." Cay wiped his hand over the wet diagrams he'd drawn on the table as if to erase the suggestion. "I already told you. We lost the key."

"Well, even easier than picking the lock would be breaking the cabinet open with a pry bar. Unless you don't want anyone to notice."

"It's an heirloom."

Illo sniffed. "You think he's sleeping around, do you? You're looking for evidence? Letters from his boyfriend?"

"No." Cay gave Illo his firmest stare. "Don't be silly. If you must know, I lost the key, and I don't want him to know. But Adrio loves me, and we're very happy. And it's been a while since I saw any of my old friends, so this seemed like a good excuse to have supper with you."

"Sure," said Illo again. He shook his head and drained his cup. "You never should have married him," he said, reminding Cay exactly why he hadn't seen Illo in so long. "He's not your kind."

"Why?" asked Cay flippantly. "Because he's a nobleman and I'm a potter's son?"

"No. Because he's a palm tree dropping coconuts upon the water."

"What in the deep hells is a coconut?"

"I don't know. It means he's honorable. He gives. People like you and me, we take."

At one time, Cay would have argued with this, but since he was asking for lockpicking lessons behind his husband's back, he didn't think he'd be convincing. He just said, "Do you mean that he's like the swan, and I'm like the duck?"

Illo laughed. "Exactly right, Cay. You're learning." He tipped his cup to show its empty bottom and raised his eyebrows, and Cay smiled weakly and signaled for another round of wine.

In spite of Adrio's prediction, Cay was awake at dawn when his husband left home.

He didn't go down to say farewell. In the gray light of morning, he sat at his window, looking down at the bustle in the stable yard below: the carriage, the horses, the servants loading Adrio's luggage. He rested his cheek on his folded arms and watched his husband, in a dark green cloak, misty rain beading on his hair, make ready to leave.

He wanted to go down to adjust Adrio's cloak over his shoulders and make sure he had something to eat on his journey. Wish him safe travels, promise to think of him every evening, and give him a kiss to remember while he was gone.

He opened his eyes from this fantasy to see Adrio's carriage pull away with a clatter and disappear around the corner.

Cay *would* miss him. Cay was stupid, stupid, stupidly in love with him. He cursed his soft, loyal heart.

What sorrow should a swan love a golden-headed duck.

He didn't know what it meant. He knew Adrio liked duck for dinner. He remembered the day during their courtship, when they'd freed the ducks in the lake. They'd driven out to the lake several times since to look at the ducks and try to pick out which ones were *their* ducks.

Had Adrio been thinking of their lakeside kiss when he'd made his comment about ducks and swans? Did he know how painful it was for Cay to remember his kiss, that evening in the pink sunset when he'd begun falling in love? Was that the point, to cause pain?

At one time, he'd have said Adrio was incapable of deliberate cruelty, but he no longer knew. Perhaps he'd never known the real Adrio at all. After all, Adrio didn't know the real Cay.

No. Cay's heart knew Adrio was a good man. No matter what happened, Cay simply could not stop believing that Adrio was good and worthy of goodness.

He just didn't love Cay anymore.

At breakfast, Lirano brought him a note: Hob Fierar, the envoy from Muntegri, requested a meeting with him.

"Please send him a response," said Cay. "I cannot see him today nor tomorrow; offer him a meeting the next day."

"What excuse should I give him, my lord?"

"Do not give him an excuse. Tell him I will see him the day after tomorrow." It wouldn't do to give Hob Fierar the impression Cay was cowed by him. "Also, please send a card around to Lord Noresposto. Ask him if I might call upon him soon."

"Yes, my lord."

"Thank you. I will be working in my suite today and would prefer not to be disturbed. Should the envoy from Muntegri visit, tell him I am not at home."

"Yes, my lord. Would you like me to bring tea to your rooms?"

"That would be lovely. Thank you. And . . . Lirano? Do you know of a tale about a swan falling in love with a duck?"

Lirano's face grew impassive. "Perhaps, my lord."

"Will you tell it to me?"

"I would rather not, my lord."

Cay smiled at him wryly. No, it wasn't a very kind thing to ask. No doubt the servants had taken sides between them, and Lirano must be professionally loyal to them both. "But if it is in a book or something, perhaps you could find it for me?"

Lirano continued to look dyspeptic. Cay sighed.

"Never mind. I'm certain it's unimportant. You may go."

After breakfast, he began work on the first part of his plan.

He spent the day drawing purple ink on cheap pulpy paper, but this was no dress design. He'd gathered some books out of the library, including works on mathematics, history, philosophy, and several tales of adventures at sea. (With luck Lirano would think he was searching for the swan story and not look too closely.) He filled pages with sketches, plans, and notations, disguising his hand by writing with his left.

As a child, Kell had gone through a phase of writing him mysterious letters. Their father could not read them; their mother could have but indulged their games and did not. Kell could write with either her left or right hand or backward. She made up codes and rebuses. Five years her senior, Cay had been hard-pressed to keep up. But he could compose a convincing mysterious letter.

By late afternoon he was hungry, tired, his eyes dry from a day of working with pen and paper. He had a sheaf of documents that would have done ten-year-old Kell proud.

He stacked his papers, tapped them to even the edges, and folded them into a thick booklet. Then he unfolded the booklet and folded it again another way and then again another, working the creases back and forth until the cheap fibers began to fray. He swished the papers in the dust under his bed and frowned. It was too clean under there.

Cay leaned out his window, glanced around to make sure he was unobserved, kicked off his shoes, and climbed onto the windowsill. He scaled the outside of the building, which was quite easy. The exterior of Rossoulia was not ornate, but it featured symmetrical pilasters and lintels, which provided ample handholds and footholds. On the roof, Cay rubbed the papers on the roof slates, collecting city dirt and grime. Back in his room, he spilled some cold tea on his worktable and mopped it up with the papers. Finally, he folded them tightly, set an edge on fire with a candle, and then batted out the flames.

When he was done, the papers were stained and tattered and partially crumbling to ash, torn along the creases in some places, the ink smeared in others. When unfolded, certain portions were tantalizingly legible, others obliterated.

It looked quite all right, he thought. He folded the packet up tightly again and hid it in his chest underneath his clothes.

Finally, he took out drawings of the new dress design for Kell and left them about the room, in case the servants wondered what he'd been doing, and went down for a meal.

CHAPTER FIVE

The next day, Cay went to Lord Ondrei Noresposto's villa for tea.

This part of Cay's plan was unpleasant, and he felt slightly sick as he presented himself at Ondrei's door. Ondrei had been kind to him from the moment they'd met. To entangle him in this business was a betrayal. Cay knew it.

But if he was going to give false information to the envoy, he needed a plausible source. During their awful last meeting, Fierar had seized upon Ondrei as his informant, and however he wracked his brain, he could not think of a more tenable solution. So now he was deliberately drawing the attention of the enemy to his friend, with planning and forethought, and it was an ugly and mean thing to do.

But it wouldn't be the first time Cay had done something ugly in desperation, and if anyone was safe from the long reach of the Grup, it was Ondrei. His friend was insulated by money, birth, and power. Surely, this sordid business could not touch him. He would be fine.

Surely, he would be fine.

"Hello, darling!" Ondrei welcomed him to a spread of food and drink that would have put the prince's ball to shame. "I was so pleased to receive your note. Your trees are full of peaches, and your dovecotes producing eggs, are they not?"

"Indeed they are." Cay smiled at him. "I'm not here to ask for help, only to enjoy your company."

"I'm glad of it. You may always call upon me for any reason at all."

Ondrei was the same as ever: large, hearty, perhaps a little dim; a loud and flirtatious exterior covering a warm and generous heart. He plied Cay with food and drink, regaled him with the latest gossip, and consulted him about the current fashions. Ondrei loathed the current style for ruffled flounces on both gowns and shirt fronts and refused to wear them; Cay argued that, deployed judiciously, they enhanced the wearer's figure. They quarreled genially over their liver paste on toast, cheese, fruit, and cake.

"And, of course, balloon embroidery is going to be very hot this winter," said Ondrei. "I hear the tailors and modistes are working their fingers off to add balloons and other Uncanny Aviator touches."

"Really? And what does balloon embroidery look like?"

"Circles."

Cay laughed. "Well, I can certainly sew a circle. Perhaps I will join this fad and stitch circles on my lapels. I shall be all the rage."

"You make the rage," said Ondrei. "Whatever you do, society will eagerly follow."

"Perhaps, since the Uncanny Aviator is rescuing Chende, I will incorporate Chende designs."

"I've no notion what Chende designs could be."

"Patterns. Rather angular. Lucenequans like vines and leaves and nature motifs, and Muntegrise tend to embellish with lace or gems rather than embroidery. Chende do patterns of straight lines to make squares and stars. Triangles, sometimes."

"I had no idea," said Ondrei. "How do you know?"

"Oh . . . well, you know, more Chende live in Turla than in Valette. I mean, they used to, before the Grup." Cay decided it was time to change the subject. "Ondrei, perhaps you could help me with something."

"You know I am at your service, darling." Ondrei set down his plate and looked attentively at Cay.

Cay took a deep breath. "I don't ask you to betray Adrio's confidence. I know you are his loyal friend, and I would never ask you to tell me anything he asked you not to. But—" Cay cleared his throat. "But things are rather tense between us, you know, and I don't—I don't know why. I've never known why. And Winter Solstice is not so far away. We had only known each other a little for the last one, so we did not exchange gifts. But this year, I wanted to be sure of getting him something for our first Solstice together. But now, right now, it's very. Difficult." He closed his eyes and pressed a hand to his forehead. "Forgive me, Ondrei. I'm babbling."

"It's all right, Cay," said Ondrei, his voice gentle.

Cay took another deep breath and tried again. "I love Adrio. And I would like to buy him a suitable gift to make him understand I still . . . my feelings . . ." Gods, just speaking of this made a lump form in his throat. He swallowed. "But it's difficult to imagine what I could get him. It seems nothing I say makes any difference. And I do not ask you to share his confidences, but I wonder if you have any ideas."

Ondrei said nothing. Cay kept his eyes downcast, waiting.

He hadn't intended to ask about this. But last night, after all the servants were abed, he'd silently climbed the stairs and let himself into Adrio's rooms. Lighting a lamp, he'd spent two hours on his knees in front of Adrio's closed cabinet, probing at the lock with a bit of bent wire. He'd picked away at it until his fingers ached, and the little padlock remained firmly closed. Either Illo's instructions—*easy-peasy*—were hopelessly optimistic, or Cay's fingers just did not have the knack. He was mightily tempted by Illo's second suggestion—to just smash the cabinet open—but of course, he could not possibly explain the wreckage. He'd surrendered and gone back to bed eventually, but he ached with loss. The silence of his room, the place where he slept and bathed, the scent of him . . .

And Ondrei knew. Cay looked up at Ondrei through his eyelashes, and it was plain that Ondrei *knew* and would not say.

"I would very much like to be as good a friend to you as I am to Adrio," said Ondrei after a pause, "and offer you all the assistance I can. But I am constrained by my honor from giving you any help in this matter. I am heartily sorry for it, Cay, but you must ask him, not me."

Cay nodded.

"For what it's worth, I think he's being a donkey. I have argued on your behalf. And, further, I can assure you of this: although I cannot tell you his current errand, I can promise it has nothing at all to do with his feelings for you."

"Current errand? Do you mean his trip to Lodola?"

Ondrei drew a breath.

Cay opened his eyes wide. Ondrei's face wore a stricken expression.

"He didn't go to Lodola," Cay realized. "Oh. Oh." Cay pressed the heels of his hands over his eye sockets hard enough to make stars dance in the darkness behind his eyelids. "Oh, the liar. I am going to *murder him.*"

Ondrei made a distressed sound. "I have a foolish flapping mouth. Forget I said anything, won't you? Cay. Cay, don't cry."

"I'm not." Cay removed his hands and blinked the tears out of his eyes. "I'm not crying over him. Damn him. Who does he—"

Ondrei grimaced with regret. "No. No, I'm not asking you to tell me, I just— *Augh!*"

Ondrei managed a smile. "Sometimes you are very Muntegrise, darling. In Lucenequa we don't say *augh*. We say, 'Oh dear, how terribly awkward.'"

Cay sniffed and wordlessly agreed to joke, to lighten the conversation. "How like a golden stag falling into a ravine and breaking its neck."

Ondrei offered his handkerchief. "Precisely. You'll be a master of Starlight Conversation yet."

Cay took great care with his appearance for his meeting with Hob Fierar. He spent an hour touching up his hair. Enhancing his eyelids with subtle hints of makeup, he smiled a little bitterly at his reflection. He had no desire to seduce the envoy (in spite of the stupid insinuations of his stupid husband), but looking good was never a bad idea.

"What are you doing?"

Cay was in his third-floor suite, a set of rooms which at that time he almost never used, black-fingered and stinking as he massaged goo into his hair. He whirled at the voice. Adrio came into the room, nose wrinkled.

"You're home!"

Adrio had been gone for several days on some business; Cay hadn't expected him to return until tomorrow. He looked handsome and wind-flushed, slapping his riding gloves against one lean thigh. Still in his riding clothes, he'd obviously come straight to Cay upon his arrival.

"You stink like mouse piss and old onions."

"Oh!" Cay's welcoming smile vanished; he grabbed his discarded shirt and threw it over his head. "Go away! I'm disgusting!"

"You really are." Grinning, Adrio touched an exploring finger to a dribble of dye running down the side of Cay's neck, and Cay shivered at his touch. "Husband, is this dye?"

"Husband, you aren't supposed to see this."

"You dye your hair?"

Flushing, Cay said, "Obviously."

"Why?"

No, no, no. Cay's heart quickened with fear. This was bad. What a foolish deception. He should have known he would be caught out, eventually. Unable to come up with a good explanation, he resorted to distraction. Pretending embarrassment, he said, "Because I am extremely vain, and I want you to think I'm pretty." He peeked at him from under his shirt. "And I am not pretty at the moment, so go away."

"No." Adrio took a towel and gently blotted smudges of foul-smelling dye from Cay's neck and shoulders. "What a fox's song you sing. You'd be the most beautiful man in Valette if it all fell out."

"Ah, no. You're the most beautiful man in Valette. I'm only crafty. I've spellbound you with my crafty ways."

Cay was teasing, but Adrio's eyes had gone serious. He said, very softly, "Have I dishonored you, Cay, that you would dishonor me, and our marriage, with secrets? Only tell me, and I will set it right, for I would have no falsehoods between us. Even in so inconsequential a matter as the color of your hair."

Damn. Quelling his impatience, Cay smiled at him as prettily as he knew how. "How dare you call my hair inconsequential."

Adrio was not diverted. "You once told me you have your mother's hair. You said you and Kell don't look alike because she takes after your father and you take after your mother."

What a stupid thing to say. He'd need some embarrassing confession, some painful childhood secret, to make Adrio comfort him instead of picking at his lies, and soon. But at the moment he was too flustered to think. He changed tack.

"Perhaps someday I will tire of being so very, very obviously a black-haired Muntegrise among you golden Lucenequans, but not just yet. It is only pride, love. Don't fret. Now go." He pushed Adrio a little with his fingertips. "Go and relax for a quarter of an hour. Let me enhance myself, and I'll see you when I'm done."

"I'll go," agreed Adrio. But he leaned closer and brushed his lips against Cay's, a soft kiss, a promise of more. "But attend: there's no secret you could tell me that would make me love you less. Do you hear me, Husband?"

Cay smiled weakly. "Yes, Husband."

"And, did I have a secret, I would want to be able to trust your love to remain as true."

Cay could not quite meet his eyes. "Adrio, the dye will eat into my head if I don't wash it out soon. I will welcome you home properly, I vow, once I've washed up, but now you must save your sweet words and go away."

When Hob Fierar arrived, Cay was dressed in soft dark clothes of his own design. The perfect tailoring of his deceptively simple suit emphasized his waist and shoulders. He wore no adornment but his wedding ring.

"Lord Cay." The envoy bowed. "I hope you have something for me."

"Not here," said Cay. Rain drummed on the windows, so he threw a cloak around his shoulders before stepping outside, closing the door behind them. "Is there some private place we might talk?"

"We can imitate your lord husband and take a reserved room at a tavern," suggested Fierar. "He does not seem to be in Valette right now. Where has he gone?"

"Not *here*," Cay repeated.

He covered his head with the hood of his cloak and walked through rainy streets, down the hill toward the water, to a small, respectable inn near the docks, frequented by fishermen and stevedores. He went in first, asked for a private room, and hung up his cloak by the smoking fire while he waited for Fierar to join him.

The envoy came in, shedding his dripping hat. "Now, Lord Cay. Enough stalling."

"I have no desire to stall," said Cay shortly, "only to be private. My lord's servants have big ears." He took from his pocket the stained, half-burned packet of papers he'd prepared, but before he handed them over, he said, "Envoy Fierar. Attend to me, please. My husband is entirely innocent of all of this. What I learned, I learned from someone else."

Fierar smiled. "If you are honest with me, there is no need to fear. Where did you say Lord Adrio had gone?"

"To Lodola. My discovery was made yesterday, after he left."

"Go on."

Here it was, the moment he betrayed his friend.

"I found these notes when I visited Lord Ondrei Noresposto for tea. He was burning them in his fireplace when I entered the room. He'd intended to drop it into the fire, but it fell on the hearth and went out; when he left the room for a moment, I snatched it up and put it in my pocket."

"What is in those papers?"

"See for yourself." Cay handed them over.

Fierar carefully unfolded the stained, torn, half-burned packet of papers and spread them out on the table.

There, in cheap purple ink, were drawings and plans. Drawings of ships, baskets, and smoke-balloons rigged with sails and rudders. Drawings of cannons and buckets of hot oil. Graphs and charts marked with mysterious numbers and symbols. Around these images were notes in shaky, messy handwriting: descriptions of different weights of silk, descriptions of sewing and weaving techniques, speculation on the best kind of smoke to produce levity (*Straw? Tobacco? Dampened sackcloth? More experimentation needed*) and dozens of mathematical equations. The papers were illustrated with arrows and numbers and notes: *Air flow*, *Rate of levitational force*, and *Carrying capacity*. All of it was dirty, smeared, the ink dissolved in places, the paper itself charred in others. Illegible, but suggestive.

Hob Fierar studied every page silently, bending close to try to read the inscriptions. After a long silent while, he wheeled to look at Cay, who was forced to smother his smile of pride.

"Are you telling me," said Fierar slowly, "Lord Noresposto is the one who flies Chende workers over the mountains into Lucenequa?"

"Certainly not. I am telling you Lord Noresposto had these papers in his possession."

"And you claim they just fell before your eyes yesterday? The very answer to the question I asked you?"

Cay shrugged. "I was fortunate."

"Indeed." Fierar smirked. No doubt he assumed Cay had stolen or blackmailed the papers from Ondrei. There was a Lucenequan saying: *The scorpion believes the butterfly will sting.* Cay said nothing.

"These equations," murmured Fierar, tracing a forefinger over the crumpled pages. "Do they say how to make the smoke-balloons? How to navigate them?"

"I cannot understand them," said Cay with regret. "I have no idea what they say."

Fierar was talking to himself more than to Cay. "This—this diagram here, with the compass. Does it show how the balloons can be steered against the wind? Because in summer, the prevailing winds are almost always from the southwest. Balloons would be carried easily north, not south. But if one could steer them, to go where one would . . ."

Thrilled that Fierar was following the clues he had put in the papers, Cay said, "I've no idea. But sailing ships can sail against the wind, surely?"

"Indeed . . . And these dots . . . Is this a constellation? A star map?"

"Mm?" Cay looked at what Fierar was pointing at. The dots were almost surely droplets of tea. "Why, you could be right."

"Ondrei of Noresposto," mused Fierar. "Surely the man can't be as much of a fool as he pretends. It must be a ruse. He poses as an ineffectual fop so that no one suspects him of being the so-called Uncanny Aviator."

Cay remained silent, horrified at the direction of Fierar's thoughts. Ondrei, living an elaborate double life, concealing some secret identity? It beggared the imagination.

But if Hob Fierar's attention was on Ondrei, it wasn't on Adrio. Or the *real* deliverer of the Muntegrise Chende.

Hob Fierar straightened after a while and carefully refolded the pages. "I must show these to the natural philosophers at the University of Turla. I have tried speaking to the scholars at the university here in Valette, and they were deliberately obstructive. I could not even get them to admit it was possible. But this . . . this shows it is possible."

"You are returning to Turla, then?" asked Cay, as neutrally as he could.

"I dare entrust these to no other messenger." He put the pages in the interior pocket of his jacket. "But I will be back, Lord Cay, and when I return, I expect more."

"More?"

"More. Lord Noresposto is either the Aviator or knows who he is. Which? Where does the Aviator keep the smoke-balloons? From whence does he launch? Where in Turla does he land them, and how does he do so unnoticed? Is there only one balloon or a fleet of them? An armada? I must know more, Lord Cay."

"I found this only by purest chance," said Cay.

"Of course," drawled Fierar.

"No, truly. I am not Lord Noresposto's confidant—"

"Then become his confidant," snarled Fierar. "Become his lover."

"Sir, everyone knows Lord Noresposto does not have lovers."

"Then drug him. Spy on him, blackmail him. Do what you must, Lord Cay, and find me answers." He tapped his breast with his hand, patting the papers in his pocket. "Do it. If the snows hold off, I'll be back in a month. Give me answers, Lord Cay, or I shall use what I know, and all of Valette will know what Lord Lodola's pretty husband really is."

Fierar turned on his heel and headed for the door.

Cay could not let him walk away on that note. The man was Grup. The violence of the coup was still in Cay's mind: the searches, the executions, the shots fired into crowds.

"One more thing, sir," said Cay.

Fierar paused. Perhaps the formality of Cay's tone caught his attention, or the way Cay stood.

"You have repeatedly made threats against Adrio Santauro, Heir of Lodola. Understand me. If you touch him, I will touch you. If you harm his reputation, I will destroy yours. If you damage his property, I will burn your home. And if you hurt him, I will kill you."

"Lord Cay!" Fierar raised his eyebrows and fluttered his hands in a mockery of fear.

"If you know my past, you know not to make an enemy of me," added Cay.

Fierar sneered and left without a word.

Cay's knees were trembling when he left the inn. His head floated with a strange combination of relief and elation and terror.

He'd done it. He'd fooled Hob Fierar. And better—better than he'd hoped for—he'd sent Hob Fierar away. The envoy was leaving Valette, leaving Lucenequa, and going back to his masters in Turla. He'd cast absurd suspicion upon a friend, he'd distracted attention from his husband, and he'd made himself safe.

For now.

Cay didn't want to go home, so he walked toward the university. Perhaps he would catch Kell between classes, buy her food, tease her about her social life, and ask her to try to explain fluxions to him again. And if she was not available, he could climb up to her dorm room and wait. Or he might walk around the old stone streets of the university quarter, look up at the ancient towers, and pretend he was a poor student, consumed with worries about an exam, a paper, or a boyfriend.

Rain pattered on his shoulders and back as he walked, soaking into the wool of his cloak. It was a warm misty rain, not unpleasant on his cheeks, and the wind from the southwest smelled of salt and the sea. A Lucenequan autumn rain, nourishing the green Lucenequan vineyards and orchards, filling the broad wandering Lucenequan rivers.

In Muntegri the rain was sparser and icier. It fell harder; some autumns, it did not rain at all. Muntegri's fields were dry and full of stones and frost. Muntegrise ate potatoes and turnips, cabbages and oats, mutton and goat cheese. If they had money, they bought fruit, grain, and pork from Lucenequan traders. They must be hungry in Turla in the years since the roadblock had gone up. Or maybe someone was smuggling foodstuffs over the mountains, as well as refugees. Maybe the powerful were eating Lucenequan ham while the ordinary people grew thin.

In the mountains between Lucenequa and Muntegri, this gentle rain would be snow. This breeze was warm and wet; snow would fall on the Road and then melt. A rider on a good horse could take the Road from Lucenequa to Muntegri, through the mountains, in a snow like that.

But if the winds shifted to come from the north and autumn turned early to winter, the rain would turn to ice, and the snow would come down hard, blocking the Road more surely than any Grup patrol. Then nothing would pass between the two countries, not unless someone had indeed mastered the Principle of Levity.

If the wind blew right, Hob Fierar would be trapped in Muntegri until snowmelt. The Chende would be trapped in their Muntegrise camps, with no possible rescue, unless they truly could fly.

But Cay would be safe until spring.

CHAPTER SIX

Several nights later, Cay was awakened by a clatter of hoofbeats and a hubbub outside. Voices floated up the stairs. He rolled out of bed, pulled on his robe, and peered down from his window. Below, Lirano had thrown open the front door and was on the porch with a lantern, and the light was shining off Adrio's coach, gleaming with rain. Adrio, riding Sparrow, came up behind.

Cay's heart thumped at the sight of him—the graceful power of his body as he swung down from the saddle. He was muddy and wet, and his long hair was coming out of its queue in rattails.

Cay imagined a different homecoming: he would wrap Adrio in a warm blanket, would dry his hair in front of a fire, kiss him, ask after his hurts, and make him welcome. He did not move. Adrio handed the horse to a groom and then turned to help a slender person wrapped in a distinctive shawl alight from the carriage. Flickering light illuminated the lines and shapes woven into the shawl.

Oh. How interesting.

Cay pulled on trousers and tied the belt of his robe about his waist. He padded out to the landing and stood on the stairs, watching the commotion in the foyer. Adrio, his clothes and boots caked with dirt, shrugged off his cloak into the arms of a footman. He looked cold and exhausted, his lips thin as he pushed his straggling, wet hair out of his eyes.

Lirano was quietly barking orders—mulled wine and food for my lord; hot water for my lord; stir the fire in my lord's bedroom; put a warming pan in my lord's bed. And—Lirano looked questioningly at the small figure standing silently in Adrio's shadow.

"This is Osan Farkas," said Adrio, gently drawing her forward. It was a woman, probably in her thirties. She continued to clutch her shawl around her head. "She is a new member of the staff. You've probably all heard of refugees coming out of Muntegri. She is one, and I've offered her a job. Lirano, please make sure she has clothes and shoes and a place to sleep. We can discuss her duties in the morning."

"Yes, my lord."

Adrio swept his eyes over the other servants. "Mistress Farkas is very welcome here," he added. "If anyone is unhappy about this, you will not trouble her with your concerns but bring them to Lirano, who will bring them to me. *Not* to Lord Cay. Do you all understand?"

They nodded. Cay cracked his knuckles. It was his fault Adrio thought he wouldn't welcome this servant, but he still didn't like it.

He glided down the stairs on bare feet. Adrio caught sight of him. His face, already drawn with weariness, tightened.

Cay pressed a kiss to Adrio's unshaven cheek. He smelled like horse and old sweat. "Welcome home, my lord," he said, in his sweetest tone. Then he turned to the woman. "Mistress Farkas? I'm Lord Cay. May I take your beautiful shawl and hang it to dry?"

She hesitated, her dark eyes anxious.

"It's all right," he whispered.

She ducked her head and removed the ohahi, handing the woolen garment, intricately woven in geometric shapes, to Cay. Her thick plait of hair, now revealed, was streaky purple and lavender.

"Thank you," said Cay. "Will you tell me your clan? You don't have to, but if you like, I can find out if you have kin here in Valette."

"Thank you, Lord," she said, her voice very low and quiet. "I'm Ibai. And . . . Ibai is in blood-feud with Kordhal, so . . ."

Cay nodded. "That sounds serious."

"If the Wind blows right, I will not meet any of the Kordhal."

"I see. Thank you, I will keep it in mind." Cay nodded dismissal to Lirano.

"Come, mistress." Lirano jerked his chin at the other servants to send them to their tasks. "There's a fire in the kitchen and hot soup on the stove."

Cay turned to see Adrio staring at him with an unreadable expression. Cay quirked an eyebrow at him and said, "You're dripping mud on the floor, Husband. Take yourself off to your bath before you catch your death."

Adrio gave a polite bow—possibly sarcastically polite—and went up to his suite.

Back in his rooms, Cay listened to the silence.

It was after midnight, and all in the house were abed. Outside, the city was dark and quiet but for the thrumming of the rain. Mandru curled into a bony oval at the foot of the bed. He was not sleeping; his slitted eyes were on the window, and he occasionally twitched his crooked tail-stump.

Cay could not sleep either. Adrio was home, and Cay wanted him. He wanted to tell him about his triumph, however double-edged, against Hob Fierar. He wanted to ask him so many questions. He just wanted his company.

Surely Adrio was asleep. And even if he were awake, he would not welcome Cay. No matter how lonely Cay was for him.

Cay moved about his suite restlessly and then went out to the landing, planning to go downstairs and find a suitably dull book in the library. But instead of heading down the stairs, he went up to the fourth floor. Adrio's floor. Light shone under the door.

Without examining the impulse, Cay let himself into Adrio's suite.

Adrio glanced over as Cay entered the bedroom. He was abed but not asleep, stretched out on top of the coverlet in nothing but his dressing gown. The thin cloth lay loosely rumpled across his body. He cradled a cup in the center of his chest.

Cay sat at the foot of the bed, pulling his bare feet up and tucking his robe around his toes. The bed was big; there was plenty of room between them. But they were together in one bed again for the first time in months.

"Cay." Adrio's voice was low, a little rough. "I'm tired."

Cay leaned back against the bed's high wooden footboard. "So am I."

Adrio sighed and sipped his drink.

The house was still around them—it was late, quiet, and they were alone together. The bedclothes were soft, velvety, and warm, and Adrio smelled of wine, rosemary soap, and clean skin. His lips were soft, surrounded by stubble, and dark shadows of fatigue hung around his eyes.

Sometimes, Cay knew, Adrio could not sleep. Some nights, when he was very tired or stressed, anxious and melancholy thoughts cycled through his mind and he would lie awake. He would drink to find relaxation, with only middling success. Vigorous lovemaking worked better, a remedy Cay had been happy to provide, once.

Oh, but what a fool he was. How he ached with desire for his husband. He met Adrio's gaze, wondering if he were thinking the same thing—but Adrio turned away toward the rain-streaked window.

"Where did you find the Chende woman?" asked Cay, after a while.

"Begging. I brought her here on impulse. Thank you for being kind to her."

"I am often kind," said Cay. "Why wouldn't I be? Because all Muntegrise hate the Chende? Or is it because I am by nature petty and mean and love discord more than peace?"

"Ah." Adrio closed his eyes. "You found the poem."

"Yes."

He'd come across it in *The Best-Loved Works of the Great Cinna*, a two-hundred-year-old book every Lucenequan child read in school and at home. Cinna's poems and fables were full of animals, plants, and interesting legendary creatures, charming enough to appeal to children. They were apparently admired for their accurate portrayal of the natural world, and they all contained little moral lessons, suitable for impressing good principles upon young minds. Cay had not read many of Cinna's works because he found the high-minded tone a bit cloying, but every Lucenequan knew them by heart.

The poem read:

See the swans, how they cleave to their loves,
And should one die untimely, a swan in solitude speechless mourns.
Meantimes in that same pond the golden-headed drake
Creepeth from his nuptial bed to visit one mistress and another.
His wife knows well her husband's journeys,
And slatternly she receives the attentions of suitors.
When her heart grows angry she lays her eggs in the nests of her rivals,
For golden-headed ducks love pain and anger, and sowing discord
More than they love peace.
And should a swan love a golden-headed duck,
What sorrow!

"When you said that to me, I thought you were thinking of the time we freed the ducks in Lake Paluda. Do you remember?"

"I remember."

"I'm annoyed." Cay rested his chin on his folded arms. "Because it was a good memory, and you've spoiled it for me. And also because I am not the fucking duck. If anyone is the swan in this relationship, it's me."

Adrio closed his eyes. He rubbed his fingertips over his forehead as if trying to smooth away the deepening crease between his eyebrows. For a moment, his mouth twisted as if in pain. He whispered, "I know."

"You—" Cay glared at his husband. "You know?"

"It was cruel." Adrio's voice was husky from the alcohol. "You're the swan, and I'm the one who was deliberately cruel. That is who *I* am, not you."

"Adrio," breathed Cay, astonished. "How drunk are you?"

Adrio sat up suddenly, his eyes snapping open. "Do you remember when you mocked me? When you mocked me for my pretended honor?"

It had been their first real argument.

They were walking home through the dark streets of Valette from Fonsca's house, where they'd attended a party. The spring night was beautiful, scented with orange blossoms, and Cay loved walking with Adrio. In a teasing mood, he complained about Fonsca's dislike for him.

"He'll come around. Once he is convinced we love each other, he will be your friend as well as mine. It would be dishonorable not to."

"And Fonsca is honorable?"

"Oh, very." Adrio laughed, and Cay nudged him.

"What is amusing, Husband?"

"I am remembering how we met, Fonsca and I."

"How?"

"We fought a duel."

"Be serious."

"I am quite serious. Shall I tell you the story?"

Cay did not remember all the details of the convoluted tale of teenage misbehavior that followed. It involved a night of roistering, a misplaced pair of gloves, a hasty accusation of theft followed by a challenge to a duel of honor.

"But I was in a bit of a delicate position," he went on. "Naturally, I couldn't win the duel."

"You couldn't?"

"Absolutely not. In the morning I found my gloves, so I knew I was in the wrong. Winning the duel would assert my rightness, which would clearly be dishonorable."

"I see," said Cay, although he didn't. "Why not simply call it off? Would an apology have been dishonorable too?"

"No, that would have been appropriate. But I was sixteen and wanted to fight." Adrio grinned. "So we met, and we fought until I'd made it clear I was at least his equal, and then I threw away my sword

and declared that Fonsca's skill had proved my allegations about the gloves false, and then I apologized. And then he might in honor have run me through, but instead, he scarred me, here." He pulled back his hair.

"He cut you?" Cay leaned in close to look at the small white scar near Adrio's left ear.

"Mm-hmm. Then we bowed to each other, and he loaned me his handkerchief to mop up the blood. We've been friends ever since."

They walked on in silence, turning a corner. The red door of Rossoulia came into view. Cay snorted. "Adrio. What possible good could come of either of you being injured or killed over a pair of missing gloves?"

"Ah, it's a way of settling disputes without involving authorities or courts."

"So the winner is always right, and the loser wrong? How is it fair?"

"It isn't about winning. Indeed, I didn't win. It's a test in which both parties might emerge with honor intact."

"Or one dead. What if he had tripped and knocked himself on the head? Would the world have said you were in the right, although the gloves were in your pocket?"

Adrio shook his head, smiling indulgently. "Cay. Even at sixteen, I was too much a man of honor to permit that. Is there no dueling in Muntegri?"

"Perhaps among the nobles. Tradesmen are too busy trying to earn their bread to engage in such games."

"I suppose. Well, of course it's contingent upon the circumstances. Fonsca and I had both trained in swordplay, so it was a fair match. Had one of us been lacking, we would have found a different arena: wrestling, or marksmanship, or Starlight Conversation. It is a point of honor to find some equitable way to meet."

"Unless you just want to win."

"It's not about winning," repeated Adrio, this time with a note of frustration.

Cay shook his head. "So losers always say."

His tone was light as he said this—they'd both been in a happy mood all evening. But Adrio fell silent and said nothing.

Nothing, until they were home, in their suite, undressing for bed. Cay sat at his mirror, removing his cosmetics, while Adrio sat on the bed, unlacing the cuffs of his shirt.

"You're wrong," said Adrio suddenly. "I'll admit the cause of the duel was ridiculous—two boys fighting over a pair of gloves—but the ritual of the duel reveals true character. In the space of one duel, I recognized Fonsca's integrity, his uprightness. And he recognized mine. It allowed us to resolve the difference in a way that satisfied both of our senses of what is right and wrong, and neither seriously hurt. Do you not find it admirable?"

"I suppose. As far as it goes," said Cay, studying him in the mirror. "But in a real fight, one does whatever one must to survive."

"It wasn't a fight. It was a duel. An affair of honor."

"And honor is a pastime of the rich. It only makes sense to a person who's never faced real hardship."

"No, you have it backward. Honor is what remains to you when everything else has been torn away."

Cay smiled—or perhaps it had been more of a sneer. "So says a man who has never had more than his trousers torn away in his life."

Adrio's face flushed with offense. "You assert honor only means something to me because I have not known hardship? And honor is irrelevant to you because you have? Do I understand you, Husband?"

"Essentially." Cay turned to face him. "Surely you see how the ritual could be turned into a weapon. What if you wanted to steal Fonsca's gloves? You could challenge him to a duel, and as the winner, take them."

"Then it wouldn't be a duel. It would be a mugging."

"But all would call you an honorable man, and you'd have the gloves."

"I would know. Honor is a public face, yes, but it is also a matter of private integrity. Lack of integrity will always show on the face."

"I've never heard you say a more naïve thing."

They'd quarreled then, a short, bitter quarrel. They'd gone to bed without touching and slept, and in the morning, made love without apologizing for the night's ugly words. Neither had ever referred to it again. But looking back, Cay thought it must have been the first harbinger of the serious breach to come.

Cay's cheeks burned at the memory. Adrio's eyes were red-rimmed and a little wild.

"I shouldn't have spoken to you so," he said. "I was being cheeky."

"You were right. It's easy to have honor when you're warm and safe."

Cay shook his head. "I still think that's true. But there's no shame in being warm and safe. I shouldn't have thrown it in your teeth."

Adrio glared at him. "*You* have never claimed to have any sense of honor."

"I was not raised with such notions."

"But you're kind to me. I, with my vaunted honor, am deliberately cruel. Why is that?"

Cay shook his head; he had no answer, except *Because I love you, and you don't love me.* But he didn't say it. Adrio seemed so bitterly unhappy; he had no idea what to do to make it better.

Adrio rolled to his knees, liquor sloshing over his fingertips. He tipped his head back and drained his cup, throat working as he swallowed the remainder of his draught. He tossed the cup to the floor and stared Cay in the eye as he brought his hand to his mouth and sucked the drink from his fingers.

Chills raced over Cay's skin at the hot expression in his husband's eyes.

"You should leave," growled Adrio. "For if you stay, I am going to take you."

He said the words as if they were a threat. Cay lifted his chin. "I think I'll stay."

"You shouldn't." Adrio reached for Cay, and in one swift move had him down on his back on the bed, his movements sure but his hands gentle. He braced on his arms over Cay, above and around him, but not holding him.

"You should run back to your room," murmured Adrio, so close Cay could smell the wine on his breath. "We have established I am neither honorable nor kind."

This was a mistake. Cay knew Adrio was out of control. There was nothing loving about Adrio at this moment. If *he* were an honorable man, he would recognize Adrio was unreasonable and incautious with drink and leave him. He would preserve Adrio's dignity and privacy and go.

But Cay's entire body was singing with anticipation, his blood rushing through his veins in rapid throbs, making his breath shallow and his cock ache. He didn't want to be alone with this *want*; he couldn't leave his husband wanting. And he'd never claimed to be a man of honor.

"You are heavy-hearted tonight," he whispered, "and I would ease you."

"Ah." Adrio cocked his head. "So you would do me a kindness, then?"

Ignoring the heavy irony in Adrio's tone, Cay's replied breathlessly, "I would be happy to."

Adrio touched him at last, placing a hand to his throat. His fingers curled around his neck to nest at Cay's nape, under his hair, and his thumb stroked under Cay's jaw. His hand was warm, hard enough that Cay felt his pulse against it. Intoxicated, Cay melted into the touch, closing his eyes. Adrio's hand tightened slightly, and a shiver streaked down Cay's spine.

"I'm going to regret this." Adrio's whisper tickled the skin of his neck, and he shivered, excitement tingling through his veins.

"But what if we decided . . ." Cay's voice faltered as Adrio pressed a sucking kiss to his collarbone. Cay arched his neck and closed his eyes. He focused all his attention on the sensation of Adrio's lips and tongue, hot on the hollow of his throat. "What if we agreed . . . we won't regret it? This once."

Adrio lifted his head, and Cay surged up to meet his mouth. But before they could kiss, Adrio unwound Cay's arms and flipped him over a little sharply, shoving him face down into the mattress. Cay went willingly, his body supple and passive, as Adrio kneed his legs apart and knelt between them.

Adrio was ungentle. He pushed Cay's hair up and kissed his nape, neck, and shoulders. His stubble and the sharp edge of his teeth rasped Cay's sensitive nape while he stripped off Cay's robe, baring him. Cay moaned in pleasure, his arousal undeterred by Adrio's brusque movements. Adrio's lips were always soft, no matter how roughly he kissed, and his hands on the sensitive skin of Cay's ribs left trails of shivery fire.

He had missed this so much. He hadn't been touched in months. Cay lifted his hips so Adrio could push his trousers down. He felt rather than saw Adrio shuck out of his robe, then skim his hands down Cay's back to palm his ass. Adrio's loose hair brushed his skin before he bit Cay's neck and pressed his erection hard against Cay's tailbone.

Cay murmured and tried to turn over, wanting to touch him, to kiss him, but subsided when Adrio growled, "Be still." Adrio groped in his bedside cabinet for oil, spilled it shakily over Cay's body, and began to rut there, between his buttocks. Cay lifted his hips in welcome, but Adrio did not breach him; he took his pleasure in sinuous grinding along and between Cay's cheeks, against his tailbone. He clasped Cay hard in his arms and rode him, his cock heavy and hard, dragging heat and moisture and friction against Cay's body.

Cay clenched his fists in the sheets but kept his body malleable. Adrio was using him for his own satisfaction, giving nothing back, not even the touch of his hand. Cay was more than willing to be used this way, but he wanted more—a kiss, a caress. Some little intimacy, along with the heat.

He didn't get it. One of Adrio's hands tangled in his hair and pressed his face to the velvet coverlet, the other hand hard on his hip, holding him still for Adrio's purpose. Cay tried to move with him, to give pleasure; tried to writhe against the sheets, or to get a hand under himself, to partake in it, but Adrio gripped him tight and used him hard.

Like a greedy man using a whore in an alley. A dirty whore, the kind one didn't care to caress or penetrate or kiss.

Ah, but even so it felt so good, and he had missed it so much. The sound Adrio made just before his climax was familiar and much-loved, as was the way his body tightened, the pulse of his cock, the hot surge of his spend against Cay's sweating back. Cay hummed with the borrowed delight of it.

Adrio's body relaxed, panting, pressing Cay down into the velvet coverlet. He lay still under Adrio's heavy body, nearly delirious with his own desire, flexing his fingers, imagining what they would do now Adrio's first urgency had been satisfied. Now he would use his mouth, or his hands, to give Cay his gratification. And it wouldn't be teasing or playful, but soon, ah, soon, his husband would take care of him.

"*Damn*," muttered Adrio.

Adrio rolled off him and flopped over onto his back. Cay propped himself up on his elbows, tremblingly eager for his turn.

But Adrio's expression froze him. His eyes were closed, the heel of one hand pressed against his furrowed brow, his lips pulled tight over his teeth. It was an unguarded grimace of pain and regret. Adrio turned his face away; Cay could only see his cheek and jaw and the strong tendons of his throat. So quietly Cay was certain he wasn't intended to hear it, Adrio whispered, "Shouldn't have done that."

Cay blew air from his lungs and squeezed his eyes shut against a rush of white rage. He had just permitted—invited—his husband to give him a sordid little fuck, as fast and anonymous and impersonal as it could be between a man and his husband. Because Adrio wanted it. Being a fool, Cay had even liked it.

And now Adrio had the unmitigated nerve to *wish he hadn't*. To refuse to reciprocate, as if Cay really was merely a whore.

"I cannot believe you," hissed Cay, furious. His fists clenched, his fragile happiness crushed to splinters, Cay rolled out of bed and to his feet. Unsteadily, he groped for his robe and belted it over his nudity, ignoring his stiff prick and the sticky lees of sex on his body.

Adrio began to speak, no doubt to deliver some elegant aphorism about clouds or flowers to mean *I warned you*, and Cay interrupted sharply, "Don't. Don't speak to me, Adrio."

Head held high, he walked out, closing the door (without a slam) behind him. He trotted down to his own suite, and flattered himself that if a servant had seen him, they'd see nothing furtive or ashamed in his posture or face.

Only when his door was closed and locked behind him did his shaking knees fold, and he collapsed, head in his hands.

He would not cry. He didn't want to cry over Adrio anymore. He didn't want to be in love with Adrio anymore. He didn't want to be a man who kept saying yes, and yes again, when he knew he should say no. He hated this pitiful creature he'd become, who kept wanting, kept being pushed away, and who kept coming back.

No more.

He didn't know how to stop. But he was going to figure it out soon. Not tonight, but soon.

The following days were dreary with rain. Life returned to its routine—if one could describe the tense air in the house as *routine*. When he and Adrio breakfasted together, they did not speak. More often than not, Adrio left the house before breakfast to go about his mysterious business, and Cay would spend his days drawing, sewing, or visiting with Kell. In the evening, Adrio often escorted him to a social engagement, and only then did they ever touch or even look at one another. Adrio refrained from delivering cutting insults, possibly because Cay refrained—or tried to refrain—from mooning at him like a lovesick puppy. He kept his chin at a proud angle, his mouth shut, and the fading bruises on his neck covered with high collars, cleverly embroidered with tiny silver balloons.

He anticipated, with every moment, the return of Hob Fierar. What would he say to the man? What would he do? He seemed to have exhausted all his ingenuity in those forged papers. Now he could do nothing but wait and fearfully wonder what to do next.

Everyone in Valette society was wearing balloons: not just embroidered circles, but enameled balloon brooches, earrings, and hair ornaments. The Uncanny Aviator had become a hero of Lucenequa, not because anyone cared about the fate of the Chende prisoners, but because the Aviator's daring exploits were a black eye on Muntegri. Some believed the Aviator was a beautiful woman; others, a handsome and dashing man. She flew smoke-balloons, her long tawny Lucenequan hair blowing in the breeze. He disguised himself as a Muntegrise nobleman and infiltrated the Muntegrise court. She could turn invisible, wrapping her body in black silk imbued with the Principle of Disguise. He seduced the Muntegrise prison guards with his sensual beauty, so they willingly opened their doors for him. She was the queen, or he the king, of the Chende: a monarch in exile.

This last made Cay giggle.

"Sir, do the Chende *have* a monarch?"

"Everyone has a monarch," said the young lordling telling this tale.

"Indeed?"

Without looking at him, Adrio gently stepped on his foot, and Cay said no more.

The weather changed, as it sometimes did in Lucenequa in the autumn. The rain stopped, the skies brightened, and the rivers coming down from the mountains were swollen with snowmelt. The ground grew pregnant with moisture, and plants pushed eager green shoots through the pavers. They would all freeze again; the cold would come, nipping the green leaf-buds from the trees, but for now, the warm air blew up from the south, scented with false spring.

"So why couldn't a smoke-balloon fly into the wind, the way sailing ships do?" wondered Cay aloud.

Not immune to the illusory springtime cheer, he'd bought apricot-cakes and wine and took them around to Kell's dormitory room at the university. He was not supposed to be here—no nonstudents were allowed in the dorms after dusk—but the regular ornamental projections on the building's façade were almost a joy to climb, and he'd scaled the walls and wriggled through the window often. He liked this room: a small rectangle with two narrow beds, one chair, and cases stuffed with books. It was cold and smelled a bit of unwashed sheets, but Kell had found a home here. Cay's shy little know-it-all sister now had know-it-all friends, people who respected and understood her, and she'd blossomed.

A small gathering of students had joined them to enjoy the treats: Kell's roommate Isa, Isa's girlfriend Bienta, and a boy called Giuro. Cay was lounging on Kell's bed, with Kell sitting cross-legged at his ankles. Isa and Bienta cuddled on the other bed, and Giuro sat in a rickety chair. If Cay did not mistake, Giuro eyed Cay's place on Kell's bed with envy.

"No keel," said Kell, through a mouthful of cake.

Cay wrinkled his brow at her. "The keel is the bit sticking down into the ocean?"

Giuro rolled his eyes. "First of all," he said, "they're not smoke-balloons; they're heat-balloons. Smoke isn't the levitating Principle, it's heated air, which rises above cooler air."

"It does?"

"Think of a kitchen where the oven has been going all day," said Bienta. "If you raise your hand above your head, you can feel the layer of warm air above you."

"True." Cay didn't spend much time in kitchens, but recalled the heat rising off his father's pottery kiln in a visible shimmer, up toward the high ceiling. "So the smoke isn't part of it at all?"

"The smoke probably makes it less efficient," said Giuro. "It's a matter of differing levels of pressure."

"Which brings us back to your original question," said Isa. "A ship can't go directly into the wind, but if the sails are set at an angle to it—" she gestured vaguely with her hands "—then you get higher air pressure on one side of the sail and lower air pressure on the other, which draws the ship forward."

"And that's why you need a keel," said Kell. "It creates resistance with the water so the ship doesn't get pushed about by the wind. Which a balloon, lacking a keel, would."

But what did heat have to do with pressure? Cay's lack of comprehension was probably clear on his face. Giuro rolled his eyes again, this time looking pointedly at Kell.

Cay's most innocent expression hid his desire to knock the boy's teeth in. He regularly smiled into the eyes of dowagers who saw him as a whore who had fucked his way into the nobility. He could certainly meet the gaze of one rude undergraduate. But he disliked the way Giuro kept leaning over to touch Kell's knee or her shoulder, offering her more food and keeping her glass filled. She was entitled to a young man, but must it be *this* young man?

"So it's not possible," he repeated, "because the balloon is in the sky, and even if it did have a keel, it would also be in the sky, so it wouldn't work. Right?"

Giuro sighed loudly. "So many people don't understand that *sky* is not empty space. It's full of matter—air, which has weight and density and pressure. Air is subject to natural forces, the same as water and earth. A balloon is entirely at the mercy of the forces of air, whereas a sailing ship may make use of the differential between the Principles of air and water. It's a very basic concept."

"Lots of people weren't taught those concepts, Giuro," said Kell, as if noticing Giuro's aggressive tone for the first time.

"Fish don't drown."

"Ooh," murmured Cay. "Starlight Conversation."

"I don't know about fish," said Kell, "but you're being awfully shitty to Cay. All he did was ask a question."

"I just don't understand why you want to spend time with people like him," Giuro snapped. "Just because he's rich doesn't mean he's smart."

"My brother is too smart!"

"He's your *brother*?"

"Of course he's my brother! Why else would he keep coming around here?"

Isa and Bienta began to giggle.

Cay grinned at Giuro. "Two people with Muntegrise accents in one Valette dormitory room. So many people would never guess they're related, but it's a very basic concept."

The waiting came to an end the next day.

Cay and Adrio were firmly behind their masks at luncheon when a pounding came at the door. As soon as a servant opened it, Fonsca Calareto burst into the breakfast room, flushed and disheveled, shouting Adrio's name.

"What is it?"

"They say they have caught the Uncanny Aviator."

"*What*? Who?"

"That Grup envoy fellow. Fierar. He has captured a man he says is a spy. Adrio, you won't believe who."

"Who?" whispered Cay, a lump of dread frozen in his chest.

"Ondrei."

"Impossible," growled Adrio, but he was on his feet, striding toward the front door.

Cay scrambled to his feet and followed.

Adrio was pulling on a cloak and gloves. "Where—"

"The envoy is at the palace now," Fonsca said. "He is waiting for an audience with the queen. If we're lucky, we can make it—"

Adrio's eye fell on Cay, who was also reaching for his cloak. "You stay here," he said.

"No."

Adrio looked as if he would argue, but Cay set his jaw, and Fonsca said, "We haven't time for this. My carriage is waiting."

"All right," growled Adrio. He strode out the door, Cay at his heels.

Chapter Seven

The Sunlit Palace was not just the residence of the Queen of Lucenequa and her large family. Once a fortified castle, the massive building had gracious rooms for public social events—salons, ballrooms, parlors, and so on. Behind those was a maze of narrow hallways and mundane offices inhabited by clerks, lawyers, accountants, and officials: the center of the business of ruling the kingdom. Fonsca's carriage deposited them at a back entrance, not the grand public gates, and it was through the back hallways Adrio led them.

Evidently familiar with this space, he brought them through the cluttered maze of offices from back to front until they arrived at a grand hall. At the end was a pair of tall, broad doors flanked by liveried servants—an audience chamber. Adrio strode to the doors, nodded to the servant, bearing every year of his noble ancestry around him like a cloak, and the servant did not stop him from walking right through. She did eye Fonsca and Cay, both born commoners, who remained outside the doors. Fonsca gave her some money, and she allowed them to shamelessly listen. She was, after all, doing the same thing.

The furious voice of Queen Vallila III rolled easily out into the hallway: "Be very clear with me, Master Envoy. By what right do you lay hands upon my cousin, Lord Noresposto?"

Hob Fierar's voice was quieter, higher, and less easy to hear. Fonsca, Cay, and the servant all leaned in.

"By a nation's right to protect itself from saboteurs and spies, Your Majesty. I am my Lord Protector's ears and hands in this kingdom. Lord Noresposto is in league with the Uncanny Aviator."

Cay pressed a hand over his eyes as if he could hear more clearly by blocking his vision.

"Leaving aside the question of *the Uncanny Aviator*," drawled the queen, "your jurisdiction to arrest and question ends at the border. You were granted certain diplomatic privileges when you were invited here, as I'd hoped to return our nations to some semblance of a neighborly relationship. But you have far exceeded those privileges, and you will return my kinsman to his home, unharmed, at once."

"The evidence of his guilt is clear."

"Immaterial. A citizen of Lucenequa, however common or noble, may move freely about this realm without being seized by Muntegrise forces."

Cay had to note Hob Fierar's courage: he did not back down. "Unless, according to section six of the Accords of Podfluvial, the Lucenequan citizen is engaged in activities that would upset the balance of power between our two nations. I believe the development of invisible flying machines more than meets the standard."

There was a long silence. Cay glanced uneasily at Fonsca, wondering if the queen, twenty-nine years old and only on the throne for a year, knew about the Accords of Podfluvial. Then she said, "I believe the balance of power between our nations was quite upset almost seven years ago, when the Grup put to death the descendants of the royal family and erected roadblocks to prevent free commerce. Cease to speak of irrelevancies and address the issue of your illegal seizure of my cousin."

"Ah," said Fierar, his tone now conciliatory. "Perhaps I was mistaken. I believed I acted within my authority. Alas, Lord Noresposto has already been removed and is en route to Muntegri even as we speak. It is too late to recall him. If I have overstepped, I beg forgiveness. It was only a sign of my zeal to protect my nation from a new and terrible threat."

"Forgive me this interruption, Your Majesty." The voice was Adrio's. "May I ask a question of the envoy?"

"Proceed, Lord Lodola."

"Master Fierar, correctly? You believe Ondrei Rege, Lord of Noresposto, is an aeronaut who flies at will over the Elurez Mountains to Muntegri?" Adrio's voice was relaxed and humorous.

"No, Lord Lodola," said Fierar. "He is the aeronaut's accomplice, who aids him and knows who he is."

"And what led you to this amazing conclusion?"

"Two things." Fierar did not seem daunted by Adrio's mockery. "For one, three nights ago, he abruptly left his home and rode forth, without any retinue, in darkness. My agents were surprised by this and followed him. He rode north toward the mountains—"

"On what road?"

"The road to Noresposto, my lord."

"Noresposto is Lord Ondrei's country estate."

"Indeed. He did not go to Noresposto, however. He passed through his seat and continued north, toward the mouth of Lehoia Pass."

"He has another house in the foothills."

"He did not go to Wind House. Rather, he left the road and took shelter in a noisome mountain shed, which once perhaps had sheltered goats or sheep. There he was observed by my people in a secret meeting. Such was his stealth, we were unable to ascertain the identity of his associates, who fled. We did take him, however. He refused to supply a reason for his movements."

There was silence. Cay tried and failed to imagine Ondrei in a goat shed.

The queen put in, "How came you to be spying upon Lord Noresposto, sir?"

"We have known Lord Noresposto was involved in the plot for some time," said Fierar. "These documents were found upon his person earlier this year. They are, I think you will agree, quite damning."

Then came the sound of rustling papers. Cay, overcome with horror, nearly fell down.

"These . . . these were found on Ondrei's person?" Adrio's voice had gone soft with astonishment. "How? And when, and by whom?"

"These few pages are copies," said Fierar. "Part of a much larger sheaf of documents. The original is in the hands of the lord chancellor's university in Turla. As you can see, these pages contain illustrations of smoke-balloons and calculations for how to make them fly. The other pages were covered with mathematical formulae, which are being deciphered." His voice dripped satisfaction. "If Lucenequa is developing this military technology, then Muntegri must regard your proffered peace negotiations as a farce, and my masters must and shall know of it."

More shuffling of papers. Cay leaned against the wall to hold himself upright.

"Your Majesty," said Adrio eventually, his voice oddly strained. "This cannot be true. I have known Lord Noresposto since childhood, and I will vow he has never looked at a mathematical formula in his life."

"I agree he is not the author of the papers," put in Fierar, "nor the originator of their ideas. But these were indeed found upon him by one of my agents here in Valette. It follows that he knows their author. It is in the interest of Muntegri, and of peace itself, to question him further."

"Question him?"

"Respectfully," said Fierar. "We have great respect for Lucenequa's nobles."

The queen spoke. "Enough. The question is not whatever nonsense is in these papers or what private business took my cousin to his bai. The question is whether I will imprison and hang you for your extraordinary and illegal actions."

"Your Majesty, diplomatic imm—"

"Silence. You will remain free *for the moment*, but only because you have work before you. You will send to Muntegri. My cousin is to be returned to me at once. As well, send my words to your lord chancellor. We regard the taking of our kin from our lands as a gross offense, a violation of our borders, and an assault upon the very peace you claim to safeguard. My cousin Lord Noresposto will be returned to us, and if he is harmed in any way, Muntegri will answer for it. You have one week."

Cay kept his eyes trained on the window as Fonsca's carriage carried them back to the house. His knees had turned to water, his breath was coming shallow, and his stomach sloshed with acid.

"Vallila may growl, but she has no teeth," Fonsca was saying. "Lucenequa cannot fling her armies up the Muntegri Road in winter. Ondrei won't be released until he's wrung dry, no matter what the envoy does."

"I know," said Adrio.

Cay closed his eyes.

"Cay's gone all green," said Fonsca. "What's the matter with him?"

"He is very fond of Ondrei."

Cay's heart ached at the gentleness in Adrio's tone even though it was probably a show for Fonsca's benefit.

He must be brave now. He must bring to an end all secrecy and throw himself on Adrio's mercy. For Ondrei's sake, he must find the courage to tell Adrio everything.

The carriage pulled up outside Adrio's house, and the servant opened the door. Cay began to alight, then glanced back at Adrio, who was not moving.

"I'm going along to Fonsca," he said. "We must discuss this. I don't know when I'll be home."

"No, my lord," said Cay, speaking for the first time, "I must have a word."

"Later."

"Now." He met Adrio's eyes as steadily as he could.

Fonsca's eyebrows went up. Adrio, clearly eager to be away, hesitated.

"This can't wait," said Fonsca.

"Nor can I," said Cay. "My lord. You *must* hear me."

Something in Cay's face or tone seemed to move him. "I'll be over later," Adrio said to Fonsca, and came with Cay into the house.

"Send the servants out and come to my rooms," said Cay, and ran up the stairs to his suite.

He took off his shoes and sat cross-legged on the floor in front of the fire.

He had cried so many tears, but now his eyes were dry and hot. His shame and guilt, and his terrible, terrible fear, curdled like a bad meal in his stomach.

I must be brave now.

At last Adrio came in, still wearing his traveling cloak. "I've told the staff to remain in their quarters for an hour, except for Cook. There's bread in the oven, and she refuses to leave it. But we will not be interrupted."

"Thank you."

Adrio pulled the laces at this throat and tossed his cloak to the bed, where it slithered heavily to the floor. He leaned his hip on Cay's work table and folded his arms. "Now, be quick. What's this about?"

Cay popped his knuckles, one after the other. "I hardly know where to start."

"You shouldn't do that to your hands."

"I know." He clenched his fists and put them on his lap. He forced the words out of his mouth. "I met the envoy from Muntegri at the Harvest Ball. He tried to recruit me into gathering information for the Grup. I ignored him."

Adrio inhaled a deep breath, and then slowly let it out. "Go on."

"The next day he came here."

"You gave him tea."

"I did. Yes. And he blackmailed me. He demanded I give him information about you." His mouth was so dry his voice sounded creaky. "He seemed convinced you were involved in military planning. He wanted me to get military secrets out of you and give them to him. He said if I didn't do this, he would—"

Pop, pop, pop. He cracked all ten knuckles. Finally, he said, "He told me he would tell you, and everyone, some things about me. These things would damage you in society if they were known."

Adrio stared at him for a long moment. Cay did not look at his face, frightened of the contempt he would almost certainly see there. Finally, Adrio said, "I see. And how did you reply?"

"I made up a tale about a hero who rescued Chende in smoke-balloons."

Cay dared to glance up at Adrio, who was running a hand over his mouth and jaw. "You made up the Uncanny Aviator story on the spot?"

"It was not so big a story then," he said. "But Ondrei had made a joke at the ball, and Kell had said something about smoke-balloons at breakfast that morning—do you remember?"

"Yes."

Cay tucked his hands under his thighs, sitting on them, and went on, "I babbled a lot of nonsense. It was stupid. It was *nothing*. I just wanted him to go away. But soon, everyone was talking about it, and it got bigger—you embroidered the story yourself. So did everyone. And Fierar, I don't think he actually cares about the Chende refugees, but he sees the smoke-balloons as a military threat and demanded more information."

Adrio studied him for a moment. "You could have told me you were being threatened."

Cay bowed his head. "I wanted to. But you— I lost my nerve."

"Did you not trust me? Upon my honor, it is my duty to protect my husband, regardless of how things stand between us."

"I know." Cay's voice was small. "It's not that I didn't trust you. But you dislike me so much, and I couldn't bear it."

"So instead of speaking to me, you became Hob Fierar's agent."

"*No*." He jerked his head up to earnestly meet Adrio's eyes. "I *lied*. Since the story about the Uncanny Aviator had distracted him so successfully, I decided I would give him more lies. Anything to keep him at bay, to keep his eyes from you and whatever you were doing. So . . ." Cay squeezed his eyes shut, took a steadying breath, straightened his shoulders, and went on. "I made those papers. I made the drawings and copied mathematical formulae from books. I disguised my handwriting." He smiled a little.

"They were *good*, Adrio! I almost thought, if you could see them, you'd be proud of how good they were."

"You thought I'd be proud?" His voice dripped scorn.

Cay ducked his head. No. Clearly the idea Adrio would ever be proud of his efforts was a foolish one.

Adrio went on coolly, "And how did the envoy conclude these plans belonged to Ondrei?"

There was the splinter, festering at the heart of the matter. Trying to keep his voice steady, he admitted, "I told him so."

A long pause. Then: "Ondrei. The man who has ever been your true friend. Who has defended you to me a hundred times. You falsely accused Ondrei—"

"I thought he would be safe!" he cried. "I thought Ondrei could not be involved in any clandestine activity, so it would do no harm if Fierar's spies watched him! And he is the queen's cousin, so even if they did suspect him of something, they wouldn't dare touch him!"

Adrio's expression was one of disgust. "I know you mock the concept of honor, but I cannot believe you would be capable of such baseness."

"I had to get them from someone, and it couldn't be you! I couldn't say I just found them on the street! And if he hadn't gone haring off to a goat shed on the Noresposto Road in the middle of the night, it would have worked." Cay stood and began to pace, gesturing wildly as he spoke. "How could I have predicted such a wild start? How could I have imagined Fierar would dare to lay hands on him on Lucenequan soil, no matter what he did? Anyway, Fierar was so excited he left and went back to Muntegri, and I hoped the snows would keep him there all winter, and I'd have a bit of time to think. But then he came back. And Ondrei . . . I don't know. I thought he was untouchable. I'm sorry." He took a long gulp of air and turned to face his husband. "I'm sorry. I'm so sorry, Adrio. I would never knowingly do anything to hurt Ondrei. Or you. It was just—it was meant to be a distraction. You have to believe me."

Adrio's face was expressionless. After a long, painful moment, he said, "I'm not sure I have to believe anything of the kind."

Cay stared at him, mute.

Adrio glared at him, thinking, forbidding in his anger, and Cay realized he was cracking his knuckles again. He forced himself to stop.

Finally, Adrio said, "I assume the tale you didn't want the envoy to tell concerned the murder of Dizut Ingok?"

It was the last thing he expected Adrio to say. The name *Dizut Ingok* in Adrio's voice. The perfectly accurate Chende pronunciation sounded so strange in Adrio's Lucenequan accent.

"Where did you hear about Dizut Ingok?"

"Do you deny it?"

Cay stared at him, but he wasn't seeing his husband.

He was seeing—

A man with a locked cabinet. A man who was involved in some sort of secret work with his friends. A man who left for weeks and came back sunburned or muddy. A man who loved adventure stories. A man who had once bought a wagon full of caged ducks so they could swim.

A man who knew about the murder of Dizut Ingok.

"You're the Uncanny Aviator," said Cay.

Adrio's face was like stone, his eyebrows perfectly even. His lack of reaction cemented Cay's certainty.

"It's you. You and Fonsca and Ondrei." Dizzy, almost, from the force of his realization, he ran his hands through his hair. "There's nothing uncanny about how you free the Chende, of course—you probably pretend to be Muntegrise and buy them, a few at a time. You do my accent well enough. And you've made some kind of pact or treaty with the Maquhi Clan to bring them through the Lehoia Pass over the mountains. You just walk the refugees past the roadblock through the Pass, guided by the Maquhi Chende. Probably some of the refugees want to stay in the mountains, but the ones who don't, the ones who aren't used to mountain life or who belong to clans in blood-feud with the Maquhi, those you bring here to Lucenequa. One of them works in our kitchen. What did you offer to the Maquhi Clan for passage?"

Adrio sank into a chair.

"Cay," he breathed. "How do you know all this?"

"I didn't. I just figured it out. It's true, isn't it?"

"*How do you know?*" shouted Adrio.

Cay flinched. "N-no one knows about Dizut Ingok," he stammered. "Except me, and the Grup, and the Maquhi Clan. And you didn't hear it from me or the Grup, so you must have heard it from the Maquhi. Why would you be in contact with them? You've no business with them. Unless you're going through the mountains. You can't go through Lehoia Pass without paying the Maquhi Clan. No one can, not even Chende of other clans. But you have the money to pay them. So you're the one bringing the refugees to Lucenequa."

They sat in silence for a long moment. Cay's mind clicked over the new information: Adrio. The Chende. And Adrio had known about Dizut for months and had never said anything.

"You always claimed Kell was the smart one," Adrio said quietly.

Bitterness made him snap, "Sorry to disappoint, Husband. Is the old man still the chief? Gizon Ingok?" Adrio didn't reply, and Cay barreled on, too angry to remain silent. "*This* is what happened to us, isn't it? Months ago, Gizon spun you a tale of his golden heroic grandson Dizut, and of the vicious brat who murdered him—"

"Betrayed him to the Grup," interrupted Adrio. "Who hanged him for the ravens to eat, for his family to find rotting in the sun. The old man wept, telling me."

"How heartwarming," said Cay, not bothering to hide his revulsion.

"You've kept this secret from the day we met," Adrio growled, "and Gizon Ingok exposed it. You arrived in Valette in spring, with the first wave of refugees, before the roadblocks went up. And then that summer, you went back north, up to Lehoia Pass, to do your bloody work. Do you deny it?"

Cay clenched his fists. His stomach was in knots as he hugged his body and labored for breath.

"Explain it to me." Adrio was in a fury, his face flushed. "Explain how Gizon Ingok, chief of the Maquhi Clan, knows your name? How do you know his? How did you know where to go in the Lehoia's maze of canyons? How did you know you would find the Maquhi Clan there? Who gave you your information? How could you have done it unless it was a trap planned and orchestrated by the Grup?"

"So," said Cay, ignoring the questioning. "This is what happened. Gizon told you all this, and you believed him, and you never asked me. You believed him, so you kicked me out of your bed, and froze me out of your life, and broke my heart—" He gulped for breath. "And you never asked me if it was true."

"Is it?" shouted Adrio.

"Yes!"

Adrio snarled at him. "You led a troop of the Grup guards right up the Lehoia Pass to where Dizut Ingok was camped—the grandson and heir to the clan's chief. That boy's blood is on your hands."

"'Boy'?" Cay laughed.

"Are you going to claim he wasn't? How much were you paid for your act of cowardly treachery and murder? Or would you have me believe you were being blackmailed *then*, too?"

"Why should I claim anything?" Cay looked him straight in the eye, fury lending him courage. "You've had months to ask me these questions. Any time this past summer and autumn, you might have asked me. Instead, you eagerly believed the worst, based on nothing but the ramblings of an old man."

For a moment, doubt and anguish flickered in Adrio's eyes. "By the same token, you might have told me, but whenever I asked about your past, or your passage from Muntegri, or the Chende, or anything, I was met with lies. I never asked you because I knew you would not answer."

"That's—"

He broke off when Adrio abruptly closed the distance between them and grabbed Cay by the shoulders. "True. It's true. You've lied to me, distracted me, evaded my questions, pretended a false good nature to cover your real self. Your public face shows honor, your private life reveals your lack of it. And it has dishonored *me* and made my public face a lie as well."

They stood nose to nose. Then Adrio released him with a shove, and, astonished, Cay staggered back a few paces.

Adrio had never struck him. He'd never, *ever* suspected Adrio might. "Do that again," he snarled, panting with rage, "and regret it."

"And now I see the real you," Adrio said. "A dog will show its teeth."

"Then don't kick it, Husband."

Adrio visibly pulled himself together, running a hand over his face. Cay watched him warily.

"This is all beside the point. None of it matters."

It was the most upsetting thing Adrio had said yet.

"*None of this matters?*"

"No." Adrio firmed his jaw. "A good man is dead—did you know the Maquhi Clan has declared a blood-feud against you?"

"Oh, indeed?"

"And Ondrei is in a Grup prison, at your hands, and it doesn't matter *why*."

Cay bit his lip. Ah, but that last was true. How cruelly Adrio wielded the truth.

"You must cause no further damage," Adrio went on. "You know far too much, and you cannot speak to anyone of any of it." He ran a hand through his hair. "I'm going to Turla to try to rescue Ondrei—whatever's left of him. I must discuss it with Fonsca. And your friend Hob Fierar cannot know."

Adrio strode to the wall and pulled the bell cord. "I don't know what to do with you, and I don't have time to figure it out. You must stay put and keep your mouth shut until I get back. I'll see to you then."

"See to me?" demanded Cay. "What do you mean?"

Adrio didn't answer. A tap at the door and Lirano stood there, slightly flushed from what must have been a dead run from the servants' quarters.

"My lords?"

"I have important instructions for you," said Adrio. "Tonight I'll be at Fonsca's. Tomorrow, I will probably be leaving for a trip of about a week, perhaps two. I need you to prepare my horse and pack my things, the usual."

"Yes, my lord."

"Lord Cay is not to leave this house until I get back."

Cay straightened. "What?"

"No—he is not to leave his rooms."

Lirano's eyes anxiously darted between them. "My lord. What should we do if . . . if Lord Cay wishes to leave his rooms?"

"You will restrain him."

Cay ground his teeth. "Adrio, don't do this."

Adrio took in Lirano's horrified expression and seemed to judge whether his servants would be willing to lay hands on Cay. "If the staff are reluctant, hire guards. It's just until I get back."

"Very well, my lord."

"Adrio," Cay said again.

Adrio turned to him, visibly impatient to leave.

"Do not try to *lock me up*, my lord. There will be no repair. There will be nothing left to reconcile."

Again, Cay thought doubt and pain darkened Adrio's eyes. But then, his husband hardened his features and said, "I cannot afford anyone to know what you know. Not while they hold Ondrei."

"I won't—"

"You already have." He glanced at Lirano. "Lock this door and station someone outside. I'll be back in the morning to get my bags."

He walked out.

"Adrio!" shouted Cay.

But he was gone. Lirano bowed with apology in his eyes and left as well, closing the door to Cay's suite behind him. He heard the key click in the lock.

Cay stared at the door, stunned.

It was over.

Imprisoned in his home. The way Bekh Clan was imprisoned—oh, that comparison was absurd; this house was no labor camp. These rooms were made of luxury. He was afforded every comfort. And yet. His husband—Adrio—had ordered that he be *imprisoned*.

He had held on to hope for months, but there was nothing now. Nothing to be recovered, except possibly his dignity—and he had little enough dignity left.

He spun in place and imagined destroying every piece of furniture in this room. Shattering the mirror, shredding the tapestries, breaking the furniture and tearing up the rugs. And then setting the wreckage alight.

He didn't. He contented himself with finding his best shears and taking them savagely to Adrio's discarded travel-cloak. After he sliced and ripped it to pieces, he swept the scraps of wool and leather into a pile, put away his scissors, pressed his hands to his eye sockets until stars swam in his vision, and forced himself to think.

There was no real hurry. No need to flee into the night, for his husband would not care and would hardly turn over every stone to find him. So he had time to gather his wits.

He found a bag and packed it with his plainest clothes. He scooped all his jewelry and valuables into a small purse, leaving behind anything with Lodola or Santauro insignia. The earrings, the gold chains, they could be sold. He'd need cash.

When a tap came on the door, he dropped the satchel behind the bed. It was an apologetic Lirano with a meal on a tray. Pumpkin and mushroom soup, with bread and wine. Cay did not try to push past Lirano out the door or beg Lirano to let him go. To do either of those things would force Lirano to try to stop him. Instead, Cay thanked him politely and told him he was tired and would go early to bed.

He ate. He'd grown accustomed to excellent food here at Rossoulia, and who knew when he'd get another such meal? Then he pulled his clothes and belongings out of their cupboards, sorting out those things that might be light and useful. Good shoes, yes. Books, no.

As he worked, he thought of the Maquhi Clan—*"Did you know Maquhi Clan has declared a blood-feud against you?"*—and shivered. It wasn't a surprise, just a grim reminder of the horrors of

Lehoia Pass and the thing he'd done. He'd known consequences would follow. He hadn't thought those consequences could reach into his marriage, but he should have.

Adrio condemned him for it. He didn't care why he'd done it. Cay had been right not to tell him. That realization hurt so much he paused in his packing, swaying slightly, a hand pressed to his chest.

All this time, he'd been right.

After sundown, when it was full dark and the servants would all be either in the kitchens or their quarters, Cay blew out his lamp and banked the fire. He pulled off his wedding ring and placed it on the center of his table, where a servant would be sure to see it. No need to leave a note; the wedding ring would be enough.

Finally, barefoot and with his bag slung across his back, he stepped out onto his windowsill and climbed down to the alley below. There, he paused to put his boots on.

Mandru crouched on the edge of the rooftop of Rossoulia, looking down at him silently, half-tail twitching.

Would any of the servants feed the cat once he was gone? Or let him in out of the rain?

Mandru wouldn't miss him. Mandru survived. He didn't need anyone.

Cay bowed to the cat in farewell, turned on his heel, and left his home and his marriage, intending never to return.

CHAPTER EIGHT

"I can't believe he would do it," sobbed Kell. "I can't believe it."

Cay held her tightly, letting her cry onto his shoulder.

He had climbed up to her dormitory room last night. If it was against the rules for him to be here after dusk, it was absolutely forbidden to stay here overnight; but of course, he'd had to come here. Kell's roommate had tactfully taken herself elsewhere, and Cay had sat on her bed and told Kell everything.

In a way, it was like when they were children when he and Kell had shared a room. When small Kell would crawl into bed with him, and he'd tell her stories until she slept.

She'd taken the news calmly. She'd approached the problem of what they were to do next with composure and logic, helping him to see what paths were open to them. Only now, as the small high window grew pale with dawn, did she break down.

"I trusted him. I liked him. I liked having another brother."

"I know. Forgive me. I'm so sorry."

She shook her head. She was red and puffy, her face streaked with tears. "It's not your fault. He betrayed your trust too. I just— How could he?"

Cay shook his head mutely.

"I knew you were having problems."

"Did you?"

"You can't hide anything from me. But I didn't think . . . I remember how hard he tried to get you to marry him. I know you didn't give in easily. How could it have all changed? Didn't he ever love us at all?"

Of course he did. But Cay didn't say it. He didn't know anymore, and Kell deserved better than comforting lies. They would face the future together, with nothing but truth between them. They belonged to each other, always bonded by love, trust, and a long-standing partnership of defiance against their father. Loyalty to each other, in spite of those who would try to divide them, was the bedrock of both of their lives.

Someone pounded on the door, and they both startled.

"Ugh, I'll bet that's him now," grumbled Kell. She crawled out of bed, kneeing Cay in the kidney. She scooped a robe off the floor and pulled it around her as she padded across the small room. With a sense of dread, Cay wrapped his arms around his knees and stayed in bed as his sister threw open the door.

It was Adrio, of course. Adrio, damp and harried and annoyed. Lirano must have discovered Cay's escape and sent him word. And here he was, come to fetch his prisoner home again. Adrio blinked at Kell's swollen eyes and bare feet and then looked over her shoulder at Cay, wrapped in blankets, sitting up in her bed. His lips tightened with some emotion—anger or frustration.

Adrio was about to speak, and Cay braced for whatever he was about to say. Then Kell slapped Adrio across the face so hard the sound reverberated through the room, and Adrio fell back against the wall, probably more in astonishment than pain.

"I thought you were my family!"

Adrio, pressing a palm to his face, gaped at her.

"How dare you hurt my brother?" she shouted at him. "Did you think we would stand for it?" Kell was furious, her voice thick and harsh with unshed tears. "Who do you think you are?"

Someone down the hall yelled, "Shut the fuck up!"

Kell grabbed Adrio by the front of his shirt and pulled him into the room, slamming the door behind him.

"Kell," said Adrio, "I—"

Cay was interested in what he had to say, but Kell cut him off. "I'm going to the registration office today and resigning my place at the university."

"No!" Adrio appeared genuinely startled. "Kell, you can't leave the university."

"Are you *stupid?* Do you think you'll keep my brother locked in his room while I go to class and pretend nothing's wrong?"

Adrio glanced at Cay. "You told her?"

Cay just lifted his eyebrows at him.

"Yes, he told me," Kell said acidly. "He told me you're sneaking into Muntegri and freeing Chende, and you think he's a Grup spy, and you tried to lock him up. He told me you stopped loving him, or maybe you never did. Maybe you never loved either of us."

Adrio bristled. "Some of that wasn't his secret to tell, and the rest has nothing to do with you. It's between me and Cay."

"Oh, what do you think is happening? Do you think we're *staying?*"

Adrio paused. For the first time since Cay's confession yesterday, he seemed genuinely rattled. Cay hadn't been able to get behind Adrio's scornful, cold mask, but Kell had done it.

"We'll be gone by tonight," said Cay.

"Where?" Adrio's eyebrows drew down. "Why?"

"Did you really just ask why?" demanded Kell. She was so angry she was almost crying again, her voice ragged. "Did you not accuse him of murdering Dizut Ingok Maquhi?"

"You know about that?" Adrio lifted a hand, as if he wanted to wipe her tears from her cheeks. She leaned out of his reach. "He did not deny it."

"Neither do I. We both did it. If you don't want him anymore, you don't want me either."

"Kell." Adrio's voice was gentle. "Don't be silly."

"Silly?" She was nearly dancing with fury. "Everything he did, I did it too. If he's earned your *disrespect*—" her voice broke on the word "—so have I."

"That's not true, Kell," said Adrio, softly.

"And I suppose you know all about it? Believe what you want. We did what we did, and we're not sorry, and we don't need you."

"I'm— Wait." Adrio rubbed his eyes with one hand. His cheek glowed bright red from the force of her blow. He turned to Cay. "Do you intend to allow her to bear responsibility for this? She was a child."

"Don't talk to him," snapped Kell, shoving his shoulder. She was over a head shorter than he was and probably no more than half his weight, bristling with defiance. "I was there. I'm old enough to bear the responsibility for my actions."

"And you claim Cay took his thirteen-year-old sister with him when he went up Lehoia Pass to kill Dizut Ingok?"

She laughed in his face, a rough, bitter laugh. "We came through Lehoia Pass to get out of Muntegri, you idiot. The roadblocks were already up when we left Turla. We came through the Pass. Dizut Ingok was our guide."

"What?" Adrio turned to at Cay. "You came south in spring."

Cay didn't meet his eyes.

"Summer," said Kell. "The summer I was thirteen, and Cay was eighteen. How old was Dizut Ingok? Did you ask? Did you ask what happened before he died?"

Adrio huffed softly, as though he had been punched in the chest, and his eyes darkened with horror.

"Oh look," said Cay. "He believes *you*."

"I believed *you* when you told me it was spring," snapped Adrio. Then the air left his lungs in a rush, and he seemed to deflate, lowering his head. He slowly slid down the wall and sat with his back to it. His gaze flicked between them: at Cay, huddled in the bed, and at Kell, standing with bare feet and tangled hair.

"He did something?" Adrio's voice was quiet.

Cay shrugged.

"What did he do?" When neither of them answered, he repeated, "Cay, what did Dizut Ingok do?"

"If you cared," said Cay slowly, "you could have asked. I would have told you everything."

"You would not," argued Adrio. "You lied about everything. You lied about matters large and small, dishonoring me and our marriage at every turn."

Cay bristled. "I never dishonored our marriage."

"What do you call lying to your husband?"

"I call it self-preservation. Just yesterday you told me it doesn't matter why I did it. You've judged me. Why question me now?"

"So we're leaving," put in Kell, keeping to the point. "You can claim abandonment and dissolve the marriage after a year. Or you can tell people we died. Whatever you want."

"I don't understand you," Adrio said, running a hand through his hair. "Do you *want* to go?"

Cay looked away, clenching his teeth.

Kell, stronger than he, said, "Yes. We want to go."

They remained frozen in a triangle for a long moment—Kell, panting with fury; Cay, his face turned away; Adrio, sitting on the floor.

After a long moment, Adrio said, "I found my cloak."

Cay crossed his arms. "I thought about burning the house to the ground. You're lucky I like the servants."

"As you no longer like me?"

"Correct."

Adrio stared at him.

Cay threw his hands in the air. "*What?* Are you surprised? Have you not been insulting me and taunting me for months? We both know it's over. This marriage." His heart was thumping in his chest, his stomach sour with misery. He crossed his arms over his torso and forced himself to continue. "You don't trust me. You don't like me. We barely speak. You won't even look at my face when we fuck." Kell coughed; Cay grimaced at her. "Sorry. But we tried, and it was too hard. We thought we would be happy together, but we aren't. We obviously married too soon, before we knew each other well enough, and now it's over. I know they'll talk when I'm gone. They'll say I jilted you, but you can survive the scandal. It'll die down. We'll both be happier when I'm gone."

Adrio's voice was quiet as he said, "This isn't what I wanted."

"Isn't it? Then what was the point of the cruel gifts and poems full of spite? What else were you trying to do if not drive me away?"

"To get a reaction," argued Adrio. "To get you to reveal who you really are. I had gotten nothing but falsehoods. I thought I could surprise the truth out of you."

"Oh, the roseapple tree that turns into a hangman's gibbet?" Cay glared at him. "Well, surprise. I'm no good at Starlight Conversation. I had no idea you were accusing me of murder. I thought you were just calling me ugly and unwanted."

"I know." Adrio ran his fingers through his hair. "The only thing I learned was that you loved me and I was breaking your heart."

He sounded regretful. Cay softened for an instant.

Kell did not. "When you came here this morning, what was your plan? To drag him back home and lock him in a cellar?"

Adrio lowered his eyes. Was that true?

"No," said Cay. "I will not permit it. I will not stay and endure your hatred for the rest of my life. I don't know why you think it would be an option, but it isn't. I am leaving. I have already left."

"Cay, please. I—" Adrio squeezed his eyes shut, and when he opened them again, his face was set with determination. "I must go," he said. "The weather is clear, but it could turn any time, and if I am to get Ondrei out of Muntegri, I must be on the road today, now. I cannot delay. But Cay . . . Cay, I would speak further."

Cay said nothing.

"Maybe you're right. Maybe we were too hasty. But I did, always, want to know you. I still do. Wait until I get back, at least."

Cay kept his head down, his eyes averted. Kell crossed her arms.

Adrio added, "I'm sorry. I must go, and I wish—I hope you will still be here when I get back. Or, if you must go, please send me your direction when you find a new place, and I will find you. Please, Cay. We must talk."

"Must we?"

"We haven't. And yes, we must. I would hear you, whatever you want to tell me. At least we can understand each other."

I begged you to talk to me. Cay was on the verge of tears, *again*. How much would he cry over this man?

"He doesn't owe you an explanation," said Kell, and at the same time, Cay said, "All right."

Kell shot him a scornful glare, her jaw mulish. Cay said to her, "You have exams. You should finish your semester, at least. Complete the courses you're taking now. It's only two weeks."

"I'll be back within two weeks." Adrio jumped to his feet. "Cay, I will be back. I can't—I won't let this go without understanding. Please."

"All right," Cay said tiredly. "But no matter what, I'm leaving at the end of Kell's term."

Adrio pulled Cay's wedding ring out of his pocket. He offered it to Cay, who closed his fists and shook his head. Tight-lipped, Adrio pocketed the ring, then bowed to them both.

"Kell, I will see you again too."

"Lucky you."

He sighed, turned, and was gone.

"Ugh, it's the crack of dawn. I'm going to sleep." Kell flopped onto Isa's bed. After a moment, she said, "You don't have to say yes to him every time. Especially not now."

"I know. It's the only answer I've ever had for him, though."

"It would do him good to hear no every once in a while."

"I know."

Cay went home.

He was fuzzy-headed as he walked across the city from the University District to Rossoulia. Hungover, not from drink but from too much emotion in too short a time. He still wasn't sure if he'd made the right decision.

"You don't have to," Kell had said. "We can be gone tonight."

But she should stay in school. And Adrio had said he wanted to talk. He hadn't wanted to talk in so long. How could Cay walk away from his marriage without at least one last conversation? How could he leave without knowing what happened to Ondrei?

The villa's red door was opened by Lirano, who made a low, prolonged obeisance at the sight of him.

"Please don't be troubled," Cay said, to the top of Lirano's head. "The offense was Lord Adrio's, not yours. He put you in a difficult position."

"Thank you, my lord." Lirano was still bowing. "Are you—Will you and he—"

"Is he gone?"

"Yes, he took Sparrow and rode out early this morning."

"Not the coach?"

"No, sir, he rode."

"Well, we must wait for him to return before we discover what is to become of us," sighed Cay. He removed his cloak and held it out to Lirano, which served to jolt the servant out of his confusion; he took Cay's cloak and folded it over his arm.

"I see, my lord. Thank you. Do you need anything, my lord?"

"I'm starving."

Lirano looked relieved to be given a useful task. "We were not expecting you back, but we have bread and ham and preserved apricots. I'll bring you a plate."

"Thank you."

"You're welcome." Lirano hesitated, and added, "I'm glad you are here, my lord."

Cay smiled at him tiredly. It was temporary, his stay here at Rossoulia. They might talk, he and Adrio, but his life here was over. He and Kell would start over somewhere else. They'd done it before.

But it was nice that the servants still liked him.

After food and a long sleep, he woke in the gray hours of the morning and could not sleep again.

Adrio would be on his way north. Somewhere—probably at Wind House—he would stop and stable Sparrow and take a sturdy stripe-legged Chende horse up one of the steep mountain paths to Lehoia Pass, where the Maquhi Clan of the Chende awaited him. Did he go alone? Or did he have a Maquhi clansman guide to help him through the maze of canyons and trails? Perhaps he took a crew of brave fellows with him, men and women who loved adventure, when he went to free the Chende from their Muntegrise camps.

For the first time, Cay had time to imagine Adrio as the Uncanny Aviator. He smiled, closing his eyes and pressing his face into his pillow.

Of course it was Adrio. Of *course*. A brave man, an idealistic man, a man who loved adventure novels. A man born to money who wanted to earn it. A man reckless enough, confident enough, to risk capture, torture, and execution by the Grup. That man might ride straight up to the gates of a Turla prison camp, masquerading as a wealthy Muntegrise, and hire five or ten Chende servants. And he might bring them back to their clansmen in the mountains or, if they had none, down into the green and fertile lands of Lucenequa.

What a romantic, dangerous, stupid, beautiful thing to do. And it was so simple. Why had no one figured it out sooner? But of course, most people didn't care about the Chende, thought Cay bitterly. Hob Fierar didn't care. He was obsessed with the idea of the smoke-balloons, and how they might fly armies over the mountains. The queen wanted Lucenequa to be a tolerant society for the Chende, but she cared far less about them than about her kidnapped kinsman. For Lucenequans, the Chende were but tragic victims in someone else's romantic story—the Aviator's.

Adrio cared. Adrio had decided to do something about it—to spend his money, to risk his life and liberty.

Cay did not have that kind of daring. His goals had always been smaller: Kell's safety and his own. It was not indifference on his part but a kind of fatalism. What difference could *he* make? If Adrio had such doubts, he didn't let them keep him from acting. Cay wondered if the difference between them lay in the circumstances of their lives. Or was it simpler? Perhaps some arrangement of the stars or whim of the gods had granted Adrio a courageous spirit, and Cay with a timid one.

Why would a courageous man allow his mind to be poisoned against his husband? Adrio had once begged Cay to marry him. He'd claimed he didn't care about the scandal or the gossip; he had loved Cay and wanted him in his life, and Cay had loved him too much to refuse.

Why had Adrio allowed Gizon Ingok to taint his love?

Did it matter why? He'd have his entire life to wonder.

Cay rolled over restlessly, staring at the cloudy sky through his window. He and Kell would go south, perhaps. Harodj was a port city where the ships from the Isles came every spring, bringing blown glass and metal and peppery wines. There was a university in Harodj. They probably wouldn't be able to afford for Kell to attend, but who knew? They could both find work. They could put Valette behind them.

After it was clear he wouldn't sleep again, Cay got out of bed and pulled on his robe. The lockpicks were in its pocket. He went up the stairs into Adrio's suite and Adrio's little office. It was morning; the servants were about, making breakfast, cleaning. He would probably not be interrupted, but if he were, what of it? There seemed no longer any need for stealth. He knew the truth, Adrio knew he knew, and the marriage was over. He no longer had to hide what he was doing.

He dropped to his knees in front of the locked cabinet. He'd knelt here several times with his lockpicks, sweating over the godsdamned padlock, with absolutely no luck. He took a deep breath, let it out, and inserted a pick.

Perhaps it was because it didn't really matter, or because he had decided if the lock couldn't be picked he would smash open the cabinet and damn the consequences, but after a few moments, the tip of his pick caught onto a ward. He held his breath and applied pressure. There was a *snick*, and the lock popped open.

"Oh!"

He opened the cabinet and pulled out a fat leather-bound ledger.

He found a meticulous journal of Adrio's activities as the Uncanny Aviator, written in his familiar, untidy handwriting. He'd been incredibly busy. Here were the names of all the Chende he had rescued, including tribal affiliations. Expenses: food, travel, bribes to buy the silence and cooperation of various Muntegrise. Names of those who had stayed in the mountains and those who had come to Lucenequa. As Cay had suspected, both Lord Ondrei and Fonsca Calareto were involved, providing money and goods, but it was Adrio alone who went up to Muntegri and brought the refugees out.

Wonderingly, Cay read how Adrio had found places for many refugees in his bai of Lodola and arranged apprenticeships for the youths as servants or stable hands or clerks. He'd even bought farms for some of the families. He paid for tutors and was planning to sponsor one young man at the university. He seemed fond of these people, keeping track of their progress and noting their successes.

A whole section was devoted to gifts given to the Maquhi Clan, the Chende who lived in Lehoia Pass. He had dealt with Krutiv Ingok Maquhi, the eldest daughter of Chief Gizon Ingok. To them, the adventurers had supplied in abundance things to ease life in the high passes: preserved food, salt, spices, tuns of wine, bales of wool and linen and leather, charcoal, alfalfa hay and corn for the animals. Medicines, books, knives. By these means, Adrio had undoubtedly made the Maquhi one of the most prosperous of the mountain Chende clans. Ondrei, whose holding of Noresposto was just south of the mountains, was the most frequent liaison with Krutiv, arranging supplies to be stored in a certain inconspicuous shed until the Maquhi brought their ponies down the Lehoia Pass to collect them.

It was clear from these pages Adrio admired the Chende, though his admiration was sometimes tinged with confusion or disapproval. Most of all, Adrio was curious about them, eager to learn about their traditions and customs, which he recounted in detail:

The Chende Clans who live in the mountains are reputed to be fierce and wild, prone to unreasoning savagery. The Chende I spoke to from Lucenequa fear the mountain clans and are hesitant to travel through the Pass, in spite of my assurances.

Is the Wind the Chende god, or just a common Chende figure of speech?

I believe they use kites as signals—visible in the sky, even from other mountain passes. How much information might be conveyed with a kite?

Adrio was particularly fascinated by the blood-feud:

It is a Chende rite of vengeance, ever portrayed as the summit of barbarity. But I have learned the custom is one of great solemnity, never invok'd for any capricious or trivial offence, and is clad in adamant rules of what the Chende call "honor."

Upon some profound violation of the law—murder, rape, assault upon a defenceless person, for example—the wronged person's clan publiquely demands justice. For this, they use words of debt, payment, &c.; but these are unmoneyed people, and for them, payment must be made in blood. The clan of the accused may at once make amends, usually by whipping, or maiming, or executing the perpetrator.

Only in the rare event no satisfactory payment is made will a feud between the clans be called; and then the offended clan may wreak vengeance upon the offending.

And when the debt is paid (how do they conclude this?), peace is restored, with no enmity on either side. This is a great point of Chende honor. A clan may not call a blood-feud to avenge the payment of another blood-debt. The Chende know well this would perpetrate an unending cycle of violence and retribution. Continuing enmity after just payment of a debt is seen to be false and dishonest, a marque of weakness or even insanity.

It seems obvious to me the ritual of the blood-debt might readily be turned to base purposes. Yet I am reminded of something C said about duelling. Honor prevents abuse of the duel—I suppose one must trust that Chende honor prevents abuse of the blood-debt.

C would call me naïve. But C has little respect for the Chende, or for honor. I know how well honor guides my hand, so I must suppose Chende honor also guides theirs, though I little recognize it.

I wonder what recourse they have when the rules are broken?

"Huh," said Cay aloud.

Here was a version of Adrio that he'd lost sight of: a thoughtful man, a man who was willing to see the best in people and things, even if it were contrary to his upbringing and training. Perhaps a little too in love with honor, but not a fool.

Cay turned a page and skimmed through several more pages full of details of Adrio's operation. Then, tucked into the back of the ledger, he found several folded pages that appeared to have been torn out of a different notebook. Curiously, he unfolded these. Adrio had written *About Cay* across the top.

He took a deep breath, released it, and tucked the torn pages into his pocket. He returned the ledger to its place and relocked the cabinet. Then he rose stiffly up off the floor and headed back to his room.

He needed to gather his courage if he was going to read *About Cay*.

Over the next fourteen days, Kell remained at the university, studying for her exams, and Cay haunted Rossoulia like an anxious ghost. Desperate for occupation, he used his lockpicks to open and close every lock in the house.

The weather stayed clear, and the passes through the mountains remained open. The way was clear for Adrio and Ondrei and any pursuers who might stop them. If Cay did not keep busy, he would collapse with anxiety. Were they safe? Had they been killed, betrayed, or captured? It was all too easy to imagine scenarios of danger and violence for them both. So he tried to read, he tried to draw, he tried to sew, and he picked locks.

He quickly got the knack of the single-ward locks, which secured drawers, cabinets, and lockboxes. A little concentration helped him master the more complicated ones. Once he found the knack of it, he had little trouble—it was, as promised, easy-peasy. Every lock, from his own jewelry box to the cook's pantry to the gardener's shed, eventually yielded to his patient touch. He was aware of servants following him discreetly from room to room about the house, watching him test door after door. His only failure was the front door, not because the lock was too complicated for him, but because the bolt was so heavy it threatened to bend his homemade lockpicks rather than shift.

The Chende servant woman, Osan, even brought him her battered keepsake box, which he unlocked and returned without opening.

"Thank you, my lord."

"Mistress." He hesitated. "When you were in Muntegri, in the prison, did you know anyone from the Bekh?"

She didn't speak, her eyes dark and cautious, not meeting his own.

"I'm sorry. I don't mean to pry or bring up painful memories. But when I was a boy, I knew an old woman named Urgeg Viki Bekh and her clan. I hoped for news of them."

Hesitantly, her voice low, she said, "There were many Bekh in the camps. But no old women. No old people, my lord. The camps are for people who can work."

"No. I see. And a younger man, Bahen Op Bekh?"

She shook her head. "No, my lord."

"Ah. Thank you."

"How did you know them, lord?"

He smiled, pocketing his lockpicks. "It's a long story."

He now knew, more or less, what Adrio was doing during his "business trips," and it was almost impossible to think of anything else. Where had he gone? Did he know where Ondrei was being held? How? Did he have informants? Did he have spies? Did his familiarity with spies and secret deeds make it easier for him to believe Cay himself was an informer? Had Ondrei been tortured? Had Adrio been captured? Was Adrio in pain, or dead, even now?

The university term ended. Kell got excellent marks. Adrio did not return, and Kell and Cay did not leave.

"My lord, I've misplaced the key to the buttery. Can you help?"

"Of course."

"Oh, my lord, the woodshed lock is stuck. Will you have a look?"

"Certainly."

He went to the back stable yard to open the well-oiled, perfectly maintained woodshed lock.

About Cay, Adrio had written.

Nesting in his bed with blankets wrapped around him, Cay sipped his wine and thumbed the dirt smudges on the first page of these notes. The handwriting within was messy, as if written in haste.

It must have been the summer of the Coup in Muntegri. Cay went up the Muntegrise Road from Lucenequa. There he found a Muntegrise patrol. Pleading some ill-usage, he led the Muntegrise up Lehoia Pass to a canyon where they found Dissut Ingoc Makhi. They fell upon the sleeping boy and imprisoned him & in the morning hanged him. This was told me by Gisson Ingoc, chief of the Makhi. He gave no reason why Cay should have done this thing, nor can I imagine one.

I met Cay six years later.

The next page was more tidily written, and the page cleaner.

At Wind House. Midnight.

Wind House was Ondrei's old house in the foothills. They had honeymooned there. It was the site of some of Cay's happiest memories—not just memories of passion but of the luxury of time alone together with nothing to do but talk, sleep, read. The luxury of *marriage*, of affection that was not secretive, of passion that was not illicit. The luxury of knowing they were family now and always would be.

There Adrio had put to paper his hypotheses regarding Cay's guilt or innocence.

H1: Cay is innocent.

Gisson lied or was mistaken.

Gisson was drunk.

He is old and not entirely strong in his mind.

In his grief and in his cups, may have exaggerated.

H2: Cay is guilty.

Gisson was not contradicted by the other Chende.

He knew Cay's name. How could he have known it?

He had no way of knowing I was married to Cay, so this was no attempt to manipulate or control me.

I can think of no reason to concoct such a tale.

Cay does not like the Chende. He changes the subject whenever they come up.

Cay never speaks of his past. It has struck me many times, how he changes the subject or exploits my feelings to avoid it.

Lucca says there are Grup spies among the refugees from the coup in Muntegri.

Cay can disguise his handwriting. He dyes his hair, uses paint to change his looks. I have seen him manipulate people into thinking he is more naïve and foolish than he is. How unlikely is it I, too, have been manipulated?

A long space, and then:

I cannot imagine why. Why would Gisson lie? But why would Cay do it?

I cannot bear to think why. I can only wonder at how.

How could Cay have known where to find the boy Dissut? How could he have known how to bring the Muntegrise up the Pass? The Pass is a labyrinth. I have travelled it, and I would not know how or where to bring them. He must therefore have been shown.

Who would show him? Why would they show him? Why would he comply?

Why would Cay—a refugee from the Grup—betray the Chende to the Grup? Why was he in the mountains at all?

Why?

That was all.

Cay drained his cup.

It had been painful to lose Adrio's love. Reading his logical reasons for it, in his handwriting, was fresh agony. And the injustice of it was infuriating: Adrio wanted to know why? Why? Why?

Why not ask him, then?

By the fourteenth day, Cay had searched every inch of Adrio's suite. He learned that the staff politely but emphatically did not want him in the kitchen. He was so jittery that he could not concentrate on sewing, drawing, or reading. He had taken to scaling the exterior walls of the house to relieve his anxiety and tire himself enough to sleep. So he was on the roof when a servant led a horse up to the back of the house. They moved slowly, the horse's red head bobbing with every limping step.

He dropped through a window into the attic and ran down the stairs and out into the stable yard, where Adrio's horse Sparrow stood, head low. He'd been unsaddled, and patches of dirt and sweat darkened his sides. Coreia, the head groom, knelt at the horse's feet, running her hands over his legs and clucking. There was no sign of Adrio.

"Is he here?" Cay demanded.

"No one here but this poor beast," said Coreia shortly, lifting one of Sparrow's hooves. "I'd like a word with whoever rode him to lameness."

Confused, Cay repeated, "But isn't he here?"

"The horse was walked over by one of Master Calareto's men," said the groom holding Sparrow's head. "My lord is not here."

Cay walked across the city, past the great bronze dolphin fountain, past the palace. On his way, he passed the small but elegantly-appointed house granted by the queen to the Muntegrise envoy. A servant swept the front steps, but the house itself seemed dark and quiet.

He went to the house of Fonsca Calareto. Though patches of white frost clung to the shadows between buildings and under balconies, the sun was warm on his shoulders, and he was sweating lightly by the time he reached Fonsca's door and pulled the bell rope.

The door was opened by a servant. "May I help you?"

Cay slipped nimbly past her and strode into the house.

"Sir! Please stop!"

"Don't worry," he said over his shoulder. "Master Fonsca and I know each other well." He glanced into the front parlor and the dining room as he passed, both empty, and continued on down the hall.

Fonsca had walked freely into Cay's home many times, but Cay had only been here for social events, only when invited, and only on Adrio's arm. Behind the receiving rooms facing the street was a smaller, private conservatory. Its door was closed, but Cay threw it open and walked in.

"Sir!" protested the servant on his heels.

The conservatory was a pleasant room, less formal than the front parlor, with old, comfortable divans and windows opening onto the small back garden. The furniture had been moved since the last time he'd been here. One of the divans was turned so its back was to the door, its cushions to the sunlight shining in through the window. He didn't have a moment to wonder about it because Fonsca was rising from a chair, his face taut with annoyance.

"What in the deep hells are you doing here?" demanded Fonsca, blocking his entrance into the room. "Tria, why did you let him in?"

"I'm sorry, sir, he—"

"Don't scold *her*," snapped Cay. He turned to the servant with an imitation of Adrio's lordly manner and said, "You may go."

She looked at Fonsca and, at his sigh and nod, vanished.

"Where is he?" Cay demanded.

"I have no idea."

Cay surveyed him. Fonsca stood with his fists clenched, his handsome mouth set in a kind of pout. "His horse has returned. Is Adrio here? Is he hurt?"

"The Muntegrise are known for their uncivil and coarse manners," said Fonsca. "You are the very illustration of the text."

Cay snorted. "Leave my personality aside for now, as well as your dislike for me. Adrio is my husband. Tell me your news of him."

"I have no news."

"We must play cards sometime, but not today." Fonsca glare intensified. Cay took another tack, gentling his tone, widening his eyes. His face had softened hard hearts in the past. "Please, Fonsca. I beg you, please, tell me what word you've had."

"None. And do not bother to play this pretty music for me, for I am deaf to it."

"You are deaf to reason," snapped Cay. "Do you suggest the horse came to you on its own? Adrio married me. It was his choice, and surely he would choose for me to know his fate now. You know he would not cherish my ignorance."

"He might not, but I do. Indeed, I think he would not choose for his fate to be reported directly to the Grup, via your good friend the envoy."

Cay flushed. "I am not a Grup informant."

"And yet you inform the Grup," Fonsca said. "I have no news for you, Lord Cay, and if I did, I would take it directly to Hob Fierar. It's good business to omit the broker in the middle."

Cay pressed his fists over his eyes, wrestling with fury and despair. He didn't know what to do: walk out like a kicked dog or punch Fonsca in the face like a madman. Neither course would get him closer to what he needed, but what else was there?

A drawling voice said, "Honestly, Fonsca, no need to be *such* a cow."

"Ondrei?" Cay opened his eyes and blinked the water out of them.

Ondrei Rege, of Lord of Noresposto, rose from the window-facing divan. He wore a blue robe pulled tightly across his barrel chest and swayed on his feet, bracing himself with one hand on the back of the divan. He scolded Fonsca: "You no more think he's a willing traitor than I do."

"He is a gentle beast, said the man of the bull that gored him," said Fonsca.

"Oh my gods," cried Cay, coming toward Ondrei. He wanted to throw his arms around him, but there were stark gray bruises and scabbed cuts on his face, and he was standing on one foot as if the other pained him. And, of course, Cay had done this to him.

Cay dropped to his knees, bowing his head. "My Lord Noresposto. Please forgive me."

Ondrei said nothing but sank back into his seat with a grunt of pain.

Cay felt tears prickle his eyes. "I had no idea you were involved. I had no idea the envoy would dare touch you. But of course—of course—this is no one's fault but mine."

Ondrei said softly, "Well, Cay. How shall we climb down from this branch?"

Still kneeling, Cay examined him. The sunlight from the window fell upon the divan, and Ondrei had clearly been napping there. His feet were bare, his hair damp, and in the open V of his shirt, Cay thought he saw more bruises. "Lay back. Please. You look awful. How badly are you hurt?"

Ondrei dropped back onto the cushions. "A little sore."

Cay sat beside him on the divan. "Do you need anything? Are you in pain?"

"No. I'm all right." His tone was dryly ironic. "They seemed to realize my ignorance of invisible flying machines was entirely unfeigned, so they stopped."

"Oh, Ondrei." This man might never be his friend again. The idea was unbearable. "Please. I am so very sorry."

Ondrei sighed. "We took pains to ensure you didn't know, so it's no one's fault but ours."

Fonsca cut in: "You forgive him so readily, then?"

"I don't know. Maybe I must ask forgiveness of him." He put a hand on Cay's. "Adrio came and got me out. He released me but was himself captured."

Cay's breath caught in his throat.

Ondrei hung his head. His eyes were shadowed, one half-hidden behind a painful-looking black bruise. His voice was low and rough. "He thrust the reins of his horse into my hand and ordered me to flee; he said I must go or we would both be taken. To my shame, I obeyed him, and now I can't stop imagining what else I might have done. Had I done something clever and brave, we might somehow have won free. But I didn't. I mounted and left him behind, and now I am here and he is not."

Cay pressed his lips together and tried to breathe past the tremor in his heart. Adrio was in the hands of the Grup.

But Ondrei was gray with guilt and sorrow, and Cay understood him all too well.

"Ondrei," he said, very softly, clasping Ondrei's hands. "May I tell you something? Something I have told almost no one?"

"If you wish." Ondrei spoke with his customary politeness, but his face was gray and lined with tension. Of course, he was exhausted, angry with Cay, and full of guilt and pain; he didn't want confessions. Cay smiled at him, acknowledging the strain between them.

"As you know, my parents were killed in Turla," he said. "I was seventeen when the Grup seized power, eighteen when my father was killed. I didn't defend him. I didn't attack the man who killed him. I hid with my sister and held my hands over her ears, so she wouldn't hear what was happening. And I have often thought of all the things I might have done differently; how I might have leaped from my place and stopped it, or distracted his attacker, or somehow helped him. How my father would be here today if only I had acted differently."

Ondrei raised his head.

"Sometimes the world moves too quickly," Cay went on. "Later you think of all the options there might have been, but in the moment, there's no time. You must make the best choice you can, knowing only what you know. No one would judge you if swift disaster overcomes you."

"Oh, Cay," murmured Ondrei.

"I forgive you without reservation." He squeezed Ondrei's hands and forced a smile. "And I hope we will be friends again someday. I'm so relieved you're home safe. And when Adrio returns, I think he will scold you for worrying."

There was a long silence. Ondrei closed his eyes, but he did not sleep; one hand rested on his chest, and he tapped his fingers there, as if lost in thought or memory.

Something about the story Ondrei had told nagged at Cay. It didn't quite make sense. Cay examined the man's injuries, trying to deduce what had happened to him: scraped knuckles, a broken fingernail, a smudge of dirt behind his ear, missed by his bath. Behind him, Fonsca sighed with boredom.

He realized what was bothering him.

"But you did not ride all the way back from Turla on Sparrow, surely." The horse would be dead after such a journey, not merely lame.

"No," said Ondrei. "I wasn't in Turla. They were holding me—"

"Ondrei," warned Fonsca.

"Oh, shut up, do," said Ondrei. "He deserves to know. I was held in Bortorra by Emaro, that moss-covered oak, that dung fly, barely five miles from Wind House."

Cay blinked at him. "What? Bortorra?"

"Bortorra is the country home of Emaro of Hasca, my near neighbor. Hasca is just on the other side of the river from Noresposto, to the west, but we do not socialize. The details of the feud between Hasca and Noresposto are too tedious to recount, but Emaro seems quite devoted to hating me and snubbing me socially. Imagine my shock to be taken to a bedroom in his summer home. Locked in, but fed and feted like an old family friend until Hob Fierar of the Grup arrived to tenderize me like a tough steak." He sniffed. "The man is allied with Muntegri, whether because he agrees with the Grup or because he seeks vengeance upon my family, I do not know."

"Treason," breathed Cay. He glanced at Fonsca. "You've sent this information to the queen?"

Fonsca said nothing.

"Noresposto is but two days' ride from here," added Cay, his brain scrambling to assimilate this news. "Why— It's been two weeks?"

"Adrio thought I was in Muntegri, like you," said Ondrei. "We didn't have time to talk, but I think he must have gone up Lehoia Pass to talk to the clan, or even all the way into Muntegri, to speak to his contacts, before he learned I hadn't crossed the mountains at all."

"But—"

"I don't know how he found me," interrupted Ondrei. "We didn't have time." He frowned, touching the bruises on his face. "And then I left him and may have killed his horse hurrying home."

Cay straightened, and then turned. "Is the queen sending a party to rescue him? To arrest the traitor and seize the envoy and bring Adrio home?" Fonsca studied his fingernails. Cay found himself on his feet, wringing his hands. "Answer me!"

He did not. But Ondrei said, "Too risky. If the envoy sees a troop of soldiers marching up the hill, he might make haste to bury the evidence—Adrio."

"Then you are planning a rescue mission, surely? Fonsca! We could be there by tomorrow night!"

Finally, Fonsca answered. "We are not hounds after a hare. Ondrei needs sleep, and I need to talk to the others and make a plan. And you will return to your burrow and stay out of it."

Cay opened his mouth to protest but then looked at Fonsca's obdurate expression and thought better of it.

"Adrio would want me to stay out of it, wouldn't he?"

"Absolutely he would."

"He really would, you know," said Ondrei, in a kinder tone.

"I do. I know." Cay lowered his lashes. "And what could I do, anyway?"

"Nothing." Fonsca nodded firmly. "You should wait at home."

"Of course." He met Fonsca's eyes. "I will wait at home. Will you send word to me if you hear news?"

"Certainly I will," said Fonsca.

Gods, what a terrible liar.

Cay said his farewells to Ondrei and set off for home. As he passed the envoy's house, he noted again how dark and quiet it seemed. Perhaps Hob Fierar was still not in Valette. Which meant Hob Fierar was probably at Bortorra. Perhaps even now, *right now*, Hob Fierar was torturing Adrio for information about the Uncanny Aviator.

Cay broke into a run.

CHAPTER NINE

The following evening, Cay descended from Adrio's coach in front of the livery stable in the village of Sarea, part of the demesne of Lord Emaro of Hasca, in the foothills of the Elurez Mountains. Lirano had driven him here after obscuring the coach's identifying crests with dull black paint. They'd come with all possible speed, spending coin liberally to change horses several times along the way.

As he waited for Lirano to finish his business at the livery, Cay surreptitiously rolled his shoulders and bent his knees to stretch his hamstrings. He didn't know about Lirano, but he was tired from the journey, and his body ached from trying to sleep in the rattling carriage. But he knew his night's work had just begun.

It was cooler here in the foothills than in Valette. Sarea was the last village on the road up to Lord Emaro's summer home, Bortorra. It clung to the banks of a lake, cupped in the steep rocky hills. In spite of the golden light of a glorious sunset, the village seemed a poor place. Its lanes were narrow and dirty, a damp stink rose off the water, and the walls of the little shops and inns were stained gray with what appeared to be mildew.

"They say someone's up at Bortorra," said Lirano, leading two hired horses out of the livery. Lirano knew this place, for he was born and raised here in the north. He seemed to walk differently here than in Valette, his shoulders looser, his accent broader. "In summer Lord Hasca's retinue and their families are all in residence for the fishing and the cool air. But in winter, they follow the sunshine south, and all these shops should be empty and boarded up. But the man at the livery said food deliveries are going up the hill once a week."

"Do they know who's there?"

"Naught but gossip. Are you sure you don't want me to come up to Bortorra with you?"

Cay smiled at Lirano with genuine gratitude. The servant had joined him on this escapade without a second's hesitation, and his steady competence had cleared away all kinds of obstacles that Cay couldn't have predicted. "I am grateful, but no. You must stay down here and keep safe. I'll bring my lord down to you."

"Very well." Lirano patted a horse's nose. "These are good beasts. Not beautiful, perhaps, but sound and fresh. Ride the mare and save the gelding for my lord; he's a bit full of himself."

The horse or my lord? Cay kept the joke to himself. "Thank you." He took the reins. "Remember what I told you. Give no one your name, or mine, or my lord's. I have no idea what I'm going to find, but the Hasca's loyalty is to the Grup, and the people here all owe him their livelihoods. You must trust no one."

"I'll remember," said Lirano.

"With a bit of luck, we'll be back by morning."

"I'll make sure I've got fresh carriage horses ready to go."

"Good. And if I'm not back by noon tomorrow, go straight to Valette, and tell Fonsca Calareto everything."

"I'll wait a few days, my lord."

"Don't wait too long; you'll draw suspicion. And don't assume all is lost if we don't come back this way."

Lirano nodded. And then he bowed, clasped his hands together, and kissed his knuckles: a countryman's old-fashioned gesture of gratitude. "Stay safe, my lord."

"You also. And don't worry," he added lightly. "I'm cleverer than I look."

"Yes, my lord. I know."

The dun mare might have seemed a reliable beast to Lirano, but Cay soon hated her. She strode out from the village at a steady, swift pace, but once the road started to go uphill, she slowed to an amble. Unless Cay constantly urged her on, she stopped to graze. Perhaps she detected his anxiety; perhaps she objected to his inexperience as a rider; perhaps she just wanted to go home. Cay suspected she was deliberately delaying him out of a spiteful nature. Meanwhile, the gelding on his lead constantly tugged to go faster, or slower, or in a different direction, or balked in alarm at every fluttering leaf or night-bird call.

The night was cold enough to show their breaths like smoke, but Cay was sweating by the time they neared the top of the hill, cursing under his breath and feeling as though he'd carried the horses, rather than the other way around. They came around a bend, where the estate's wall and gate were silhouetted black against the dark sky. He sighed with relief.

His plan, if one could call it a plan, was to tether the horses outside the wall and approach the house stealthily on foot. There he would see what could be done. He had never been to Bortorra, and knew nothing of what he would find. He had a pocket of money, a dagger, his lockpicks, and his wits. He would (somehow) release Adrio, and they would ride back down to Sarea and away.

Easy-peasy.

He startled when, in the full dark, the sound of his horses' hoofbeats changed from the dull thud of dirt road to the sharp-ringing clip-clop of a stone-paved drive. The capricious gelding, upon hearing or feeling the stones beneath his feet, threw up his head and blew sharply out his nose with alarm, a now-familiar routine the horse would have to be coaxed out of before he would proceed.

"Come on." Cay attempted to keep his voice sweet and encouraging. "It's only pavers, pretty, you can do it."

He was apparently not convincing. The gelding huffed and executed an unexpected sideways maneuver, whisking his lead out of Cay's hand. For a moment, he stood with ears and tail high, and then, realizing he was free, wheeled and trotted back down the road toward the village. Something in his motion suggested ridicule and contempt.

Cay sat in the saddle, stupefied, watching him go.

The mare he sat upon made to follow the gelding. He reined her in and attempted to direct her toward the gate. But she had no intention of being left behind by her companion. She flattened her ears, wheeled in a tight circle, and tossed her heels in the air.

Cay hit the ground with bruising force. He lifted his head to see her cantering away, tail raised like a flag of victory.

"Fuck."

He stood, rubbed his sore shoulder, and began to walk up the road, cursing himself and picking gravel out of his forearms as he went.

Apparently Adrio was an adventuresome fellow, well-accustomed to breaking people out of prisons and spiriting them away. If Cay could get to him—and he would bribe, seduce, or kill in order to get to him—perhaps *he* would have some ideas.

Cay hurried as much as the darkness and the steepness of the road would allow. He paused to rub dirt on his face and hands, hoping to darken his skin and roughen any sheen of sweat, and then slipped through the iron bars of the gate and snuck up the drive to the house.

Bortorra was an ancient stone tower surrounded by irregular outbuildings. Probably, like Wind House not far away, it had once been a fortification against Chende bandit raids from the mountains and had since been renovated as a residence. The restoration had not robbed it of its military character: it was a near-cube, three stories tall, stone and mortar, irregularly studded with arrow-slits. On the third floor, the arrow-slits had been enlarged. No doubt the renovated windows marked where the living quarters were: inconvenient for the staff, but with a good view of the lake.

A light glowed golden in one of the windows on the southwest corner of the top floor.

Cay crouched in the blackness between the wall and a terra cotta pot that probably held flowers in the summer; now it was filled with a scrubby mass of weeds. No one was about; it must be nearly midnight, and the house was dark but for that one lit window.

Adrio, he thought, hugging himself and shivering against the cold. Ondrei had said he'd been kept in a bedroom, not a cellar or a dungeon. Perhaps Adrio up was up there, in that southwestern bedroom. Perhaps he was reading a book, or writing a letter. Perhaps he was perfectly fine.

Cay surveyed the building, trying to plan the easiest route from the ground floor to the southwest window. Entering through the front door and up the stairs was tempting but surely foolhardy. Up the outside of the building seemed safer. As a boy, he had scurried up and down the walls of the Six Circles of Turla like a squirrel. Most of the tower's exterior was a flat vertical plain, lacking ornaments for handholds, and there was an unhelpful overhang between the second and third stories. And he was older now, a bit out of condition, and sore from riding and from falling outside the gate.

Still. Old stones and mortar probably provided finger and toeholds, and if he could get to the top of the stables first, he could nearly halve the vertical climb. He thought he could manage it.

And then, please, and thanks to all the gods, he would see Adrio.

He snuck toward the stables, flexing his fingers and rotating his shoulders in preparation for the climb. He heard the crackle of flames from above, and orange light flickered at the top of the tower. Wondering if the place was on fire, he looked up and saw the strangest sight.

On the tower's roof, surrounded by a scaffolding, a strange, moving black shape blotted out the stars. In the fluttering light of a fire, it seemed to swell and distend in an unnatural manner, like a monstrous blister. Cay watched as the surface of the thing bulged outward, pressing up against the wooden slats of the scaffolding.

It was a balloon.

Breathing hard and slick with sweat, he hauled himself up to peek over the tower roof's low parapet. Bortorra's masonry walls hadn't been repointed in decades, if not centuries; Cay had tucked his boots and stockings awkwardly into his belt and nipped up to the top in no time at all. Now, concealed by darkness and the sheer unlikelihood of anyone being where he was, he saw a surprising bustle of people on the roof, lit by flickering lamps. There were also piles of materials: bales of cloth, stacks of wood, and so on. He climbed over the parapet and, still barefoot, folded himself into the center of a large coil of rope to watch.

Fortunately, everyone had their eyes upon the balloon.

It was a large bag of thin black fabric, held erect by a rickety-looking rectangular scaffolding. Its open mouth was suspended over a large round wicker basket, to which it was attached by lines. It was extraordinary to see, a cloth sack billowing and swelling like the throat of a frog, seeming to pull upward through some uncanny force of its own. Air, obeying the Principle of Levity, rose as if from a hot oven, filling the bag. For inside the basket, on a sort of high table, was a kiln, and two people labored there, one feeding charcoal and the other using bellows to brighten the fire. Sparks flew upward into the cloth sack, which grew and grew. Its fattening surface pressed outward on the bars of the scaffold, and before Cay's eyes, the basket beneath lifted off the ground. The upward motion was gentle at first, but soon the balloon seemed to be straining skyward like a horse eager to escape, the lines keeping it attached to the scaffold quiveringly taut.

"Good!" crowed Hob Fierar. He, and several other people, were gathered around, silhouetted against the firelight. "Beautiful! You've done it!"

Cay bit his fist against a wave of visceral hatred at the sight of the Muntegrise envoy. He indulged in a brief, violent fantasy of the balloon suddenly becoming a solid, heavy mass, falling on top of him, crushing him from life.

"No, sir," said a woman. All the workers seemed to defer to her, and Cay concluded she was the leader of this project. "It inflates, it lifts, but it all goes wrong when we try the sails."

"Show me."

The foreman called, "Lay along the sprits," and workers sprang into action, some of them climbing the scaffolds, others lifting long wooden staves and attaching them to the basket.

Cay's eyes widened.

He had drawn this. In his imaginative pictures, the balloon's basket had been shaped like a ship, with a keel and long booms stretching out to either side, and triangular sails, full with wind, stretched from the booms to the top of the bag. He watched as workers clambered up the scaffolds with unwieldy bundles of black cloth, watched the way the wicker basket wobbled in the air, and then sank from the weight of the booms and sails.

"More fire!" called Hob Fierar. The workers in the basket began feeding the fire again, the man with the bellows sweating in the firelight. Slowly, without its previous eagerness, the balloon lifted off the ground once again.

"Drop the frames," ordered the foreman. The workers swarmed down from the scaffolds, unclewing them at each joint. The scaffolds fell backward, and the balloon remained erect without support, a majestic oval of black silk suspended in the air, its sails hanging lax at its sides. But it would not rise further, though no part of it touched the ground. The servants in the basket worked furiously with charcoal and bellows, faces shining with sweat in the firelight, but in spite of their efforts, the balloon hovered there, a few feet of air between its basket and the tower's roof. They could work no faster; the balloon, burdened by wooden booms and yards of sail, would climb no further.

Hob Fierar bellowed again for more fire, but the foreman said, more quietly, "No. Enough." The workers at the kiln stopped, visibly heaving for breath. The balloon remained inflated but sank down to gently touch the roof.

"Get a drink and rest," the foreman told the workers, then turned to Fierar. "It's simply too heavy. The heat of the kiln isn't providing enough levitational force. A larger burner would produce more heat but would be heavier still."

"What can be done to make it lighter?"

The foreman shook her head. "We've already lightened the pannier. If we replace the booms with lighter wood, like balsa, they won't be strong enough. If we replace the sails with lighter fabric, like muslin, they won't hold the wind. There must be something we're missing."

"The Heir of Lodola is holding out on us," agreed Fierar, stroking his chin.

"He must be," agreed the foreman. "This isn't working."

"I will question him further. He will tell me or regret it."

He strode away and disappeared through a door.

Cay cursed under his breath and crept through the darkness to the parapet. Swinging over, he berated himself: he should have gone to the southeast bedroom, to Adrio, rather than getting distracted by the spectacle of the balloon. He could have had him away while Hob Fierar was occupied here on the roof. He lowered himself from the parapet and searched for toeholds.

Climbing, especially climbing down, could not be done in haste. Painstakingly, gritting his teeth with frustration, Cay inched downward until he was level with the lit window. The air was cold, but fortunately the south wall of the tower still held the day's heat, keeping his fingers and toes viable, and there were excellent footholds here, the mortar between the stones crumbled with centuries of weather and neglect. If he wedged his toes in, he could stand relatively comfortably, giving his hands and arms a rest.

He descended to the side of the lit window, hooked his fingers into a deep crack between stones, settled his weight on the balls of his feet, and leaned to his left to peer inside.

The room was brightly lit. It was a bedroom, small but comfortable, simply furnished with a bed and a stand with a basin and ewer. A lantern glowed brightly on a table. Adrio sat in an upholstered chair, apparently none the worse for wear. Cay, who had been prepared for anything from bruises to burns to amputations, breathed with relief. Adrio's clothes were a bit more rumpled than usual, his hair unkempt, but he appeared uninjured and even comfortable, sitting with one leg crossed over the other knee. With the air of a man welcoming a guest to tea, he was smiling up at Hob Fierar, who stood before him.

The window would be a mirror to the men inside. Cay tested all his holds to make sure they were safe, and then reached over and tugged the window with his fingertips. It was open, just a bit—Adrio always kept his bedroom window open just a bit—and he gently, quietly, pulled it open further.

It was clear why Adrio hadn't been tortured. Because Adrio was talking.

"Well, I really couldn't say." Cay could clearly hear his voice. "*I* never had that problem. No, I could scarcely keep mine from bolting up into the sky. But, of course, different materials have different levitational virtues. It is not the weight of the materials, as I've said before, but levitational virtues inherent in every material. My first balloons were made from linen, and they scarcely rose at all, although they were very light. Only when I switched to silk could I get it more than ten feet off the ground."

Cay listened with astonishment as his upright and honorable husband delivered this mountain of fabrication and misdirection. His face was open, eyes shining as if with sincere interest in the problem of the balloon.

"You're using silk, you said?" continued Adrio. "It's the best material I've found. What are the spars made of?

"Wood," growled Fierar.

"Yes, I know, but what *kind?*"

"Pine."

"That's probably it," said Adrio, nodding. "I used cedar."

Hob Fierar strode forward, seized a handful of hair at the top of Adrio's head, and slapped Adrio sharply across the face. Cay sucked in a breath. Adrio did not move, and for the first time, Cay saw his hands, which seemed to rest comfortably on the wooden arms of the chair, were bound there by the wrists.

Fury blew through Cay's mind, clearing away all hesitation. Adrio's bound wrists, his exposed neck, his courage and helplessness in Hob Fierar's hands. Cay was so angry he thought he could crush the stones of Bortorra's walls in his hands. Adrio was *his*, and Hob Fierar would pay for this.

"You propose to send me on a hunt for *cedar?*" Fierar snarled, wrenching Adrio's head back. "I suggest you stop toying with me, my lord. I will have answers from you if I have to pull them out with your guts."

Adrio clenched his fists, then stretched out his fingers, clearly attempting to keep calm. No turmoil showed in his pleasant voice. "But the answers are not in my guts. They are on my tongue, and I am telling them to you. I saw the beating you gave my friend Ondrei; I've no mind to endure the same."

Fierar sneered. "Your friend Ondrei did not test my patience with nonsense." He released Adrio's hair with a shove and straightened. "But you're right, I need not be rough with you. I need only send word to my men in Valette to bring your husband here, and I suspect your tongue would loosen."

A muscle moved in Adrio's jaw; he was clenching his teeth. After a moment, he said, "I tell you, there's no need for anything of the sort. I am giving you the information you need. The weight of the materials isn't actually important. What matters is their levitational properties."

Fierar paced. Adrio stealthily flexed his fingers and tugged at his bonds. He immediately stopped when Fierar turned around to face him.

"And how are the levitational properties of materials to be determined, before I spend months trying to source cedar spars?"

"I don't know. I'm not a natural philosopher. In my notes was a list of materials and their levitational index. It must have been one of the pages that was destroyed."

"And that list—"

"Came from a book of my father's. I found it in the library at Lodola," said Adrio, with the air of a man patiently repeating something he'd said many times already. "Which burned in a fire nearly ten years ago. Those notes were the only copy I had."

"Then why was Noresponto burning them?"

"I don't know. I doubt he knew what they were. I left them at his house carelessly, and I think he merely threw them away."

"That's not the impression Lord Cay got."

"Lord Cay knows nothing."

Fierar snorted. "I believe you. He is no brain, but what a beauty! Those big eyes, those lips?" He leered at Adrio. "Did you know he threatened me if I hurt you? Such a fierce kitten. Perhaps I should send a message to have him brought to me. Would you treasure him as much if his pretty face were scarred? If his big eyes were blind?"

"Sir," said Adrio again, slowly, "I am telling you everything I know. Silk bag, mahogany pannier, cedar spars. She will fly. She will cut through the air like a yacht on a calm sea; you will be able to sail her anywhere except directly into a strong wind. I cannot tell you more than I know."

"I wonder." Suddenly Hob Fierar strode toward Adrio again, pulling a knife from his belt.

"Enough," whispered Cay. He reached out and pushed the window open further.

"How would your Cay treasure *you*, if you were scarred or blinded?" Fierar rested the blade of his knife under one of Adrio's brown eyes.

Cay climbed silently into the room, narrowed eyes trained on Fierar.

"Cedar," Adrio said huskily. "Silk and cedar and mahogany. I—" His gaze fell upon Cay, crawling through the window, and his eyes widened. His mouth opened, but no words emerged. Then he snapped his focus back to Fierar. "*Actually*, there might be one more thing you could try."

Cay slipped closer, pulling his dagger from its sheath. His bare feet were silent on the worn rug,

"Go on."

Cay seized Fierar's shoulder, yanked him around to face him, and plunged his dagger toward the center of his chest.

Though he'd taken Fierar entirely by surprise, the man's fighting instincts were fine, for he flinched, wrenching his shoulder from Cay's grasp and dropping his knife with a cry of surprise. The tip of Cay's blade tore his shirt and shallowly slashed his skin, but then Fierar seized Cay's wrist in a two-handed iron grip.

He was strong, bigger than Cay, and he bared his teeth savagely as his fingers dug into Cay's forearm hard enough to make Cay yelp with pain. Cay clung to the knife desperately, knowing he'd be dead if he dropped it.

There seemed to be a lot of blood and sweat, making his hands slippery. Cay's grip on the dagger weakened. He heard Adrio shout.

With his left hand, he pulled one of his lockpicks out of his pocket and jabbed them at Fierar's eyes. They weren't sharp, but Fierar jerked back, off-balance for a moment. Cay wrenched his right arm free and drove the dagger wildly at him. It punched into Fierar's throat, just above the notch in his collarbones.

Blood sprayed Cay's face, hot and meaty-smelling, and he recoiled. Fierar made a breathy sound like a kicked dog. And then Fierar was on the floor, motionless, the dagger sticking obscenely out of his neck, and blood was *everywhere*. The smell was of blood and urine and something else, an iron-rich musk Cay supposed was the smell of death itself. Cay cried out in horror and staggered back away from the corpse. He tripped over his feet and stumbled against a wall, nearly knocking over the washstand by the door.

"Where did you come from?" breathed Adrio.

"Home," said Cay, and then turned and vomited painfully into the washstand basin.

When the spasms passed, Adrio, still bound to the chair, said his name.

"Just a moment." Shaking, Cay dunked his bloody hands directly into the water-ewer and washed them, then splashed water on his face and fingered it through his hair, trying to cleanse away the sensation of life-blood hot on his skin. The water went pink, and he mopped his face with his shirt.

He pressed his lips together, trying to be calm, as he turned around to survey the room. The movement made his head swim; his breath came in fast pants.

Nothing remained of the envoy but a heap on the floor, sodden with blood. Cay could not quite bear to look at it, so he stared at Adrio, trapped in his chair, saying Cay's name again and again. He gulped down nausea, wiped his hands on his shirt, picked his way past the mess and the pools of stinking blood. He thought he'd vomit again if he touched his own weapon, embedded in the body, but he found Fierar's knife on the floor near Adrio's chair. He picked it up and went to Adrio's chair to cut his bonds. His hands, he noticed distantly, trembled.

"Gods, Cay." Adrio's voice was breathless. As soon as his hands were free, he stood and wrapped his arms around Cay.

"I'm all dirty," Cay protested weakly.

"I don't care." Adrio's arms around him tightened, his hands running up and down Cay's back, and, shivering, Cay relaxed against him, resting his cheek on Adrio's shoulder and closing his eyes.

"I warned him not to touch you," he said, nonsensically, into Adrio's shirt. "It was his fault. I always warn them first, but they never believe me."

Adrio squeezed him. "Are you hurt?"

"No." The warm clasp of Adrio's arms around him was helping to ground him, to reconnect him with his body. "You?"

"Are you certain you're all right?" Adrio cupped his face and stared down into his eyes. "Cay?"

Cay nodded.

"Good. That's good." Adrio closed his eyes and pressed his forehead to Cay's. "You are splendid," he whispered. Then Adrio released him and straightened, stepping away. "And now I must piss." He went over to the narrow bed and pulled a chamber pot out.

Cay politely turned his back, staring at the wavery reflection of his huge-eyed face in the dark window as Adrio relieved himself.

"They didn't keep me tied up often, or long, fortunately, or I'd be dirtier than you by far." Adrio's voice was strong and cheerful but not quite steady.

Still trembling, Cay put a hand on the wall to keep from swaying. "Are you hurt? They haven't beaten you, like Ondrei?"

"Oh, no. No, but then, I've been giving up information as fast as I could invent it."

He heard Adrio refasten his trousers and turned to see him smiling a little. His hearty cheer was a mask, Cay thought; he was trying to bring Cay out of his attack of nerves.

"Well. You have rescued me handily, and avenged me too. Where is Fonsca?"

"Still back in Valette, as far as I know."

"You didn't come together?"

"He did not include me in his plans. I have Lirano and the coach down in the village, waiting to whisk us away."

"Good. And the mounts to get us to the village?"

"Ah," said Cay. "I tried. But they ran away."

Adrio's eyebrows went up. "The horses ran away?"

Uncomfortably, Cay sat on the bed and pulled his boots and stockings out of his belt and began to put them on over his scraped and dirty feet. "I was able to approach unnoticed on foot," he said.

"And scale the wall unnoticed too," said Adrio. He went to the window, glanced down, and grimaced. "How are we to get out of here?"

"Perhaps we could steal some horses from the stables?"

"Guarded. We'd be shot on sight." He gestured at the corpse on the floor. "We must be quick. Someone will come in search of *this* before long."

"Then we'll walk to the village. We'll leave the road and cut through the hills."

"It'll take too long. First they'll search the house and grounds, then ride straight to the village and post men there. They'll find Lirano and lay a trap for us."

"Then we must be faster. What if we create a diversion, to draw the guards away from the stables?"

"That's how I got Ondrei free, and I was caught. It won't work a second time."

Irritated, Cay said, "Well, I don't know, Husband. Perhaps *you* could contribute some ideas, since spiriting people out of prison is your specialty?"

"If I knew how to escape, without horses or keys or useful assistance, I'd have done it already!"

Cay glared at him. "We'll scout out the stables," he said. "Perhaps it's not so dire as you think."

Adrio glanced at the window, and his voice softened. "Cay," he said, "I'm sorry, but truly, truly, I cannot go down that wall."

"Oh." Flustered, Cay patted his pockets for his lockpicks. "No, of course not. We'll go through the house. It's the middle of the night; perhaps no one will be about."

"The door's locked."

The lockpicks were on the floor, of course. It was difficult because Cay wanted to avoid the blood. If he looked too closely at the body on the floor, he would remember the blood on his face, the way it sprayed, and his stomach would heave—no, there was no time. He found the picks, rinsed them in the pink water of the ewer, and knelt to probe the lock to the front door.

"When did you learn to do that?" muttered Adrio.

"From my Grup masters, no doubt," growled Cay. "Now shut your stupid mouth and let me concentrate."

His shaking hands made opening the door more time-consuming than it should have been, but once he had it open, Adrio took the lead. It seemed he had completely memorized the layout of the house, though he had only been here a few days. He blew out the lamp and led them unerringly through dark hallways, past the main stairway, to the servants' stair at the back of the house. It was a stone spiral, narrow and pitch-black, the steps worn smooth from centuries of footsteps. They crept down from landing to landing, soft-footed. On the stairs just above the main level, they froze: they heard people in the room just below them.

"How long is Master Fierar going to be?" grumbled the first voice. "I would sleep sometime this week."

"Go to bed, then," said a second person.

"He said to wait for him while he got answers out of the Aviator."

Cay silently tugged Adrio's sleeve. Cautiously, they began to climb back up the spiral.

A third voice said, "Then he'll be there all night. That fellow's tongue is slick as the port side of an anchovy."

Cay bit his lip to keep in a hysterical giggle.

"It has been a while," said another person. Cay thought it might be the woman who was in charge of the balloon project. A chair scraped on the floor. "Stay here. I'll go see."

Adrio and Cay silently fled up the stairs, staying one spiral ahead of the sound of footsteps coming up behind them. Since Adrio's room was on the top floor, they went past it to the roof.

The balloon was still inflated, though sagging; it loomed into the sky like an enormous eggplant, blotting out the stars. The crowd of workers was gone, but a few people still sat about, chatting, clearly waiting for further instruction.

Cay and Adrio hid behind a stack of timber.

"What do we do?"

"I don't know."

Trapped. Nowhere to go, nothing to do but wait for discovery and capture. Cay had been a fool, impulsive, and led by his heart instead of his head: as always.

"I'm sorry," he whispered. "I'm sorry I lost the horses. I'm sorry I didn't have a better plan. Fonsca refused to include me, and I just couldn't bear to wait in Valette, and . . . I should have. This is my fault."

"No." Adrio's whisper was velvety in the darkness. "No, do not apologize to me. I didn't imagine I'd ever see you again. But you came for me. I'm grateful . . . And I am humbled by your courage." He huffed a laugh. "I can't believe you climbed that wall."

"You know I like to climb."

"I also know you were planning to leave and never come back. Yet here you are."

"Much good I've done either of us," grumbled Cay, his face hot.

Adrio silently slid his hand into Cay's and laced their fingers together. "Thank you anyway."

After several minutes, a distant shout from the building below. The sound of a window or a door being thrown open. More voices. The workers on the roof perked up. And then, shattering the night, a bell began to clamor.

"They've found him," said Adrio.

The workers rushed past them to the door and ran down the servants' stairs, leaving Cay and Adrio alone on the rooftop, with the silent balloon looming above them.

Adrio released Cay's hand and stood. Cay looked up at him. Adrio was staring at the balloon.

"No," said Cay. "It doesn't fly."

"It flies."

"No. I watched them test it before I came to you. It could only get a few feet off the ground."

Adrio turned from the balloon, a wild light shining in his eyes. "It won't fly because of the masts and sails and things. I tried to talk them into putting a rudder on it too. We'll have to take all that stuff off." He grinned. "It doesn't steer, but it flies."

"*Adrio.*" Cay gaped at him. He was serious.

"Come on. We'll have to be quick."

They worked together, fast and silent. Adrio held a section of the scaffolding upright while Cay climbed up and cut the sails loose from the top of the balloon. The heavy silk slithered to the ground. Cay jumped back down, clambered into the wicker basket, and began feeding charcoal into the kiln while Adrio unhitched the heavy spars and dragged them away. He threw a bag of charcoal and a few discarded cloaks into the basket, climbed in, grabbed the bellows, and began to pump.

The balloon seemed to ruffle itself, shaking its feathers like a falcon released from its hood, and the flagging bag of the balloon stretched and filled. They rose from the ground and stopped with a stomach-swooping lurch when they reached the extent of a line tethering the basket to the roof. Pulled by the balloon but restrained by the line, the basket tipped. Cay dropped into a terrified crouch and clung to the rim.

"Give me the knife!"

He passed Adrio the knife, and Adrio leaned out and cut the tether.

The balloon seemed to spring skyward, and the basket rocked, and Cay's stomach turned upside-down. He squeezed his eyes shut and gripped the rim until his knuckles went numb.

"Look, Cay!"

He opened his eyes. The basket drifted, impossibly, through nothing but sky. Adrio was standing, peering down over the edge of the basket.

Cay peeked over the rim. The roof of Bortorra dropped away, smaller and smaller in the distance, as the balloon rose into the sky.

"Oh my gods," moaned Cay. "We're going to die."

"Look," said Adrio again, pointing.

The grounds of Bortorra were alight and aswarm—people with lanterns and torches were running about. Searching the grounds, searching the buildings. Searching for Adrio and Cay.

Not one of them turned their eyes upward.

Adrio and Cay sailed up and up, above their heads, until an easterly breeze caught the balloon and took them, slowly and silently, away.

CHAPTER TEN

As Bortorra dwindled in the distance, Cay gathered his courage and his limbs and creaked to his feet, knuckles white on the rim of the basket. Beneath his feet there was nothing—hundreds of feet of nothing, and far, far below, the hard ground.

But air was not nothing, as Kell's irritating friend had said. The air seemed alive, pulling them upward and pushing them eastward, obeying laws of its own. The wind was cold and fresh in his lungs as he took in the view. It wasn't fully dark up here. The indigo sky was spangled with stars, and the eastern horizon was beginning to brighten, a line of azure above the black hills. The mountains to the north loomed, an almost-impassable barrier, their snowy sides glowing in the starlight. When he peeked downward, the world was a map: roads, rivers, villages, pastures and fences, and barns, all reduced to brushstrokes on paper, tiny and astonishing.

Adrio stood straight in the basket, the wind blowing through his hair, watching Cay's timorous explorations.

Cay said, "The bag will catch fire, and we'll burn to death."

"Possibly."

"Or we'll run out of fuel and fall out of the sky."

"I hope not."

"Or we'll be blown out to sea."

"We're going east. We'll run out of fuel and fall out of the sky long before we reach the coast."

"You've lost your mind."

Adrio smiled, wide and delighted. "We are the Uncanny Aviator. Together we have bedeviled the Muntegrise and escaped in our invisible smoke-balloon."

"Slick as the port side of an anchovy," said Cay. Adrio threw his head back and laughed.

Adrio added fuel to the kiln and turned to pump the bellows. Cay curled up in the corner of the basket, wrapped a cloak around himself, and watched as Adrio experimented with opening and closing the vent at the top of the bag to make the balloon rise or fall. His exertions must have been keeping him warm; Cay was freezing. After the first shock of flight faded, he began to feel his weariness. The two-day journey from Valette to Sarea, the fall from the horse, the climb, the— Well, he was exhausted.

"Feel that?" said Adrio. "If we go too high, the wind shifts northward. I'd rather not crash in the mountains. But if I drop us down, we'll start going east again. I just have to keep from going too high or too low."

"How do you know what you're doing?"

"I've been reading about it." Adrio smiled. "You can learn a lot from books, Husband."

"You cannot learn how to *fly* from books, Husband. How did you know this would work?"

"Well," admitted Adrio, "I couldn't think of anything else to try."

"Oh my gods, you didn't know."

"Look." Adrio pointed. Cay peeked over the rim of the basket. "Look at the clouds above us. Do you see how they're flat on the bottom? It's as if they cannot go lower. As if the air moves in layers. Different winds in different layers. Up above, the clouds go north; down here, we go east. I read about it, and now we're in the air, I can see it."

Hesitantly, Cay asked, "How do the layers of air stay separate? And how can you make the balloon pass from one layer to another if the clouds cannot?"

Adrio didn't answer.

"Is that a foolish question?" wondered Cay.

"No. It seems an excellent question to me. I have no idea."

"Kell will know," Cay suggested sleepily. "The Principle of Clouds."

"Perhaps the Chende know. They say, 'If the Wind blows right,' when they hope for good fortune. Perhaps tonight, the wind blows right."

Adrio was so handsome, with the wind in his tawny hair and the light of the coming dawn on his face. Cay hadn't seen him so happy in ages. It made Cay's soul feel a little cleaner. He tried to forget he was filthy, exhausted, and miserable with cold; his toes were scraped, and there was gunk under his fingernails and blood in his hair. He tried, instead, to bask in Adrio's happiness.

After a long while, Adrio tidily coiled and stowed the vent line, and then came and sat beside him, wrapping his arm around Cay's shoulders and tucking him against his side. Cay shuddered with relief at his warmth and melted against his body.

"Flying frightens you," said Adrio, "but you climbed up the side of a tower to save me."

He shrugged. "It's not the same. When I'm climbing, I'm concentrating on what I'm doing."

"This seems less frightening to me," said Adrio. "Because there's nothing *to* do. All we can do is let it happen. So . . . let it happen."

Cay leaned his head tiredly on Adrio's shoulder. The stars shone on them, and the night was quiet except for the wind.

"Thank you for rescuing me, Cay," murmured Adrio, so softly Cay could hardly hear it. "I've had time to regret the things I've said to you, the last few months. I'd consider myself well-served if you were in Harodj by now."

Cay shifted, tucking his icy hands under his armpits. He didn't know how to respond to an Adrio who was nice to him. Gratitude, probably. Which was not the same as liking or respect.

He said, "I only learned how to pick locks after you left." Adrio said nothing, and Cay smiled bitterly. "You're wondering if I'm lying. How can you trust anything I say, after all? You think I'm a Muntegrise spy."

"Well, I don't think so any more."

"Because I—" The words congealed in Cay's throat. He coughed to get them out. "Did I prove my innocence when I killed Hob Fierar? Perhaps I should have brought you a Muntegrise corpse as a courting-gift. Or, no, because you also think I'm a heartless killer. Perhaps it's all right if I murder my own countrymen but not the Chende?" He shrugged. "I don't understand what you think."

"Neither do I," muttered Adrio. "You kept so many secrets."

"Are you really chiding me for keeping secrets, O Aviator?"

"I would have told you," protested Adrio.

"Well." Cay rested his cheek on his knees. "Perhaps I would have told you too, if you'd given me the chance. We'll never know."

"I gave you every chance. I asked about you, and your past, and what you wanted, and you just smiled like a poppy and changed the subject."

Cay closed his eyes. He didn't want to fight. He felt Adrio sigh, and relaxed into him, leaning his head on Adrio's shoulder. He was warm all along where their bodies were pressed together, where Adrio's arm was around him, and the rest of him was cold and aching with soreness.

After a while, Cay said, "Shall I tell you a secret, then?"

"Will you?"

"All right. I never hated the Chende. I like them. I always have."

He felt Adrio's eyes on him. "You what?"

Thirteen-year-old Cay sat cross-legged on the dirt floor of a tiny stall in a Turla marketplace, picking the glass beads out of cheap costume jewelry and sorting them by size, shape, and color. All around him, the marketplace seethed and sang—shouting voices, music, barking dogs, the smells of people and cooking and fire and sewage. The jewelry Cay was breaking down was almost certainly stolen.

A hand came down and ruffled his hair. "It's getting late," said Urgeg Viki Bekh. "You should go home to your supper."

"I don't want to go home. And I haven't finished." Cay dropped a glass ruby into a saucer of other glass rubies. He looked up at Urgeg—a gaunt old Chende woman, her hair a mix of gray and silvery-lavender. She would make him leave unless he could get her talking. "Why don't you live in the mountains?"

"Why don't you?"

"I'm Muntegrise. Chende live in the mountains."

Urgeg snorted and tugged Cay's hair. "I've never even been to the mountains, boy."

"Why? Did you feud with a mountain clan?"

"No one will buy my wares up there."

Urgeg's assistant, Bahen Op, chimed in: "We were here before the Muntegrise were."

Cay glowered at him. "No, you weren't."

"We were." Bahen was whittling something ornate out of wood. "All our songs say Bekh is a plateau clan. We followed the snow-deer with our horses and dogs and never went to the mountains. We stayed when the Muntegrise came and killed the deer and made it against the law for us to own horses."

Cay had never heard of snow-deer or of Chende who rode horses across the great plateau of Muntegri. "But the Muntegrise are here now. Don't you want to go to the mountains?"

"Why would we?"

"Maybe they'd be nicer than the people here," mumbled Cay, ducking his head, using his fingernails to pry an amber bead out of its tarnished setting.

"Probably not," said Bahen cheerfully.

Later, after Cay finished breaking down the jewelry and Urgeg had fed them both bread and butter, Bahen showed Cay what he had made: an intricate set of nested wooden spirals small enough to sit in his palm.

"What is it?" Cay turned it over in his hands.

"Hold it this way." Bahen set it in Cay's cupped hand. "Now, watch." He blew on it, and its central spiral spun around and around.

"What's it for?"

"You put it above your door so you can see what the wind is doing."

It was beautiful. Cay blew on it, setting it in motion, and then asked, "Can I have one?"

"No." Bahen took it from him. "It's a Chende thing. Your father wouldn't like it."

"I ran away a lot when I was younger," Cay explained. "I began roaming the city, climbing down the city walls to the Sixth Circle. The slums. Lots of dangerous places for children: gaming dens and brothels and beggars. People who can't afford to be anywhere else. And of course, the Chende of Turla lived in the Sixth Circle. Clan Bekh began protecting me, keeping the pimps and the drug-dealers away. I suppose they took pity on me. There was a Bekh merchant—she ran a pawnshop, except most of the things were probably stolen—who let me hang around and help. She saw I was interested in buttons and fabrics, so she They arranged for me to meet a Muntegrise tailor on the Fifth, and he visited my father to see if he'd let me become his apprentice."

"I had no idea," marveled Adrio. "I thought you hated them."

"No. I spent as much time with them as I could. They were kind to me, and I'm indebted to them. Those Chende I knew in Turla."

"Why did you run away from home?"

Cay sighed and snuggled more closely against Adrio's side. "I think that's why I never told you. Because then you'd ask why I ran away from home. Why I apprenticed with a tailor, instead of my father."

"Will you not tell me?"

Cay sighed. *Why not?* "I was a baby in my mother's arms at my parents' wedding. My mother said the man who sired me had died, and her new husband, Cou Olau, pledged to raise me as if I were his own. I didn't know all that, of course, when I was a little boy. I adored him. I followed him around and went into his workshop, and watched him work. He would let me play with the clay. I was going to apprentice with him. One day I was going to be his partner. I used to pretend I was already a potter, working by his side."

Adrio turned his head to nuzzle Cay's hair.

"I was five when Kell was born. She looks just like him. More and more every year. And every year, I was looking more and more like someone else. And he . . . he stopped liking me. He didn't want to see me, or talk to me, or have me around anymore. He stopped teaching me his trade. He would punish my mother if she seemed to favor me, even if he was just imagining it. And he wanted Kell to stay away from me. He told her I was a bad boy. A bad influence, and she shouldn't be like me or listen to me."

Adrio's hand was in his hair, stroking. "Your mother never defended you?"

"Only behind his back. Kell did, though. When she got old enough. She took my side every time. Well, you've seen how she defends me."

"I can still feel it," joked Adrio, massaging his jaw.

Cay smiled. "So that's how it was in my home. Nothing I did could earn my father's favor. So I would leave. I dreamed my sire wasn't dead and I'd find him there on Six—stumble across someone who recognized me and would claim me. Which I never did, of course. Whoever he was, I never found him."

"I'm sorry," said Adrio after a while. "It must have been a hard childhood."

"It wasn't terrible." His voice was husky from talking, and he cleared his throat. "I had Clan Bekh. They always welcomed me. And my father . . . He wasn't a bad man. He provided for us. He . . . he died bravely."

Adrio rested his cheek on Cay's head.

"You grew up with secrets. How I wish I had known that. Why did you keep all this from me?"

"I hardly know. I didn't decide to. I've always kept it secret. And . . . I suppose I'm at such a disadvantage, without you knowing I'm a bastard as well."

"I don't mind, Cay."

"I know. But I do. I mind being your poor common-born husband, sometimes, though I know I shouldn't. And also . . . I don't like to talk about him. Because I loved him, and he didn't love me. And now he's dead, and I miss him. It's hard to explain. I didn't think you would be very sympathetic."

"Oh, Cay. I'm sorry." After a while he added, "Perhaps do I understand a little. I still miss my father too. My parents had a dynastic marriage, and they weren't happy. He was the one who told me to marry for love, not for Lodola."

"Well," said Cay encouragingly, "you will have a chance to do it right. When Kell and I have gone, you'll court someone different. Someone who's really good, not just good to look at."

Adrio paused for so long before he responded that Cay wondered if he'd heard him. He glanced over; Adrio's eyes were on the sky. Finally he said, "You still intend to leave, then?"

Cay blinked. "Of course. Nothing has changed."

"Has it not?"

"No. It was decided the moment you imprisoned me."

"*Tried* to imprison you. It was hardly a successful attempt."

"Do you imagine that matters?" snapped Cay.

"No." Adrio's voice was low. "No, I suppose I am being flippant."

Cay studied his face. "Our marriage is over." It hurt to say, but it was best to be plain. "But we can both begin again, wiser this time. You'll find someone who makes you truly happy. You deserve to be happy."

Adrio did not reply. After a while, Cay murmured, "Look how beautiful the sky is."

Together they watched the dawn paint the sky rose and gold.

When he opened his eyes again, the sky was deep blue with morning, and the tops of trees whisked by.

He jerked upright. "We're falling!"

"We're landing," said Adrio.

"We are?" They were much closer to the ground; the fire in the stove was banked, and Adrio held the line to keep the vent open. As the balloon gently lowered itself toward the meadow below, Cay admitted Adrio's mastery of the thing was impressive.

"You can't see it now, but Wind House is just behind us, on the other side of those hills," said Adrio. "I tried to land closer, but we kept getting blown this way. Still, we can walk a few miles and then have a meal and a bath and a bed. How does that sound?"

Like paradise, he began to say, but then one corner of the basket touched ground, and he squawked and was thrown against the side. They skidded and hopped across the field over the ground with teeth-snapping force, dragged by the wind. They might have bounced along for miles, if the balloon hadn't snagged on a copse of junipers. The basket came to an abrupt halt, tilted at a precarious angle three feet in the air, and dumped them out. Cay rolled and lay on the ground, shaking.

"Are you all right?"

"Dizzy." Cay sat up, rotating his sore shoulder. Adrio, who had landed neatly on his feet, was trying to tug the balloon out of the trees.

"You're hurt?" asked Adrio. "Your shoulder?"

"From when the horse threw me."

"You didn't tell me the horse threw you."

"Well, it had to get rid of me before it could run away. It was a lot like what just happened, actually."

He stood cautiously and stretched. Huddling in the cold in the balloon's basket for hours had left him sore in every muscle and stiff in every joint.

"Let's leave this and get somewhere warm," said Adrio. "Can you walk?"

"Of course."

He could limp. It was not far, but it was mostly uphill over uneven ground, and by the time they reached Wind House, Cay was sweating through his clothes and certain he stank like a goat in the summertime. A bloody goat. There was something gummy and black under his fingernails and in the creases of his palms that he suspected was dried blood, and stains on his clothes, and his temper was as foul as his smell. Adrio noticed and left him alone, matching his limping pace until Wind House came into view.

The sight of it didn't improve Cay's mood. The happiest days and nights of his life had been spent in this beautiful round tower-house, golden stone with arched windows, nestled in the foothills and surrounded by gardens. He'd been so full of hope— or perhaps *hope* wasn't the right word. Confidence. His Adrio loved him, was willing to challenge all Lucenequan society to be with him, so what could ever hurt him?

The door of Wind House flew open, and Mella came out. She and her husband Nesso and their children lived here year-round, tending the house and grounds and keeping all in readiness in case Ondrei or his guests wanted to visit. Mella looked alarmed at the sight of them, and no wonder.

"My lords! How in the world did you come here, afoot? I had no word!"

"It's a long story, mistress," said Adrio. "But may we impose upon your hospitality? We are in need of shelter."

"You are both most welcome. What do you need?"

Cay hung back while Adrio rattled off their wants: a message to Ondrei, food, baths, clothes, and a place to stay for a day or so while they recovered.

"I can have baths hot in an hour or so, and in the meantime, we've fresh bread, cheese, and hot stew."

Cay piped up. "Thank you. It sounds marvelous, but I would render any bathwater unfit by touching it. Who would like to hose me down?"

He was escorted to the kitchen yard pump, where he stripped and was doused with icy water by the servants' giggling children. He welcomed the scouring cold, and Mistress Mella's strong yellow soap. He scrubbed the hard soap wedge over his skin and combed the stinging suds through his hair again and again, shuddering at the memory of blood and the smell of death.

Clean, blue with cold, and wrapped in a borrowed robe with a towel around his head, he padded into the kitchen to find Adrio eating and drinking with Nesso. "Come have some food," he said, but Cay shook his head.

"I just need to sleep in a bed that isn't moving."

He expected one of the servants to escort him to a room, but Adrio got up, took him by the hand, and led him to a bedroom. It was not the same room they'd stayed in during their honeymoon. This room had a balcony overlooking the mountains, not the gardens. Cay gazed longingly at the bed, deep and wide, and covered with a red quilt. A clean nightshirt was folded neatly on the pillow. He turned to look at Adrio, who, for some reason, was still there.

They weren't married anymore. Only technically. There was the formality of Cay leaving, of Adrio filing his claim of abandonment, but it was over already.

He waited.

After an awkward moment, Adrio bowed his head. "Sleep well." He turned to go.

Only after the door was closed behind him did Cay drop his damp towels, pull on the nightshirt, and crawl beneath the blankets to sink into the warm bed.

In his dream, Cay pushed his dagger into Hob Fierar's throat so slowly he felt everything through the hilt. The skin, layer by layer, parted to the blade, then the thicker meat of muscle, the gristly pipe of the airway—all separate and horrifying sensations. What had, in life, taken barely an instant now seemed to drag out for hours. The dagger pressed on eagerly, grinding against bone, and blood sprayed and flooded and spattered out, coating him—

He woke with a gulp of air.

There was no blood, no dagger. No filthy stench. He was in a deep bed, clean and warm between smooth sheets. The room was dark. Dim moonlight streamed through the window, casting shifting shadows over the curved stone walls. He had slept the day away.

Adrio lay next to him, though he was invisible in the dimness. Cay knew the sound of his breathing, the scent of his skin and hair. For an instant, he thought he was still dreaming; a dream of his honeymoon and Adrio's love. But Adrio was lying on Cay's right arm, and his hand had gone numb. His happy dreams never featured such discomforts.

"Are you all right?" murmured Adrio.

Cay wiggled. "My arm."

"Hm?" Adrio shifted so Cay could free his trapped limb, then rolled over and wrapped his arms around Cay's waist, nuzzling his bristly cheek against Cay's chest before lapsing back into sleep.

Cay flexed his hand, waiting for the pins and needles to subside, trying to believe it would be better if Adrio weren't in bed with him. It would only make it harder to leave. He should find somewhere else to stay rather than remain here in this shifting darkness, surrounded by the warmth of Adrio.

Instead, Cay stroked tentative fingertips through Adrio's silky hair, then traced down his nape. He wore a loose-collared nightshirt, linen from the feel of it, and Cay slid his hand into the collar to stroke his shoulders. He couldn't see them in the darkness, but Adrio's shoulders were broad and smooth, with patchy freckles. Cay had liked to kiss those freckles, once. He could almost feel them—the skin on Adrio's shoulders was bumpy. Curious, Cay rubbed a thumb over one of the bumps.

Adrio woke with a jerk and a hiss of pain. Cay yanked his hand away. Then his eyes opened wide in the darkness.

"That son of a dog," snarled Cay.

Adrio sat up. "What is it?"

"Are those scabs on your back?" Adrio said nothing, and Cay insisted, "Did that bastard whip you? Light a lamp, and let me see your back."

"Oh, no. No, it's nothing. Go back to sleep."

Cay gritted, "My lord. Husband. Answer me. Were you whipped?"

"It wasn't bad, truly. It'll heal." He reached for Cay's arm.

"Does it hurt?"

"No." Cay ground his teeth, and Adrio added, "Only a little."

"I'm going to go back there and stab him again."

"Come on. Lay down." Adrio tugged him, and Cay allowed Adrio to arrange him on his side and to hug him from behind, chest to Cay's back. Adrio combed his fingers through Cay's hair, soothing him, and Cay closed his eyes, trying to breathe through his tangle of emotions: anger and love and hurt and confusion.

After a while, he said, "Why are you here? You didn't want the servants to know we sleep in separate rooms?"

Adrio tightened his arms around Cay's middle. He said, after a moment, "I missed you."

Cay laced his fingers in Adrio's and held Adrio's hand against his heart. "You didn't miss me a month ago."

"I think I started missing you as soon as we married."

Because he had been disillusioned, Cay supposed. He had been disappointed. He said nothing; there seemed to be nothing left to say. They lay quietly for a while. Adrio's body was warm, and Cay could feel the steady rhythm of his breathing.

"You saved my life," said Adrio. "I'm still astonished by it. You left me; you still intend to leave me. Don't you?"

"Yes."

"And yet you risked your life to save mine, with no thought to the risk, wanting nothing of me. It is . . . It is the very definition of *honor*."

"I didn't do it because it was honorable," said Cay.

"I know." Adrio shifted in the darkness, perhaps running his hands over his face as he did when he was thinking.

Suddenly furious, Cay sat up, folding his arms even though Adrio could not see him in the darkness. "Adrio, what is the use of all these gentle words? I told you when you locked me in my room that there would be nothing left. Where is the husband who did it anyway?"

Adrio sat up too, ready to defend himself. "Right here. And I don't believe there's nothing left."

"*Why*? What are we but two men who married too soon, knowing each other too little?"

"Two men who loved truly."

"Hah." How he wanted to believe him. He steeled his heart. "No. I think you married me thinking I was sweet-natured and would look pretty in your bed. You started having doubts when you realized I'm not very sweet, actually—"

"That's not—"

"And perhaps the pressure of the scandal was more than you expected it to be, so—"

"No. No." Adrio slapped the bed with one palm. "None of that is true. I did not give a damn about the scandal, and I hate it when you're sweet. I wanted you, all of you, all of your maddening—" Adrio took a deep breath. "*You.* I kept waiting for you to stop pretending and to talk to me, and you never did."

"I planned to tell you!"

"No. You lie, and you distract, and you maneuver, and you deny truths I can see with my own eyes. I doubted my own senses sometimes because I wanted to believe your lies. You heaped dishonor upon me with every distracting lie—"

"Your peacock's honor had nothing to do with any of it."

Adrio sighed, a hot breath of frustration. "I know. I—I think I am beginning to understand. But Cay, honor . . . it is a public display, yes, because I have been born with great gifts, and I must be seen to deserve them, to embody what it means to be a nobleman. But it is a private thing too. It springs from my heart. From my sense of who I am and must be. And to be lauded for my public honor, while in private I could not convince you to give me the tiniest sliver of your trust . . . It was painful. There seemed no reason for it."

"And so you seized upon the first explanation you were offered?"

"The only one." His voice was low with sorrow. "I grant it makes little sense, but it was all I had. What could be so terrible that you would not tell me, no matter how hard I tried to win your confidence? That you're illegitimate? I don't care!"

"I didn't know you wouldn't care!"

"Can you blame me for doubting you, when you so clearly did not want me to know you?"

"Can you blame me for doubting you now?"

"No!"

They sat in bed in the darkness, facing each other in mutual hurt.

"No," added Adrio. "Not now. Not after my disgraceful behavior. But how honored I would have been, Cay, if you had turned to me with confidence. How I would have loved to be trusted by you. Every little untruth shamed me and pricked at me. And then you looked at me with such love . . . I treated you abominably, but sometimes I needed to make you stop looking at me like that."

Cay wanted to remain angry, but he felt tears pricking at the backs of his eyes. How different would things be if he had opened himself fully to his husband? It simply hadn't seemed possible at the time. He protected his heart by letting others see what they wanted to see. He'd begun doing it as a child, pretending to be his father's son.

"I did want to talk to you." Cay's lips felt stiff as he forced this admission out. "I didn't know you felt it or you minded it. I didn't know. And then you didn't like me anymore, and I thought it proved I was right not to confide in you in the first place. But I was trying to protect myself and my sister, and you just resorted to meanness. It's not the same."

Adrio sighed. "But I still don't understand who you were protecting yourself *from*. Me?"

Cay felt a pang of guilt for hurting him. No matter how angry he got, he wanted Adrio to be happy, always. He never wanted to cause him pain. "I suppose I'm not being fair," he murmured. "It's not reasonable to expect you to be as much a fool as I am."

"That's— Wait." Adrio passed a hand over his eyes. "Wait. Lay down beside me, Cay. Lay with me and relax, and I will tell you a secret, as you told me a secret last night. Doesn't that seem a good place to begin? Lay back, Cay."

"All right." He cuddled beneath the blankets again, not touching his husband but sharing the bed.

"All right. At her coronation, the queen said she wanted to recognize the dignity and humanity of the Chende people, which the former king had never done. This was of course a response to the rumors coming out of Muntegri, of the massacres of the Chende, and the Grup labor camps. She wanted to distinguish her reign from that of the Grup."

"I remember you telling me about it."

"Those rumors . . . I wanted to find a way to liberate those prisoners and bring them to a new home. I started trying to find a way before I ever met you."

"Sounds like a very honorable thing to do."

"You mock me," Adrio said mildly, "but yes, of course. A person ought to find some way to make good use of his fortune if he has one. Also, I thought it would be fun."

Cay smiled in the darkness.

Adrio went on, "Did you know, hundreds of years ago, this used to be Chende land? There was a string of Chende fortifications at the foot of the mountains to guard the passes, and Wind House was one of them. Bortorra, too. When we Lucenequans came north, we took this land and took their towers. They became smugglers and raiders in the mountains, and we made Wind House a fortification against them. Did you know that?"

"No. But I knew a Chende in Turla who told me Muntegri used to be his clan's land."

"Yes. I think they were first. But the Lucenequans came up from the south, the Muntegrise came down from the north, and now the Chende clans are in their mountains. Or serving us as our servants and laborers, or being worked in the mines by the Grup. That's how I got the idea to bring them out of the camps in Muntegri through Chende territory. Surely the mountain Chende clans would help their cousins, I thought."

"The Chende clans demand payment for passage through the passes," said Cay flatly. "No matter who you are."

"They do. I didn't know at the time." He shifted. "If it was light, we could see the mouth of Lehoia Pass through the window. It's just through the hills to the north. We Lucenequans named it Lehoia for the lions, but the Chende call it Szul, which means *wind*. They speak often of the wind."

"Perhaps they worship it."

"Certainly they respect it. So, one night on our honeymoon, you were asleep and I was looking up at the mountains, thinking about how the Pass goes right to the river that runs north to Turla. After we returned to Valette, I came back and rode up alone and met with Gizon Ingok of the Maquhi Clan."

"I remember. You told me you had some business and left me alone for a week."

"Do you challenge my honor for my lie? Well, you're right to do so. I was eager for your approval, and I was afraid the Maquhi would kick me out on my ear."

"You're lucky Gizon Ingok didn't kill you."

"You *do* know him, don't you?" Cay said nothing, and Adrio continued. "Fortunately, he is susceptible to wealth."

"I picked the lock on your cabinet and read your account book," said Cay. "I know what you've been paying the Maquhi Clan."

He expected anger, but Adrio only snorted. "So. I dealt with the Maquhi Clan, then I followed the river north to the prison camps south of Turla, hired six Chende, and led them south through the Pass. They live in Lodola now. Do you know what surprised me about it all? I was terrified the whole time."

He confessed this in a voice so low as to be almost inaudible. Cay frowned, puzzled. "You're never afraid."

"I was so frightened the first time I spoke to a Grup guard at the work camp, I thought I would faint."

"You were throwing lies in Hob Fierar's face as he was getting ready to torture you."

"I was very nearly pissing myself." He turned his head on the pillow. "When you came through the window, my gods. I have never been so frightened. All my life I'd longed for adventure, not realizing I was such a coward."

"You?"

Cay rethought what he'd seen in Bortorra, when Adrio, sitting tied to a chair, smiled up into Hob Fierar's face and made up lies about the levitational properties of cedar. Nothing about him had seemed frightened—his relaxed pose, his easy voice.

"You are no coward," whispered Cay.

"Anyway," Adrio went on, "that is my best explanation, Cay. I wanted to be a hero. I wanted to be *your* hero, but I came home with a new knowledge about myself: my cowardice. And my impotence. The camp . . . There are hundreds of prisoners, men and women and children, and I'd rescued six. I'd imagined

I would feel triumph and you would admire me, and instead, I was frightened and tired, and with all my money and planning and daring, I had helped *six people*. I could go back again and again, and still, it would be so little. So, so little."

Cay turned his head to look at him but could see nothing but a silhouette in the darkness.

"Of course I wanted to tell you everything. And I wanted you to comfort me and tell me I am not such a bad fellow. But then I wasn't sure you would. Perhaps you would be unimpressed. Perhaps you would laugh at me and my feeble attempts to be a hero."

"I would not have laughed at you, Adrio."

"I didn't know. You seemed more like a stranger every day. Whenever I tried to speak of the Chende, of Muntegri, of your past, of *anything*, you changed the subject. You weren't even honest about the color of your hair. And when Gizon told me . . . It made no sense. It still makes no sense. But I couldn't imagine how he would know your name if there wasn't some truth to it. And by then, I was so shamed by you, and so angry with you. My heart was broken, and I could make no sense of anything you did."

They were lying side by side together in the big bed, and Cay was wretchedly silent.

Adrio had been in pain. Frightened and uncertain, he had needed him. Adrio always seemed so confident; he very nearly glowed with self-assurance. But he had needed a husband's care, and Cay had been no comfort to him. Cay had been too intent on keeping his secrets, blind to his husband's problems and unavailable to him in his need.

He had utterly failed his husband—it was a hard lesson to learn, but it was true. Cay had enjoyed the comfortable home Adrio had provided, spent his money, and savored his privilege while his husband had suffered alone.

They lay in silence for a while in the darkness, and then Cay said humbly, "I should have left months ago so you could start over. I'm sorry."

"Ah," whispered Adrio. "How can you say it?" His arms surrounded Cay, and he pulled him back against his chest, hugging him warmly, pressing his cheek to the side of Cay's neck. "Don't go. Don't go. Cay. I'm confused and surprised and confounded by you. The more I learn, the less I understand, but don't leave me, Cay."

"Why?" whispered Cay. "I have been so bad a husband. You should be delighted to be rid of me."

"As you want to be rid of me?"

Cay sniffled.

For so long, he'd wanted Adrio to talk to him, to hear Adrio apologize and ask him to stay. And now he had—but this sensation in Cay's gut wasn't happiness. It was anxiety. Because no matter what Adrio said now, Cay remembered the swan poem, the earrings, and the nights alone. The acid scorch of Adrio's contempt and the sickening bitterness of Adrio's regret. Adrio had hurt him, and he did not know how to trust him.

Maybe it was too broken. Maybe it was too late. Maybe . . . he was just too tired to think of a solution to this tangle.

Adrio kissed his neck. Then he did it again, his warm lips lingering on the sensitive skin under Cay's ear. He opened his mouth, kissing slowly and a little wetly now, and Cay shivered with a dizzying surge of pleasure and arousal. Unexpected, like stepping off a curb, a little swoop of surprise and excitement inside. Cay made a small noise, half-protest, and Adrio smiled against his skin.

"Are you—"

"Yes," whispered Adrio.

"But—" He broke off with a gasp when Adrio brushed his lips against the oval of his ear. Adrio knew he loved that.

"The last time," Cay began unsteadily, trying to think beyond the tingly delight of what Adrio was doing to his neck. "The last time, you didn't—"

"I don't like remembering the last time," Adrio growled, his voice low.

"You regretted it."

"I regretted being cruel. I despised myself because I wanted you but was too weak and confused to find a way to want you without hurting you."

Cay rolled over so they were face to face. "And what are you doing now?"

Though Adrio was almost invisible in the darkness, Cay imagined he was looking into his eyes. "That night I was drunk, and tired, and . . . and a fool. I hate to think that your last memory of us together is going to be that night."

Oh. Adrio wanted a last time to say goodbye? It would hurt so much when he left—would this make it hurt more, or less?

But of course he agreed, tipping his head, meeting Adrio's lips with his own. Adrio cupped his face, his thumb stroking over the apple of his cheek as they kissed, slow and deliberate.

Cay shivered again. They were going to make love like this, with this intentional tenderness. A *goodbye* lovemaking. His entire body was alive and singing with welcome, while his heart cringed at how much it was going to hurt.

Thankful for the darkness, Cay reached up and drew Adrio down to him.

How vulnerable Adrio had been tonight. Cay wished he could see him, but perhaps, without the darkness, Adrio wouldn't have been able to confess such weakness or beg Cay for this.

This time, Adrio's kiss was deep and almost rough, and a thready moan rumbled in the back of his throat. With eager hands, he stripped away Cay's nightshirt and then gripped his biceps, his forearm, his wrist, squeezing. Cay didn't want to think, only to feel; he freed his legs from the blankets and twined them around Adrio's hips, pulling him down with his legs, reveling in the weight and size of him. Adrio broke this kiss with a sharp gasp; bracing his weight on his arms, he rucked his hips, rubbing them together. The tail of Adrio's nightshirt was wadded between them, preventing perfect contact, but still, they could feel each other's erections through the bunched cloth. Exciting and gorgeous and not enough.

"I love your prick," whispered Adrio, surprising Cay into laughing.

Adrio pulled his shirt off over his head, then rolled them over so Cay was sprawled on top of him, his hands braced against Adrio's chest. They kissed again, laughing into it. Cay lined them up by feel, just *so*. Adrio kissed him needily, gripping his ass to hold him still while he thrust upward against Cay's belly.

Cay wanted more, wanted to be thoroughly penetrated and filled and overwhelmed by Adrio. But they didn't have any oil or ointment, so he just moved with Adrio, enjoying the catch and skid of skin against skin, the heat and humidity and imperfect roughness of it, the stutter of Adrio's breath, and the pressure of his hands.

And then Adrio's fingers were questing, suggesting, sending shivers over Cay's skin and making his toes curl. "Will you let me inside you, Cay?" he murmured.

Unseen in the darkness, he made a hunting-in-the-bedside-cabinet motion, familiar as an old friend. Except this was Ondrei's house. Ondrei did not fuck, nor, probably, equip his chambers for others to do so.

But Adrio had a bottle of almond-scented oil, and he was working its cork out as he kissed Cay, and Cay pulled back enough to murmur, "Where did that come from?"

Obviously, Adrio had brought it to this room. Borrowed it from Nesso or from a helpful servant, with a wink and a grin. There was a smile in Adrio's voice as he replied, "'Tis the intrepid horse, not the swift, that wins the race."

Cay sat up. "Is this . . . Did you plan this, then?"

"You think I presumed?" whispered Adrio. "After the mistakes I've made, I presume nothing from you. But I have been stupid with wanting you, ever since you came for me in that bloody tower. Cay, do you want to stop?"

"No." That, at least he was certain of. "No, don't stop. Show me what you brought."

"Mm." Adrio's hands were on his thighs again, his hips. "It's too dark to show you. I'll have to let you feel . . ."

They kissed, sitting up in bed, and Cay lifted onto his knees to give Adrio's clever, oil-slicked fingers easier admittance. And soon enough, Cay sank downward onto Adrio's cock, the scent of almonds and arousal all around him.

He bit his lip at the burn and paused to adjust, loving the tightness and stretch.

"Oh, Cay."

Cay smiled in the darkness, concentrated on making his muscles relax, and sank voluptuously down on Adrio, seating him hard and full inside him. He began to move slowly and easily, feeling vulnerable and thrilled and loving how Adrio's heavy length opened him. So *good*. Adrio began to move with him, gently, pressing up with each of Cay's downstrokes, making them both gasp.

Adrio groaned, tightening his fingers.

They clenched and rocked and fucked, slow and oily and steady. A luxurious passionate grind, the kind they could make last for a long time. But they were too eager; Adrio gripped him tighter, and Cay rode him faster, and the old wooden bedframe began to creak in protest as they moved together. Cay arched his back, dropping backward to catch his weight on his hands, bracing himself crab-position while Adrio pumped up into him.

He had fallen into a trance of pleasure, wanting to finish but wanting to make it last. Wanting whatever Adrio wanted. Wanting to go on all night.

"More?"

"Please—"

Adrio heaved up, hauling Cay off. He threw Cay onto the bed, caught his legs and spread them wide, and pushed inside again. Deep and hard, deep enough to drive a high cry out of Cay's throat.

"All right?"

Cay made a wordless sound of surrender, and Adrio leaned over him, devouring his mouth in a kiss as he worked his hips, grunting with effort and need, pumping deeply into Cay, making him cry out and clench his fists in the bedding.

Cay was immobilized, impaled, flying with exhilaration as Adrio took him.

Perfect. *Perfect*.

Maybe it was because it had been so long. Maybe it was because this might be the last time. Maybe it was because, however much they argued and wrangled and hurt each other, their bodies meshed perfectly.

Maybe they were simply perfect together and always had been.

Later, at the edge of sleep, Cay heard Adrio murmur, "Oh, gods, how I miss you. Cay, my Cay, I don't want this to be the last time."

Cay sucked in a breath to reply—he knew not how.

"Ah, no, don't answer." Adrio's thumb brushed over his lips. "Don't say no. Please. Don't answer now—just sleep with me tonight, Cay, and don't say no until later."

Chapter Eleven

The sun was high in the sky when Cay slipped out of bed the next morning, careful not to wake Adrio. In the cool gray light streaming through the mullioned windows, he paused to peel back the sheet and inspect the red wheals crisscrossing Adrio's shoulders, the black scabs where the whip had broken the skin here and there.

The man responsible had died for it, and Cay was satisfied. He felt no guilt for what he'd done and trusted the dreams of blood would pass. It was sufficient.

He pulled on the robe and slippers someone had left for him. Stomach rumbling, he prowled down to the kitchen, drawn by the smell of food, and was given a small feast: soft bread rolls with bacon and goat cheese, stewed figs and apricots, and a pot of hot tea. He took his tray out into the gardens of Wind House.

It was cool but not cold, with beads of dew fresh on the grass. Cay curled up on a bench amid the winter shrubs and ate, enjoying the moist air on his face. He gently eased his feet out of his slippers, warmed a hand on his steaming teacup, and wrapped it around his scraped and sore toes.

Wind House perched on a high hill at the base of the Elurez Mountains. A stone wall partially surrounded the garden, but it was open to the south, and one could look out across the green-and-gold patchwork of Lucenequa, stretching down and away. The clouds, flying like mysterious balloons through unseen currents of air, cast shape-changing shadows over the plain. The garden walls were composed of the same golden stone as the house, and bare vines climbed them, thorn-studded black tendrils snaking up, spiny black fingerbones anchoring themselves to rock. A few gray leaves rattled in the cold breeze. They were rose vines, he supposed. In summer, the beauty of their flowers would charm the eye. In winter, their true nature was revealed: tenacious survivors, well-armored and willing to scratch.

He sipped.

He felt . . . fragile.

Adrio wanted him to stay, to try to be better husbands to each other. His soul was eager to agree. He had longed for Adrio to return to him, to talk to him, to explain. And he had. He had apologized. He wanted Cay in his bed and, presumably, in his life. And they might go forward happily together. Adrio might tell Cay his plans. He might let Cay help with the Chende refugees. He might grow to love Cay, at least a little, and then they might have a happy marriage.

But it had taken so much for Cay to decide to leave—so much hurt and anger—and he did not think he could put it aside. It had always been a foolish dream, the marriage of someone like Adrio to someone like him. It hadn't worked. He had hurt Adrio, and been hurt, and perhaps it was better to just let it go.

Because if they remained married, Cay would have to give Adrio what he wanted—and what he wanted was the truth. The inner truth of Cay, all the scars and thorns of his secret nature. Adrio would call it honor. He had been stupid—perhaps dishonorable—to try to conceal himself from Adrio; his husband was far too intelligent, too in love with truth, to be distracted by Cay's pretty tricks.

He would have to tell him—about his father, his mother, and Kell, and Dizut Ingok, and *himself*.

Cay's sense of honor, if he had one, came not from his parents, but from Clan Bekh and Clan Eret, the Turla Chende. His parents—his father—had wanted him to be agreeable and well-behaved, to stay out of trouble, to keep their secrets. The older he got, the more frequently he'd escape to the Sixth Circle, staying with them for weeks, playing with their children, learning their tales. Those clans had taught him another code, one (Cay suspected) Adrio would not respect.

Only Kell loved him for himself. Adrio might say he wanted to know Cay's truth, but it was an easy thing to say. He knew—in spite of Adrio's reassurance—how little it took for Adrio to reject him. How could he trust this man? How could he trust this man to trust him?

Did he have the courage to try? How would he even begin to be the kind of husband Adrio wanted? He supposed he could start this morning: bring Adrio breakfast on a tray and talk with him in the daylight. Tell him all, and face the possibility of his rejection without hiding his face in darkness, and without the distraction of lovemaking.

The idea was terrifying. He could not do it.

So he ate, drank, hugged his toes, and awaited the moment his husband would wake up and want to talk some more.

Distracted by his thoughts, Cay heard but paid little attention to the approach of horses' hooves up the gravel walk. He looked up when a string of riders came into view.

The horses had short, muscled legs and big feet, well-composed for steep mountain trails, and shaggy reddish coats to protect them from mountain winds. The riders wore woolen caps and ohahi, woven in squares of blue and yellow. He could see their purple-streaked hair where it emerged from their caps.

Cay was momentarily stupefied by the sight of Maquhi clansmen here, in the cultivated garden of a Noresposto villa, rather than in a lofty red-walled canyon, under a hot summer sky. When the thought, *They must not see me*, popped into his head, it was too late. One rider, a man, was pointing at him. Recognized him.

Cay leaped from the bench and sprinted toward the kitchen door, but one of his sore bare toes caught on a paver and he tripped. He caught himself on his palms and tried to scramble to his feet, but they were on him, a knee in his back, hard hands trying to pinion his arms. He struggled and threw a savage punch. It didn't land. Then the man was behind him, a riding crop to his throat. Cay shouted threadily, kicking, jabbing with elbows.

His breath stopped when the riding crop pressed into his airway, and he could do nothing but struggle to inhale, his head swimming.

"What in the name of all the gods is going on here?" It was Adrio's voice, roaring from the direction of the house.

The man's grip on the crop loosened, and Cay collapsed to his hands and knees, coughing. He looked up through tear-smeared eyes. His husband strode across the terrace in his nightclothes, his hair unbound, nearly vibrating with anger and the grandeur of his class. He was the Heir of Lodola, his face terrible in its arrogance and outrage.

The Chende bowed to him, all but the one who remained kneeling beside Cay, a hard hand wrapped around his wrist. Cay, massaging his throat and gulping air into his lungs, tried to assess the situation: five Chende scouts, with six horses, all bearing the insignia of the Maquhi Clan, versus one furious Heir and himself.

"Scouts of the Maquhi Clan," replied Adrio, icily.

One of the scouts, a woman, stepped forward and bowed. "I am Vuku Duli Maquhi."

"I remember you. What brings you? Aside from assaulting my—"

Adrio broke off, and his eyes widened in astonishment. Then he blinked and his face went blank; when he turned his gaze back to Vuku, his expression was again aloof and proud. "Explain yourself, Maquhi Scout."

It was exactly the reaction he'd had when Hob Fierar was questioning him, and he'd seen Cay coming in the window—a shocked reaction, swiftly concealed.

"My lord. We were posted at the mouth of the Pass, and we saw a flying thing—an oval thing. It must have landed nearby. We wondered if anyone at the house saw it. We did not expect you to be here, my lord."

"But then we saw him," added Cay's captor. "And I recognized him."

Adrio's eyes flickered down to where Cay sprawled on the terrace. "Are you all right?"

"I'm fine." Cay struggled to get his feet under him, but his arm was twisted behind his back. He tried to stand, but a sharp jerk to his arm dropped him to his knees, pain radiating up to his shoulder.

Adrio was staring at him, his face inscrutable.

Vuku asked, "My lord, you . . . know this man?"

"I do know him, and if you hurt him, I will be annoyed. Explain yourselves."

"Ease up, Haxut," said Vuku, and the pressure on Cay's arm fractionally lessened.

"This man is Cay Olau, an enemy of Clan Maquhi," she continued. "We are taking him to our chief so he can pay his blood-debt."

"Cay Olau is under my protection and in my service," said Adrio.

Adrio must not be dragged into a blood-feud with the Maquhi Clan. They might kill him. They might punish him. Certainly they would cease to help him. Cay stared at Adrio with all the intensity in his soul: *Don't tell them I'm your husband.*

"Respectfully," said Vuku, "this has nothing to do with you. He belongs to the clan."

Adrio's voice chilled. "And I tell you, by the vow I took on our wedding day, no harm will come to him."

Cay closed his eyes and sighed.

Several scouts spoke at once. "You *married* him?"

"When?"

"Have you been married to Cay Olau all this time?"

Vuku raised her voice to speak over the babble. "What you've chosen to marry is no matter to the Maquhi Clan. We are owed a blood-debt."

"What does a vow mean to a Lucenequan?" added Haxut, the man who held Cay's arm.

"What do roots mean to a tree?" snapped Adrio.

Cay raised his eyebrows at Adrio. This was not the time for Starlight Conversation.

"I know Gizon Ingok," added Adrio, "and I know Krutiv Ingok. I trust *they* would not so lightly sneer at my honor nor toss away Clan Maquhi's relationship with me. That is what you are doing in their name. Are you comfortable?"

The scouts shuffled and shared a glance. Cay remembered the record book he'd seen: the food, fuel, medicine, and supplies Adrio had given the Maquhi Clan in exchange for passage and guidance through Lehoia Pass.

But Vuku pressed her case. "You are protecting an enemy of the clan. Criminals must be punished. Do you value him over your friendship with the clan?"

"I value the truth," said Adrio. "And I know Cay Olau. He could not have behaved the way Gizon described. There must be some . . . mistake."

The Maquhi clansmen drew themselves up; Vuku dropped a hand to her dagger.

Cay closed his eyes. "Adrio," he whispered. This was a deadly insult. Matters of blood-debt were profoundly important to the Chende; to suggest a blood-debt was mistaken—or worse, a deliberate falsehood—was a blow to the honor of every clan member.

But Adrio wasn't finished. "Tell Gizon that Cay is under my protection."

"Tell him yourself," snarled Vuku. "We'll all be fascinated to hear it. We are taking our prisoner to our chief; if you wish to challenge the Maquhi Clan over a matter that does not concern you, you may do so." She turned. "Haxut Malit, put him on the packhorse. You three, go find that thing we saw in the air. We'll meet at Hemaquhi."

Haxut rose to his feet, hauling Cay up with him. Cay began to struggle but found a knife at his throat.

"If you fight me, I will slit you where you stand and count our blood-debt satisfied. Come, or die here."

Cay obeyed, stumbling. He looked pleadingly over his shoulder at Adrio, who said, in his carrying, commanding voice, "Wait. Maquhi scouts. Give me a moment to dress and saddle my horse. I am with you."

"You—"

"I will accompany you to speak to Gizon Ingok. Until then, you will keep my husband as safe as an egg in a nest, or Lodola will demand his blood-price from the Maquhi Clan."

Vuku narrowed her eyes at him. "A blood-debt called in retribution for resolution of another blood-debt is not legitimate."

Adrio showed his sharp teeth in a smile. "Unless the first blood-debt is false. Ten minutes, Maquhi scouts, and we ride."

Two scouts and Cay rode up the path toward Lehoia Pass, the Heir of Lodola accompanying them.

Adrio had reemerged fully dressed in riding clothes, with clothes and boots for Cay, which he had been allowed to put on. Adrio, as it happened, kept a string of Chende horses here at Wind House, headquarters for his refugee-smuggling activities. He and Cay rode his Chende mares. They had no opportunity to talk privately, but he was aware of Adrio riding just behind him.

The Chende horse had an easy gait but a broad back. Cay's thighs, still sore from the ride to Bortorra and the climb up the tower, ached with every clop. They rode through the day, stopping only for water and piss breaks and checking the horses' hooves. If he lived through this, he vowed he would never ride again.

But that seemed unlikely.

Up, up, out of the green hills, up to the rocky slopes where only cypress and thorny shrubs grew, up through fog and mist until they emerged into brilliant sunlight where the rocks turned red and gold. The air felt cold and dry up here, and the wind blew eddies of diamond-sparkling snowflakes from the high peaks down through the sunlight onto their shoulders.

The trail grew steep and narrow so they could only ride single-file. A cliff loomed skyward on one side and plunged down the other; far below, a cold swift river foamed through a stone channel. This was Maquhi Clan territory, marked by the strings of tattered blue-and-yellow linen flags affixed to rocks and strung across the canyon above and below. They snapped in the constant wind with a sound like handclaps. The sunlight was warm in spite of the frost growing like moss in the shadows, and both Cay and his horse were sweating as they mounted the slope.

He was numb. They would kill him. Lehoia Pass was the site of his life's worst nightmare, and he had always known they would kill him if he ever came back. Yesterday, that had been impossible, a fate only for bad dreams. The Maquhi Clan did not come down from their mountains, and he would never go up. But now here he was, and now they would kill him.

Adrio must, must, *must* go home.

He had no idea what Adrio had planned. He behaved like a hero from an oil painting: tall, shoulders square, and back straight against injustice. Heroes had no place in these cruel mountains, though. Loss, poverty, and bitterness made the Chende hard; the Maquhi clung to their dominance over the other Chende clans, and their pride would brook no defeat. What would they do with an idealist like Adrio?

He did not speak. The Maquhi Clan was not to be trusted, and he would say nothing to them. And though he was acutely aware, every moment, of Adrio riding up the trail behind him, he didn't speak to him, either. The scouts would hear every word over the thump of their horses' hooves. The Maquhi were treacherous.

So he kept his mouth shut and his wits about him as he stewed and ached.

They stopped at a stream when the sun was still bright but lowered in the sky. "We'll camp here until morning," said Vuku, dismounting and leading her pony to water. "These horses have worked hard."

Haxut lifted Cay down from the saddle. His legs barely held him up; he wobbled, caught his balance by falling against a boulder, and waited for the pins and needles to stop racing through his legs and feet. Eventually, he walked unsteadily to a patch of scrubby bushes to relieve himself. When he turned back, he saw Adrio, too, had dismounted.

He sat on a rock and watched silently as the scouts set up camp, built a fire, and tended their horses. Adrio knelt at a mare's feet and talked to her quietly as he ran his hands up and down her striped legs. She lifted each hoof for him and playfully lipped at his hair. Apparently, they were old friends. Of course, Adrio had traveled the Lehoia Pass into and out of Muntegri several times this past summer and fall. It was strange to think of it, but Adrio knew this path, this terrain, better than Cay ever had.

He watched as the others groomed the horses and tethered them to graze near the stream. Adrio and the scouts folded blankets on the ground near the fire, and at Adrio's nod, he joined them there and sank down cross-legged on the blankets. The fire was warm on his face but cold seeped up from the ground into his bones.

The shadows lengthened, and the air cooled. The only sound was the whuffle and crunch of the grazing horses and the ceaseless applause of the threadbare blue-and-yellow Maquhi Clan flags strung from rock to rock above them. Cay's joints seemed to unbuckle; he closed his eyes and wished for sleep, wished he could sink into the ground and disappear.

He heard the scouts offer to share their food with Adrio. How courteously Adrio accepted! But then, Adrio was usually exquisitely polite, even—especially—with people he disliked.

"Here." Adrio's voice was barely above a whisper. "Eat some of this."

They sat side by side, as close to the fire as they dared, and quietly they shared the food the scouts had given to Adrio: dried meat, dried fruit, chewy bread, a flask of wine that tasted suspiciously familiar: Lodola white, sweet and a little flowery.

"How are you doing?"

"I can hardly say." Cay's whisper was barely louder than a breath. "My lord, you shouldn't be here."

"Neither of us should be here."

Cay stared at him. He didn't understand. He must go home.

"Lord Lodola," said Haxut from the other side of the fire.

"Yes, scout?" returned Adrio.

"Did you see the flying thing yesterday morning? It came from the west."

Adrio frowned in puzzlement. "What sort of flying thing? Do you mean a bird?"

"No, lord," said Haxut. "We would not have come down the mountain to investigate a bird. It was a round thing in the sky."

"Oval," said Vuku. "Like an olive. Bigger than a horse."

"A round thing bigger than a horse?" repeated Adrio, with bafflement in his voice. When had he gotten to be so adept with an untruth?

"Oval," repeated Vuku doggedly. "Like an olive. Or an egg."

"And it flew?"

"From the west," said Haxut. "We thought it landed down the slope from the house."

"We all saw it," agreed Vuku.

"My friends," said Adrio, with the gentle sincerity of a shameless liar, "I have not seen this thing."

"And you?" Haxut looked at Cay. "Do you know what we saw?"

"I don't think so," said Cay. "I think I would remember if I ever saw a flying olive."

Haxut narrowed his eyes at Cay. Adrio put in, "Cay came to Wind House with me and has been in my company the last several days. Neither of us saw what you describe, and the servants at Wind House never mentioned it."

Vuku murmured to her partner, "Leave it. The others will find it. This is more important."

Haxut nodded grudgingly.

When the sky darkened and the moon rose, the scouts cast themselves down to sleep. Cay curled up too, huddled under a blanket. He was so weary but so anxious; his body yearned for sleep, but his mind whirled.

He managed a doze but woke when Adrio reached over and began stroking his hair. He rolled over to face his husband, who lay beside him and continued to comb his fingers through Cay's hair, a tender expression on his face.

"My lord," whispered Cay, "please go home."

Adrio smiled gently. "My lord," he replied, pulling one of Cay's locks straight, and then releasing it to spring back into a corkscrew, "I will not go home."

Cay glanced at the scouts, who were unmoving in their bedrolls. "You don't understand. Nothing will stay them. There's nothing you can do to stop it."

"I know them." Adrio shifted closer. His voice was low, velvety. "I know Gizon Ingok, and more importantly, I know Krutiv Ingok."

"You know what they tell you," Cay said bitterly, "and if you think the old man listens to his daughter, you're mad."

"I think the clan listens to her. And I'm getting you out of this if I can."

Cay sat up, wringing his hands. "You're only getting yourself *into* it. You must not trust their word. They're more likely to kill you than to release me." In his frustration, Cay's voice had risen; he glanced over at the scouts and dropped his voice to a whisper again. "My lord," whispered Cay, "go back."

Adrio folded his arms behind his head, his body relaxed. "If you think I will abandon you among your enemies, you have gravely mistaken me. Besides," he added, smiling the same careless and reckless smile Cay always found so attractive when it involved rescuing waterfowl and wounded dogs. "I have a lever."

Cay rolled his eyes. "You have pretty words," he said, "and the arrogance of your station. Neither of which will impress the Maquhi Clan."

"You may be right. But I meant what I said. On the day we married, I vowed to protect and serve you the rest of my life, and I will do so if I can."

"Adrio, barely three weeks ago you were trying to lock me in my room—"

At this, Adrio abandoned his pretense of laziness and sat up too. "Will you forever play that note?"

"How can I forget it? And now you're going to war with the clan? Because that's what it means."

"I know what it means."

"You don't." Cay stared into his eyes, leaning forward, and put all his conviction and desperation into his voice. "Please, as you love your honor, just listen. If you die with me, Kell will have no one. Do you hear? She will have lost everyone. Kell needs you. Please, please go back to Valette. Tell her that you tried. She will know there was nothing you could have done—she knows what they are capable of. Take care of her. Please."

Adrio snorted. "If I returned without you, Kell would go up like a granary in a dry summer."

"*Be serious!*" Cay whisper-shouted. "What does that *mean*?"

Adrio leaned in. "It means she would never forgive me, and I would never forgive myself. Husband, I vow to you I will care for our sister Kell for the rest of my life. And if I die untimely, she will be the Heir of Lodola."

Gritting his teeth, Cay said, "She doesn't need a Lucenequan title. She needs family."

"She has it. I vow it."

Desperately, Cay tried to think of something to convince him. "You'll never recover another refugee. This Pass will close to you forever. Who will save them then?"

Adrio stared at him for a long moment. Then he said, "Does that indeed matter to you?"

"Of course! Adrio! You wanted to be a hero, and you are one. You have been. I know you feel it hasn't been enough, but I read your ledger. Families living in peace in Lodola. A boy going to university. And can you imagine the ones who remain in the camp? How they must hope for your return?"

Adrio continued to say nothing, studying him. Cay must have surprised him. He fidgeted. "Just because I never tried to change the world," he tried to explain, flushing, "doesn't mean I don't respect those who do."

Adrio dropped his gaze, a soft smile touching his mouth. "Anyone can be the Uncanny Aviator. I'll hand the reins to another and back them with my fortune. But no one else can be your husband."

Cay stared at him mutely.

Adrio reached out and stroked Cay's hair again, ruffling the curls. "Take hope, for I understand more than you think I do. I understand more today than I did yesterday. In fact, I find my confusion has cleared considerably."

Cay frowned. "What are you talking about?"

Adrio's fingers snagged on a knot in Cay's hair, and he gently untangled it. "Your hair looks so pretty in the moonlight," he said, smiling wonderingly.

Cay jerked his head away. "Are you drunk?"

Adrio laughed. Like an idiot.

"Go to sleep," said Cay. He scooted out of Adrio's reach and lay down, curling up on the blanket with his back to him. "Or, better yet, get on your horse and go back down. You can't do anything useful among the Maquhi."

"I think I can." He lay down.

Cay's mind churned. His hands were free. Could he escape? Could he climb up the cliffside so quietly that the scouts would not hear him and be away? Probably not; there was a bow and quiver in the scouts' pack, and he'd be desperately exposed on the cliff wall. Even a bad shot could knock him off the cliff and to his death on the rocks below. And could Adrio climb out with him? He could not, no. Could he contemplate leaving Adrio here? No.

His restless mind struggled with possibilities, rejecting each one.

"I would hold you," Adrio whispered.

"No! Why are you amorous now, of all times?" he demanded, exasperated.

Adrio laughed quietly. The sound made an ache begin in Cay's heart.

"I don't know," said Adrio. "I suppose I feel I've discovered something important."

The tone of his voice was strange, soft. Adrio sounded happy.

He couldn't understand it. He was too tired to try.

"Shut up," he said.

Adrio rolled to his feet and walked away. Cay pressed his hands over his eye sockets, instantly regretting his harsh words.

Why was he so unkind when Adrio was being kind to him? Why was Adrio being kind to him *now*, at the end?

Adrio returned, his footsteps crunching over gravel and dry grass, and then a heavy, fur-lined cloak settled over Cay. He curled up, pulling his feet under its warm hem.

"Thank you, my lord," he whispered.

He slept deeply despite the hard ground and the fear of the morning. It seemed he had only just closed his eyes when the scouts Vuku and Haxut woke him roughly, pulling away the cloak Adrio had tossed over him. Within a few efficient minutes, they had drunk from the water bags, eaten dry bread, and prepared the horses. Cay grunted with pain as he settled into the saddle, and Haxut snorted in contempt.

"Not much of a horseman, are you?"

Cay said nothing as they started up the trail. It grew steeper, colder. There was snow now. Some industrious team of Chende had cleared a narrow trail, but snow was heaped up on either side, clinging to the slopes above them. Far below, the stream rushed beneath a lacy border of ice.

Adrio spoke to Haxut. "You recognized Cay at Wind House. Do you remember him six years ago when he came through the Pass?"

"I do."

"Will you tell me what you remember?"

Haxut sniffed. "They came up from Muntegri. Gizon Ingok ordered his grandson Dizut to guide them through the Pass. But Dizut didn't come back. Gizon sent scouts to find them—my cousin Berit among them. They spied unseen from the rocks as a patrol of Muntegrise guards from the Road hanged Dizut." He paused. "So Berit said. I didn't see. But I saw his body. I was there when they took him down from the tree."

"And Cay was there?" asked Adrio.

"Berit said she saw him there. She said the Muntegrise thanked him and gave him a coin, and he bowed to them and went away with them."

Cay exhaled through his nose. Adrio, after riding silently for a moment, asked, "You said 'they.' Gizon ordered Dizut to guide *them* through the Pass. Who else was with Cay? Other refugees from Muntegri?"

"A man and child. His father and sister, they said, though they looked not like him. I remember them."

"Ah. Were they there too, when Cay betrayed Dizut, and he was hanged?"

Haxut shrugged. "I suppose so. I don't know where else they would be."

"My lord," said Cay. "If you turn around, you could be back in Wind House tonight."

Adrio turned in his saddle to speak to him. "I know where we are. I came this way not a week ago." His tone was forbidding.

Cay met his eyes. He had, of course, allowed Adrio (and everyone else) to believe his parents had died in the riots. Not here.

Now was the time to tell him the rest. To tell him everything. Oh, it seemed so obvious now. He should've told him everything long ago. Now they were at the end, and he must speak.

"My mother died in Turla," he said, his voice strained. "Just as I always said. But my father—my father—"

Adrio pursed his lips slightly and flicked his gaze at the clansmen. *Later*, he mouthed.

Cay nodded. Adrio winked at him and faced forward again.

They were silent for the remainder of the journey.

Several exhausting hours later, they rounded a turn in the trail. Blue-and-yellow kites soared in the sky. Further up the slope, a stone tower loomed on the horizon, kites flying from its peak. It was Hemaquhi: the watchtower at the top of Lehoia Pass, the heart of Maquhi Clan territory. It bore a clear architectural resemblance to both Wind House and Bortorra, now he knew they were all Chende-made: a round tower of native red stone with arrow-slits and a square walled courtyard, paved with dirt.

There were no arched windows, gracious balconies, or well-planned gardens like at the extensively renovated Wind House. Hemaquhi was a fortress, the abode of the most powerful of the mountain clans. Powerful but still a beleaguered people, trapped in these inhospitable mountains by the kingdoms to the north and south.

The sight of Hemaquhi made him involuntarily stiffen, and the horse beneath him paused, bobbing its head.

"Be still," said Haxut.

Oh gods, this place. These sharp red rocks, those strange kites flying against an aching blue sky. The clapping of flags in the wind and the roar of the river far below. The tower, which should have been a place of refuge and sanctuary. He associated it with high summer, dry heat, dust in his mouth, and sweat-soaked clothes. He remembered betrayal, terror, blood, and the responsibility that had fallen on his young shoulders, with no one to help him.

Someone on the tower spotted them and let out a birdlike call that echoed from the rocks above to the other side of the river. Someone at the top of the tower released a kite that soared up and up, so high it looked small as a fingernail, dwarfed by the vastness of the sky.

For the first time, Cay realized the kites must serve as signals.

By the time they reached the courtyard, the clan had assembled. They were lean people with dark eyes and curly hair in all shades of violet, indigo, and plum. Their faces showed curiosity and hostility as they gathered to see the prize the scouts had brought.

Haxut, Vuku, and Adrio dismounted. Cay remained in the saddle until Haxut lifted him off the horse, his hands hard on Cay's waist. He attempted to stand, but his legs were numb. He swayed, failed to catch his balance, and fell to his knees in the dirt at Haxut's feet.

The world swirled around him; he shook his head, trying to clear the dizziness and the roaring in his ears. He heard a babble of voices and hoofbeats, and someone shouted. And then two legs in scuffed boots were before his eyes. He straightened. Adrio stood protectively over him, arms crossed.

"Are you all right?"

Cay nodded shortly, gritting his teeth against the painful tingling in his legs.

A middle-aged woman came down into the courtyard, and everyone fell silent. Like most Chende, she was slender, with large eyes, a blunt nose, and full lips. Her scarred face was grave, and she bore an invisible cloak of authority, drawing the eye of everyone present. Her purple hair was braided and wound around her head like a crown.

Adrio said, "That is Krutiv Ingok, the chief's only surviving child. I have dealt with her a great deal and found her to be a sensible woman."

We've met, thought Cay.

The Maquhi Clan chief, Gizon Ingok, had been an old man when Cay had met him six years ago—old, but still a powerful leader who'd attracted awe and fear from his followers. Cay'd gotten the impression then that Gizon adored his grandson Dizut and largely disregarded his daughter Krutiv. But Dizut was gone, of course, and Gizon was older; it had been clear from Adrio's journals that it was Krutiv who handled much of the day-to-day administration of the clan. It was she who'd communicated with the Uncanny Aviator about what supplies they needed and how to get to Hemaquhi.

Today, Gizon was nowhere to be seen. As Krutiv walked toward them, she dispersed the curious watchers with an imperious jerk of her chin. She was immediately and universally obeyed.

"Lord Lodola," she said quietly, approaching. "You are always welcome among the Maquhi, but we did not expect you so soon."

"Thank you for your welcome, Krutiv Ingok." Adrio bowed.

She stared down at Cay, who still knelt on the ground. Without a word, she turned to Vuku and Haxut, and raised her eyebrows.

"We saw a strange thing to the south while on watch and went to Wind House to ask if they'd seen it or knew what it was," reported Haxut. "We did not know Lord Lodola was there.

We saw Cay Olau in the garden and captured him. Lord Lodola insisted upon accompanying him here."

Krutiv's eyebrows went up. She slowly turned to Adrio.

"Is that correct, Lord Lodola?"

"It is."

"Well. Scouts, what of the strange thing you saw?"

Vuku cleared her throat. "It was bigger than a horse, black, oval in shape, and it flew through the air. We saw it in the sky, and we thought it landed in the hills near Wind House, so we went down to ask. But then we saw Cay Olau. The other three remained to search for it, while we brought our prisoner here."

"You say it flew?"

"Yes, Krutiv Ingok."

"Like a bird?"

"No. Slowly, like . . ." For a moment, Cay sympathized with her attempt to describe how the balloon flew. "Like a cloud," she finally said.

Krutiv looked at Adrio again. He shook his head with an air of mystification. "Perhaps it *was* a cloud," he said.

"And how did Cay Olau come to be at Wind House?"

"Not in a cloud," said Adrio, easily. "He accompanied me."

"And why?"

"Cay Olau is my husband."

Krutiv's eyebrows went up again. "You astonish me," she said. "Were you aware, when you wed him, that he owes a blood-debt to the Maquhi Clan?"

"No," said Cay. His voice came out rough; he coughed to clear the road-dust from his throat. "I didn't tell him."

Her dark eyes flicked to Cay. "It seems you took advantage of Lord Lodola's trust, then," said Krutiv. She smiled flintily at Adrio. "My sympathies. He did the same to us, with bloody consequences."

Cay managed to get his feet under him and rose, standing before her. He lifted his chin and glared at her, hopeless but defiant. She stared back stonily.

Adrio smiled pleasantly. "Not *quite* the same, I think. I would speak to Gizon Ingok Maquhi on this matter. Cay Olau is a responsibility I will not lightly set aside. Perhaps if we spoke frankly, the chief and Cay Olau and you and I, we can unravel this misunderstanding."

"You believe we called a blood-feud as a result of a *misunderstanding*?" demanded Krutiv, incredulously. "The Maquhi Clan is not so base."

"Then let us go to Gizon Ingok and speak," Adrio said. "Let us address the charges; let Cay defend himself so justice may be honorably done."

Krutiv snorted. "Our honor requires no trial, Lord Lodola. The man is convicted already by his own cruel and treacherous actions. All that is left is satisfaction of the clan's debt."

"Where is Gizon Ingok Maquhi?" he asked again, his voice carrying. "This is a matter for the chief, surely."

Krutiv turned to him in offense. "I speak for the clan."

"Is he dead?"

Someone said, "He's asleep."

Krutiv studied him. "You have been a good ally to the Maquhi Clan and are always welcome here. But we will permit no interference in how we deal with our enemies—not even from you. You would be unwise to meddle in Chende matters you don't understand."

Adrio bowed. "I value the alliance of the Maquhi Clan, and your friendship, Krutiv Ingok. I've had cause many times to be grateful for it. But just as you are a drawn blade to your enemies, I am a sanctuary wall to my friends."

"You could begin by choosing your friends more carefully," she said. "Hear me: I cut my nephew Dizut down from a tree that morning, but not before the sun had begun to bloat him, and the ants had found his eyes." Her mouth twisted. "We are the Maquhi Clan, the greatest of the Chende clans, and we will not be satisfied until our debt is repaid with blood."

Adrio, standing relaxed but ready by Cay's side, said, "I am the Heir of Lodola, and *my* concerns will be addressed to the chief of the Maquhi Clan, Gizon Ingok."

It was an impasse, but she sighed through her nose and said, "Very well. My father sleeps in the afternoons but will be awake at sundown to hear you."

"Thank you, Krutiv Ingok Maquhi," said Adrio, polite but implacable. "Until then, my guest and I call upon the hospitality of the clan."

"You may, of course, sleep in your usual room, where food and drink will be brought to you. There is a cell for Cay Olau."

"Cay Olau will remain with me," said Adrio. "Or I will remain with him."

"As you please." She nodded at Haxut. "The dungeon for them both."

The dungeon was just a cellar, cut into the living stone beneath Hemaquhi, and hastily cleared of stored items. It was cool and dry and smelled faintly of leather and onions. They were given a candle, a pallet of straw, a bucket for waste, and a jug of water. Cay thought he'd have had no water, straw, or candle if he'd been alone.

Adrio pleasantly ordered the man who led them to bring blankets, food, and wine, with much the same air as if he were checking into a hotel. The man, perhaps flummoxed by this display of lordly authority, obeyed.

When they were alone, Adrio pulled Cay into his arms. He was warm, strong—all men were warm, but Adrio's warmth was like home and safety, and Cay clung to him with all the strength in his trembling arms. It was so extraordinarily good and desperately necessary to be held by him. They stood quietly for a long while, gripping each other, feeling their hearts pound.

"Husband," said Cay, "I wish you were not playing this game."

"But I am a good gambler," said Adrio. He patted Cay on the shoulder. "You need to eat. Come on. Sit and rest."

Cay obeyed, sitting on the folded blanket, but could not face the sausages and bread. "I'm sorry I was quarrelsome last night. I should have thanked you for trying to help me."

Adrio poured water into clay cups stamped with the squares and lines of the Maquhi Clan. "Cay, don't go sweet on me now. You're only sweet when you're pretending."

"Please," insisted Cay. "I am serious now. You should go home."

"No."

"I mean . . . after this is over, go home. Don't make war with the clan, and don't think of it too much. You mustn't feel guilty. They decided to do this long ago, and it . . . it won't be your fault."

"Ah." Adrio's brow furrowed. "Don't."

"But I must. Please. Don't blame yourself, and don't grieve. Find someone to love, be happy, and forget about all of this. Except for taking care of Kell, of course."

"Cay." With gentle fingers under his chin, Adrio tipped his head up to look into his eyes. "Cay, you must stop. Sharpen your tongue, and tell Gizon, and all the Maquhi Clan, their blood-feud is without merit, and their pursuit of it is without honor."

"You think Gizon doesn't know that?" He stared at Adrio. "How do *you* know that?"

"Am I wrong? Did you not behave with honor?"

"I didn't think you believed I had any honor."

"You do. You do have honor." He reached out and combed his fingers into Cay's hair. "I believe you demanded justice for whatever Dizut did. I believe you were ignored, so you declared a blood-feud and killed him."

"*Adrio.*"

"You told me yourself you always warn them. I didn't understand. But that's one of the principles of the blood-feud, is it not? The debt isn't just claimed; it is declared first so all parties understand what's happening and why. Honor is preserved. I believe you declared a debt, and then you made Dizut Ingok pay it."

Dry mouthed, Cay asked, "And what would I know of Chende blood-feuds?"

Adrio smiled. He tugged on the handful of Cay's hair. "In the sunlight," he whispered, "it's purple as a grackle's wing."

"*What.*"

"The dye must have rinsed out when you washed it at Wind House."

Cay remembered scrubbing his hair, again and again, with Mella's strong soap. He'd always been careful before to use gentle soaps and to touch up any faded bits or roots as soon as they started to show. Not vanity, his glossy black curls, but concealment and survival. He'd started in Turla, when his purple had started coming in. He'd been ten. His mother had helped him. No one could know Cou Olau's son was Chende.

After his flight from Turla, his Lucenequan cousins certainly hadn't wanted to feed or shelter an illegitimate Chende cuckoo. It would have been harder to find a job at a respectable tailor, harder to find a place to live. And of a certainty, no handsome Lucenequan lord would have married him with streaks of plum and berry vibrant in his hair.

He stared now in horror at Adrio, wanting to protest, or deny, or explain.

"You didn't want me to know." Adrio's brow furrowed. "Even now, after everything, you still don't want me to know your real father was Chende. You have Chende blood. Do you hate them so much?"

Cay shook his head mutely, then struggled to find his voice. "I loved them."

"Loved?"

Cay's eyes filled with tears; he blinked them away. "I loved my mother and father. I truly did. But I constantly ran away from them, to Clan Bekh on the Sixth Circle, because I loved them . . . And I felt a kinship with them. Kell has my mother's brains and my father's face, but I always felt different until I was with the Bekh." He braved himself to meet Adrio's eyes. "I'm Chende. I wasn't raised by them; I have no clan. But they make sense to me."

Adrio gently cupped Cay's face. "It explains so much."

Adrio didn't mind? He didn't hate it—the fact of Cay's Chende blood? To his horror, Cay began to cry.

"My father didn't like it," he whispered.

"I like it." He kissed the tears at the corners of Cay's eyes. "I like it. I'm sorry you felt you had to hide this from me, love. I understand you so much better now."

Cay fisted the tears out of his eyes. "I don't see why it matters. I still did all the dishonorable things I did, including lying to you, obviously, and I got Ondrei captured. I am still the man you decided you couldn't trust."

"I have been thinking about it. I begin to understand what you were trying to tell me all those months ago—a nobleman can't expect a nobleman's honor from a refugee, nor a Lucenequan from a Chende. Perhaps circumstances and standards shift these things. I don't know." He glanced at the closed door of their cell. "But we haven't much time, Cay. You must get ready to fight. Put aside your weariness and stand straight. Throw the truth in their faces and make them see. I'll stand at your back."

"It won't matter," he whispered. "They already know."

"Do they? Haxut remembers your sister and father, but in all the tales he told me, Gizut never mentioned them."

Adrio stared at him, finally understanding the dice Adrio had rolled. It was so dangerous it took his breath away.

"You mistake them." He fisted tears off his face, but they kept flowing. "The Maquhi. Listen. The Chende *do* have honor— *their* kind of honor—but Clan Maquhi betrayed it six years ago. Maybe they relinquished it decades ago; maybe they've turned to stone here in their mountains. You believe the truth will win out once it is known. But they know the truth already; they will hear the truth and put a dagger in your back to keep you from repeating it."

"Cay—"

"You've sparred with your friends, but they've fought wars. You've read books— No." Adrio's brows had drawn with offense, and Cay grabbed his hands and squeezed them. "I'm not saying this to insult you or to challenge your courage. I know better. But I believed in them too. I believed they would honor their debts, and they betrayed their honor and me. You want to hold up a mirror to their shame, and they'll cut you down for it. Please. Please, go home and live."

Adrio clasped his hands. He ducked his head and kissed them, one after the other, and then rested his forehead against Cay's.

"I hear you, Cay," he whispered.

Cay tried not to sob.

"I hear you say you love me," Adrio said. "You— My gods. My behavior would shame the worst cur, and you've done nothing but give me proof of your love over and over. And Husband, though you've reason to doubt it, I love you. I love your vicious temper and your tender heart. I love your sweet face, though I know you hide behind it. I don't know what will become of us today, but I will not leave you alone. It isn't honor that keeps me here, but my heart's love. Cay."

Cay, weeping, tried to hide his face.

Adrio cupped his face, tilted it up, and kissed his wet cheeks, his forehead, his jaw. "I love you," he whispered. "Please don't doubt me anymore. I love you so."

Adrio kissed his mouth, and—as always—Cay could do nothing but yield.

Chapter Twelve

When they called him, Cay walked up the stairs out of the storeroom and into the courtyard. For a moment, he was dazzled by the late-afternoon light. The sun had descended toward the western mountains and now reflected off the sheer red cliff to the east, casting a golden glow upon the courtyard. The air was cold with evening and tasted like snow. Cay's hands were cold, his breaths coming shortly in his chest. The only sound was the clapping of flags, and high above, kites strained southward against their cords, strings taut in the north wind.

"Oh, good," said Adrio, sweeping his eyes around the courtyard. "The more public, the better."

It seemed every adult of the Maquhi was here, gathered in and around the courtyard of Hemaquhi. They crouched along the wall, sat atop it, or perched on the rocky face of the cliff above. Their faces were in the narrow arrow-slit windows of the tower. They were silent, and there were no children. Someone had taken them elsewhere.

Not a good sign.

Gizon Ingok sat in an ornate carved-wood chair at the courtyard's far end, with the glowing stone wall behind him. He was visibly older than the last time Cay had seen him, more stooped, his eyes more sunken in his lean face. His sparse hair had gone pure white. By his side stood his daughter Krutiv, straight-backed and hard-jawed.

Cay trembled and clenched his hands together, trying to stop. He could be dead in an hour; he would certainly be dead by tomorrow, and Adrio would be there to see him hang. Before, Adrio had held him close in their cell, trying to comfort him, but now in the courtyard, under the eyes of all the Maquhi, he despaired. He swallowed a rush of slick saliva, trying not to throw up.

The words of one clanless illegitimate Chende had little power against the assembled might of Clan Maquhi. He had reason to know it. They might as well hang him now.

"Courage, my lord," murmured Adrio.

Cay glanced at his husband, who was staring at Gizon, eyes shining with reckless confidence. He gulped a deep breath into his lungs and straightened his back, imitating Adrio's proud posture.

So. He would fight, to make Adrio proud of him before he died.

Head high, he walked into the sunlight, and a rustle and murmur went through the assembled men and women at the sight of him.

His kin. He had always resembled them, and when his hair had started growing in purple at about age ten, his father had barely been able to look at him. But still, Cou Olau had come here, to the Maquhi, hoping for aid on behalf of his half-Chende son.

He reached the chair where Gizon Ingok sat and bowed— enough for respect but not enough for remorse. Adrio, who walked a pace behind him, bowed a little more deeply. Krutiv, standing at Gizon's elbow, favored them with a cool nod, but Gizon said nothing, staring at Cay with glittering black eyes.

"Are you Cay Olau?" Krutiv spoke strongly, and the natural amphitheater of the canyon amplified her voice so everyone assembled could hear her.

"I—" Cay's voice came out husky. He cleared his throat and said, "I am Cay Olau."

Krutiv glanced at Adrio. He said nothing but planted his feet, hooked his thumbs through his belt, and stood tall like the hero of a play. Her nostrils flared slightly.

"We are here because our sometime friend, Lord Lodola, has married Cay Olau, who owes the Maquhi a blood-debt. Lord

Lodola suggests the Maquhi's blood claim against Cay Olau might be false, and as a gesture of our friendship with Lodola, we will explain our debt, and hear Cay Olau's explanation, before Chief Gizon Ingok." She nodded to Adrio. "Does that suit?"

"Perfectly." Like Krutiv, Adrio knew how to pitch his voice to fill the courtyard. "Lodola is proud of its alliance with the Maquhi and is troubled by this blood-feud. We would like to understand it better."

The crowd rumbled dangerously at the outrageous demands of an outsider. Cay stole a sideways glance at Adrio. His face was calm, but Cay thought he was a little pale. Adrio raised his hands, but the crowd's anger did not quiet until Gizon Ingok stood.

The old man had gotten smaller, thought Cay; or perhaps he was taller. Gizon stood unsteadily, one hand clutching the arm of the chair.

"Lord Lodola," said Gizon, not loudly. Everyone leaned forward to hear his rusty crow's voice. "My grandson is dead, and Cay Olau killed him. Maquhi's honor will not be satisfied until he is likewise dead. Why do you thrust yourself into this matter which does not concern you?"

"It concerns Lodola because I am Cay Olau's husband. My honor is no less true than Clan Maquhi's."

The crowd growled. Gizon stared stonily at Adrio. "You never mentioned your marriage in any of your previous visits."

"I was already married when you told me of the matter," said Adrio. "I was in a quandary."

"That is your problem, not ours. My grandson is dead, and he lives. That is all."

"Is it?"

"It is."

Adrio bowed. "Forgive me. I know I am impertinent. But how can a man choose between his friends and his husband? I would hear more."

Krutiv took the reins of the conversation. "For the sake of the friendship between our clans, then, let us proceed. Father, please sit and rest."

Gizon sank into his chair, his shoulders stiff with outrage.

Krutiv went on in a dry tone. "Maquhi demands blood-debt from Cay Olau for the murder of Dizut Ingok, the grandson of the chief, and my nephew. Cay Olau, did you murder Dizut Ingok?"

Trying to match her ringing tone, he replied, "I did not. The blood-feud, declared by Gizon Ingok Maquhi is false."

Another rustle ran through the crowd.

Krutiv only nodded to someone at the periphery of the courtyard. "Come forward, Berit Malit Maquhi."

A woman stepped into the center. She was a timeworn woman in a threadbare blue ohahi, her plum-colored braid streaked with white, but in spite of her age, she moved with the lean grace of an athlete. She stared at Cay for a long moment and then spat in the dust.

"Tell us what you saw," ordered Krutiv.

"I was one of the scouts who went searching for Dizut Ingok, the morning he did not return," said Berit Malit. "Erus Odgt, my partner and I—he died last winter, or he would tell you the same. We hid in the rocks and saw Dizut's body hanging. It was off the Pass, to the south, near the Road."

"He was dead when you got there?"

"Yes, but not long dead. The blood on his mouth was still red."

"Who killed him?"

"The Muntegrise. A patrol had come up the Ghian fissure from the Road to the Pass and then came south. Their footprints were clear. We followed them and saw them gathered at the mouth of the Ghian. They were going back down to the Road, one by one."

"How many of them?"

"Perhaps a dozen or fifteen."

"How had they known to come up the Ghian to find Dizut there?"

"The boy led them." The scout gestured at Cay. "This one. He was younger, but I remember him."

"How do you know he led them?"

"We saw the leader of the Muntegrise thank him and give him a coin, and he bowed to them."

Krutiv nodded. "What did you do then?"

"We came back here and told what we saw. Then you"—Berit nodded to Krutiv—"assembled a small party, and we went and cut Dizut down and brought him back here. And then the chief declared the blood-debt against the boy."

"Thank you, Berit Malit." Krutiv turned to Cay. "Do you still deny the blood-debt?"

Cay took a deep breath. "I deny it."

"Did you lead Muntegrise troops to Dizut Ingok Maquhi?"

"Yes. And before you ask, yes, I knew they would kill him. It was my intention that they kill him. In this way, I collected the blood-debt owed to me by Clan Maquhi."

The crowd murmured. Cay drew and let out an unsteady breath. After a moment, Krutiv raised her hands and silenced the audience.

"You claim you had a blood-feud against Dizut?"

"Yes."

"Liar." Gizon said the word, and it was taken up by the crowd: "Liar. Liar." Some of them began to hiss through their teeth—an unnerving sound.

"I am not lying!" cried Cay, his voice almost drowned out by the crowd. "Gizon knows I am not lying! Let me speak!"

Krutiv raised a hand, looking around the audience, and they finally subsided. "Very well," she said, but her drawling tone spoke of contempt. "Let us be silent and hear what explanation Cay Olau could possibly have for killing my nephew."

"My mother had been killed during the riots in Turla, when the Grup shot into the crowd. We found her body later, trampled."

Cay shivered. It was cold, suddenly, a cold like ice on his skin. He thought it was fear and despair until he opened his eyes. Thin snow was falling from the fading afternoon sky, pricking his cheeks and hands.

His voice was not steady. He never spoke of this. These memories, so seldom retold, had taken on a dreamlike quality. His father had not permitted him and Kell to see their mother's body up close, and at first he had thought there was some mistake. That bloodied lump, that tangle of clothes and hair, seen only from a distance, was surely not his mother. But then his father had cried, and he'd believed.

They didn't want to know about her. He needed to keep this to the bare facts.

"My father protested this killing, and they retaliated by destroying his workshop. We hid with friends, who were in danger for sheltering us, so my father said we must flee to Lucenequa, where he had cousins. But the roadblock had already gone up, and we could not get through. He brought us to the foot of the mountains, hoping we might find haven and passage through." He paused, then forced himself to go on. "I was sired by a Chende man. I do not know him or his clan. My father, the Muntegrise man who raised me, thought the Maquhi might be kind to us because, he said, my true father might be Maquhi. He was a very proud man, and it was difficult for him to beg for mercy, but that day he did. He threw himself on the mercy of the Maquhi and begged. And so we were brought here to Hemaquhi."

"I remember this," said Krutiv.

Cay nodded. "Gizon Ingok Maquhi refused to shelter us. He said there would be no passage through the mountains without payment to Clan Maquhi. And, of course, we had nothing. But then Dizut spoke up for us. He volunteered to guide us through Lehoia Pass into Lucenequa."

"I remember," repeated Krutiv.

"We set out the next morning. But I know now we did not go down the Pass. Rather, Dizut took us to the east, across the river, and up into the mountains, to a cliff overlooking the Road. We could see the Muntegrise troops down below, patrolling. Do you know the place?"

Gizon did not move, but Krutiv nodded. "That is where his body was found. But that is not the way to Lucenequa. We have often wondered why he was there."

"We didn't know the way. We went where Dizut led. He took us to the cliff above the Road, and showed us the Muntegrise troops patrolling below. He showed us the path—the crack in the cliffs, where the troop could come up, and he told us they would kill us if they came. He laughed when we were afraid. He said we had to be silent, or they would hear. And then Dizut made his demand," said Cay, his voice going hoarse. "He said my sister must lie with him, or he would give us to the Muntegrise."

"A disgusting lie," growled Gizon.

"Is it not true that the Maquhi will have payment for passage through Lehoia Pass? Was he not Maquhi?" Cay's voice grew thick with fear and anger. "My sister had just turned thirteen. She told me later she didn't even understand what he wanted, but she was afraid of the way he stared at her. My father told me to take her and run. I grabbed her hand, and we fled into the rocks, and my father stayed behind and fought Dizut."

The audience was silent. Gizon seemed bored, but Krutiv was frowning.

"Kell and I hid in a little cave, no more than a crack in the rocks, but we could hear them. My father was exhausted from our flight from Turla, and Dizut was young and strong. We could hear—" He paused. "Dizut had lied when he said the Muntegrise would come up if they heard. They fought, and they were not silent, but the Muntegrise did not come. I held my hands over my sister's ears so she wouldn't have to hear, but I heard. I heard Dizut strike him down and beat him. I heard when he stopped making any sound."

His face was cold. Snow was falling on his shoulders and hair, and tears were icy on his cheeks. He angrily fisted them out of his eyes.

Gizon sighed, his nostrils flaring. A muscle worked in Krutiv's jaw. Cay swept his gaze out over the crowd. The sun dipped behind the rocks, casting the courtyard into shadow, but the people's faces were still visible through the falling darkness and blowing snow. Were they shocked at his tale of Dizut's deeds? Did they care? He could not tell.

"Go on," murmured Adrio.

"I left my sister hiding in the cave and followed Dizut. I saw him put my father's body in the river." His voice cracked on the word *river*. He coughed. "He was swept away—my father. I had to—I had to—" Memories clogged his throat; he couldn't speak. The Chende of Turla had taught him what one must do when one is owed a debt. But when it came to it, he'd felt so helpless, so angry, and so small.

Someone in the crowd said, "Dizut *did* like young girls."

"Silence!" roared Gizon.

"'Tis true," said another, a woman. "I kept my daughters away from him."

"Enough," said Krutiv, and the Maquhi obeyed, falling silent. "Cay Olau," she said, "if you were true Chende, you would know that vengeance is not blood-feud. Private vengeance is mere murder. You murdered Dizut for vengeance, and it is false to claim blood-feud. Our claim remains true; you must pay your blood-debt."

Struggling to keep his voice steady, Cay said, "I'm not finished with my story."

She narrowed her eyes. Adrio folded his arms, and she huffed with impatience. "Go on, then."

"After Dizut killed my father, I left my sister hiding, and returned to Gizon Ingok here at Hemaquhi. I told him of the crime and begged for justice. But he laughed."

"I know nothing of this," said Krutiv flatly.

"I knew a blood-debt had to be declared to the clan. I ran back here to Hemaquhi. I don't—I've never known why Dizut stayed there. I thought he was on my heels. I thought he would find Kell if I was not swift. I still—" They did not want to hear about his nightmares or how he ran until he vomited and ran again, clutching his stomach. "I came here. It was night. No one saw me except Gizon Ingok and one guard. I told what Dizut had done. I demanded justice for my father and my sister. And when he refused me, I claimed my blood-debt to Gizon Ingok, the leader of the Maquhi."

The audience murmured.

"That . . . could not have happened," said Krutiv.

"He had dismissed the guard. I met with him alone in his room here at Hemaquhi. It was a mistake," Cay added bitterly. "I was young, and I believed he was a man of honor. I should have shouted it here in the courtyard. I didn't imagine he would keep my blood-claim a *secret*."

The crowd did not cry out this time, but their gasps and murmurs spoke of the ghastly seriousness of Cay's accusation.

Krutiv's lips parted in astonishment. "It cannot be true."

"It is true. He knows it is true. But Dizut was his grandson, so he did not care."

Gizon broke his silence. "It's nonsense."

"Where is the guard?" demanded Cay. "One other man saw me here that night." He turned in a circle, searching the crowd. "One of you saw me here."

Some were shaking their heads. Some were exchanging glances, eyes wide. Was it disbelief? Or recognition? What did it mean when a man raised his brows or a woman pressed a hand to her mouth? The woman who had said she kept her daughters away from Dizut was whispering urgently to her neighbor.

But no one volunteered. Cay had barely glanced at the guard at the time, and he recognized no one. The man might be dead, or married out to another clan, or too loyal to Gizon to speak.

"Clan Maquhi lies!" shouted Cay. He turned, despairing, to the crowd. "Clan Maquhi takes what it wants, no matter how weak or cruel. The Maquhi *is not* owed."

Krutiv's face was stony and unreadable, and Gizon sat still, unmoved.

"You *know* it, Gizon Ingok Maquhi," he said in desperation. "You know the truth, and so do I."

Krutiv asked, "What did you tell those troops to make them kill him?"

"I told them he was a bandit who had murdered members of the Grup in Turla. I told them he had kidnapped me and fled with me to the mountains."

"Lies."

"Yes," Cay said through gritted teeth. "I was a boy, and he was a Maquhi warrior. But I had my blood-price anyway." He turned to the assembled people and tried to catch the eyes of those who seemed to have doubts. "My mistake was speaking to your chief alone," he said. "There were no witnesses. No one to prevent him"—he raised his voice—"from denying a just claim against his vicious and cowardly grandson, and no one to gainsay him now."

The crowd rumbled. It was a deadly insult to the chief and to the dead man.

Cay shivered. Night had fallen, and the snow was falling more thickly. He was cold.

"A question," said Adrio suddenly, his voice booming in the stillness. "Scout Berit Malit Maquhi. When you saw Cay with the Muntegrise troops, did you see his father or sister?"

Gizon shifted restlessly, his expression black with anger; Cay thought he would tell Adrio to be silent. But he did not speak, and after a moment, the scout replied: "No, lord."

"Where do you suppose they were?"

"I didn't see them," she repeated.

"Scout Haxut Malit Maquhi. You recognized Cay when you saw him at Wind House yesterday. Do you remember his arrival years ago? How many people was he with?"

After a pause, Haxut said, "I remember the man and the girl."

"I remember them as well," said Krutiv.

"What happened to them? Where were they when Berit Malit arrived?"

"We can't know," said Krutiv.

"He was dead," said Cay. "And my sister was hiding."

"How long will we endure this questioning?" demanded Gizon harshly.

Adrio bowed low. "Gizon Ingok—Krutiv Ingok—respectfully, what is your explanation for what Cay did?" Adrio's voice was as courteous as if he were addressing the queen. "Why would he do such a thing—a youth, with a young sister and no home?"

"Perhaps," said Krutiv, "he was wicked."

Cay closed his eyes. This was hopeless; he wished Adrio wouldn't try. He heard Gizon snort.

"What happened to the man?" Adrio persisted. "Cay's sister is in Lucenequa. I know her well. But his father is not there. He never survived his journey through these mountains. And you know Dizut liked young girls. Why else was he killed? Indeed, *how* was he killed? How did Cay, a stranger, know of the fissure that led the Muntegrise troops to where Dizut camped, unless Dizut himself showed him?"

Krutiv shook her head slowly. "I don't know."

"Enough," said Gizon.

"Another question," persisted Adrio. "Dizut volunteered to guide Cay and his family without asking for payment. Krutiv Ingok, were you surprised?"

She raised her eyebrows. "I was. That is not our way."

Was this working? Krutiv appeared thoughtful. But Gizon was visibly fuming, opening and clenching his fists.

"Did Gizon speak to Dizut about it?" pressed Adrio. "Did he ask why he chose to help this family for no payment?"

"I remember," said Haxut, unexpectedly, from the crowd. "Gizon told him they must pay, and Dizut said, 'They will.' I remember because it was unusual. I expected Gizon to stop them, but he did not."

"I remember that too," said someone else.

Krutiv turned to her father. "Do you remember?"

"I don't care!" roared Gizon, making Cay jump. "How long will we listen to this? What does Maquhi care for some Turla lout and his brats? My grandson is dead!" His harsh shout bounced off the canyon walls, repeating: *dead, dead, dead.* He stood unsteadily, bracing himself on the arm of the heavy chair. "He was true Maquhi, strong and straight, with his mother's eyes and the heart of a warrior, and I will have my payment."

Cay found his voice. "That's what he said to me. When I told him what Dizut had demanded and how he killed my father. He said, 'I don't care. It doesn't matter.'"

"And it didn't!" snarled Gizon. "It didn't matter then, and it doesn't matter now."

Krutiv slowly turned to stare at her father.

Cay opened his mouth to speak, but Adrio touched him lightly, on the arm, and he remained silent.

Krutiv asked, "So you did speak to Cay Olau, that day? He did come to you with his complaint, and you said it doesn't matter?"

The old man waved a knobby hand at Cay. "He killed Dizut with his treachery. He does not deny it!"

"My chief," said Krutiv. "Did Cay Olau come to you and demand justice for his father? Did he declare blood-feud against Dizut?"

"Do you dare question me, daughter? I have led this clan for sixty years, and I say my grandson's murderer dies tonight." Gizon swept his gaze around the assembled people. "I will do it myself, if I must. Someone bring me a rope!"

No one moved.

"Answer the question, Father," repeated Krutiv. "Did the boy demand blood-payment from the Maquhi for his family?"

"No bastard downlander has the right to demand blood payment from Clan Maquhi!" declared Gizon. "*I* am Maquhi, and I deny his claim."

The crowd was muttering again. It was an ugly sound, fraught with menace. What had once seemed like a trial now seemed like a riot about to happen. They need not hang him, for a riot could kill; so had his mother been killed, exposed and surrounded by enemies.

"No!" shouted someone from the crowd. A man was standing, arms crossed over his chest. "I was there. I was the chief's guard the night Dizut died, and I saw the boy. I did not hear what they said, but the boy came and spoke, and they quarreled, and then he ran off. My chief." The man bowed low. "Forgive me. You misremember."

Krutiv raised her hands for silence, but the people were on their feet now, a roar of voices, male and female. Some shouted at the guard to be silent; others called for Gizon to take back his words. A few scuffles broke out as Gizon's supporters and critics came to blows.

It was snowing harder now, tiny flakes of ice blowing diagonally through the darkening sky. It seemed to dull the sound of the flapping flags. With a start, Cay understood what the kites and flags had been telling him: the wind was from the north, coming down cold from the plateau of Muntegri. The weather had turned at last, and true winter had come. The rivers would freeze, and the canyons would fill with snow.

"I am not satisfied!" shouted Adrio, his voice ringing above the noise. "Lodola decries the false claim of Maquhi. Do you hear me, Maquhi?"

"Silence!" That was Gizon. He was on his feet, a sword in his hand. He strode across the courtyard toward them. "I will have my debt. Now. If I have to take the boy's head off myself."

Here it comes, thought Cay. He crouched, fists clenched, teeth bared with fury and fright, as Gizon strode toward him, a warrior still, blade naked in his hand.

Adrio drew his dagger and threw it. It sank into the meat of Gizon's thigh, just above his left knee, throwing Gizon's balance off midstride. Without a sound, the old man fell sideways, and his sword clattered to the ground.

The crowd fell silent too.

"I might have struck his heart," announced Adrio. "But Lodola does not demand Chief Gizon's life. He is a great leader, who grieves the death of a beloved kinsman, and who misremembers. He will always have Lodola's respect. If Cay is unharmed—if Maquhi drops its pretense of blood-claim against him—Lodola is satisfied."

"Kill them," rasped Gizon, half-supine on the ground, his blood soaking into the dirt.

"Enough," said Krutiv. She raised her hands. "Enough. Maquhi clansmen. My father needs care, and we must all eat and rest. Go to your homes." She glanced at the low sky. "Go, and prepare your families for the cold time. We will speak again in the morning."

And with that, the crowd began to disperse, except for the people clustered around the fallen Gizon. Cay stood still, waiting. He could hear a few voices: a woman's, saying Dizut had always been a bully; a man, protesting the law of blood-feud was a thousand years older than Gizon. But they were leaving; they were walking away.

Was it possible Adrio would get away with *throwing a dagger* at Gizon Ingok?

"You madman," whispered Cay to Adrio.

"Come on." Adrio took his hand. They slowly made their way out of the center of the courtyard, trying to draw no attention to themselves. Incredibly, no one seemed to pay them any mind. Except for those carrying Gizon into Hemaquhi, the Maquhi were leaving, taking care of their business, as Krutiv had told them to do.

"Krutiv has been the power behind the throne for years," said Adrio. "They just needed a push to depose him in her favor."

"You stabbed their chief in front of their eyes, and they are ignoring you."

Adrio glanced down at him with a slightly sick-looking grin. "I guess they accepted my blood-claim."

"You are made of luck."

"Perhaps."

They put the wall to their backs. Partially sheltered from the thickening snowfall, Cay clung to Adrio's hand. They were both trembling.

"We have to get out of here before the Pass closes with snow."

"Too late, I think."

They were still huddled against the wall and debating what to do when scouts arrived on tired horses carrying a wicker basket and a mass of folded cloth.

"We found the flying thing!" announced a scout.

Chapter Thirteen

Dressed in borrowed Chende clothes and boots, Cay came down the stairs of Hemaquhi, looking for his husband.

Snow and sleet had fallen in alternating showers without stopping for three days. Now, as Cay emerged from the tower, the sun shone blindingly off glittering thigh-deep snow. The Maquhi were busy with shovels, clearing narrow pathways. It sounded like hard work. The blades of their shovels clanked and crunched as they bit into the icy drifts.

Lehoia Pass would be impassable, and the Road entirely blocked. No one in either land could travel north or south, and Cay and Adrio were trapped in Maquhi country until the thaw. They could be here for weeks or months.

Fortunately, Adrio had been right. The Maquhi had accepted the justice of his blood-claim and without further discussion dismissed their own against Cay. Gizon Ingok had voluntarily (so they were told) gone into the honorable retirement due his age, and his daughter Krutiv Ingok was now the new chief. Cay and Adrio were staying in a comfortable tower room rather than a cell, and though no one seemed exactly *pleased* about Cay's presence, no one seemed to lust after his blood, either. Chende honor would not permit anything else.

Trapped by the weather in their tower room, they'd made love again and again. Cay hadn't understood how acute Adrio's terror had been until he expressed his relief by thoroughly wrecking Cay in bed. And then they'd shared laughter and gentleness too.

Cay followed the paths through the courtyard and outside without any sign of Adrio. Men and women shoveled snow, chipped ice, and cared for livestock. Children ran everywhere, through the snow tunnels, screaming and laughing. Above the canyon he stared with awe at a house-sized array of spars and sails, which the wind pushed in a ceaseless creaking circle. He puzzled over this for a while, wondering what it was for.

But he could not find his husband until he heard the crackle of fire above him and looked up to see a familiar sight: a balloon on the top of the tower, slowly inflating.

He climbed the stairs to the top of Hemaquhi to find Adrio and Krutiv standing together. Several people were building a fire from precious charcoal, and the sack of the balloon was held open over the fire by lines held by others on the walls. It grew as Cay approached, fluttering in the breeze with a sound not unlike the ever-present clapping of the Chende flags.

Krutiv was saying, "His leg will recover, if the Wind blows right."

"I hope so," said Adrio politely.

"While I am chief, Clan Lodola and Clan Maquhi will continue as friends. If that is Lodola's will."

"Lodola would like nothing more."

"And . . . if any other clansmen want to come south, we will be more welcoming than we have in the past. Chende may come through the Pass without payment."

"You speak with great honor." Adrio bowed. "I will try to get word to those in the prison camps that should any manage to escape, they will have a safe path before them." Smiling a little, he added, "If the Wind blows right. Meanwhile, Lodola is happy to continue providing the usual supplies."

"Good." Krutiv glanced up at the swelling balloon. "More charcoal. More light wood and silk. Not black."

"Certainly. Blue and yellow? Like the kites, so all will see the Maquhi in the sky?"

Krutiv grinned. "That's right."

Cay walked up and slipped his hand into Adrio's.

Adrio smiled down at him. "I asked Krutiv about the clouds—do you remember? The Principle of Layers?" Cay nodded. "She says there *are* layers. The Maquhi have records of the winds in Lehoia Pass going back hundreds of years."

"I knew a man of Clan Bekh, in Turla, who made little devices to show the wind. He said the Bekh put them above their doors so they will always know what the wind is doing."

"We use the flags," said Krutiv, a little stiffly. "But I have heard the plateau clans make such things."

Like most Chende, she preferred not to speak to Cay directly. Honor might be satisfied, but no one particularly liked him.

She pointed upward. "Do you see how the flags up there blow from the northwest, but down there"—she pointed into the canyon—"they are closer to true north? The wind is different in different places. The flags show how fast it flows, when it turns, and where it eddies. Where it springs upward in the afternoon and plunges at night, where it runs straight, and where it breaks into rapids over the rocks. Lehoia Pass is a riverbed of wind."

"Oh." Cay thought about this. All those flags, the signal kites. So much of what he'd seen but not understood, dedicated to studying the stuff of wind. "What about the thing like a wheel? The wind was turning it around?"

"When it's icy, taking the path down to the river is dangerous. We use the windmill to bring up water."

"Really? My sister would want to study it."

"I think no one in the world knows the wind better than the Maquhi," said Adrio. He was smiling, his tawny face reddened with cold. "I'm sure of it. Who better to fly?"

By now, the balloon was full, and the clansmen were standing back, staring up at it and talking, laughing among themselves. Krutiv had a small frown on her face. "You really rode in that thing?" she said.

"We did." Adrio gave her a courtly bow. "I apologize for lying about it. At the time, it seemed like candlelight at noon."

"It simply goes where the winds take it?" she asked.

"For the most part."

Adrio explained how he'd been able to adjust the height at which the balloon flew and how he'd found different winds at different altitudes. Krutiv nodded with understanding. "The wind in the canyons is our uncle. We know how he comes and goes. But the wind above the canyons is a wild man who runs where he will."

"You shall have the tools to tame him," said Adrio. "And then, who knows what you will do?"

"I wonder if something more like a kite would be better?" murmured Krutiv. "Something we could control. I had not thought of it before."

Cay squeezed Adrio's hand. "Look at you," he murmured. "Changing the world again."

Adrio met his eyes, and his smile died. His expression grew serious. "Excuse us," he said to Krutiv and tugged Cay away by the hand.

They went down along the wall to a private spot sheltered from the wind. Adrio was grave.

"Husband," he said, "I know you never wanted anything but love, peace, and safety. I understand it better now, what you hoped for when you married me."

"I wanted you," said Cay.

"You wanted a home. One that would never be torn from you." Adrio put a warm hand on Cay's cheek. "And I, wanting to feel like a hero, made you feel unsafe there. I can see the magnitude of my crime so much better now I know your past."

"Well." Cay shifted his feet. "If you didn't know, it's no one's fault but mine."

"I don't want to haggle over blame. I want to know . . . when we return to Rossoulia, will you stay?"

Cay looked up into Adrio's eyes—dark brown but struck golden by the sunlight—and knew a simple yes or no would not do for this moment. They must go forward trusting each other if they were to go forward at all.

"You didn't just want to feel like a hero," he said. "You wanted to use the advantages of your birth to make the world better. It is one of the things I liked about you, from the very beginning. You were never content to stay safely in your wealthy house. How could I—" Cay stumbled over his words. "I'm not sure how to say this," he admitted. "But how could I expect you to, for my sake?"

"I would. To make you feel safe."

Cay's poor soft heart softened further.

"You shouldn't. You should rescue more prisoners, and help more refugees, and teach the Chende to fly. And do what your honor tells you to do. You should fill your heart with dreams and make them come true. Only, let me help you a little. Even if I only give you something to come back home to."

Adrio bowed his head and brushed their cheeks together. "Gods, Cay, I love you so. Will you come home? And stay?"

"Are you ready to brave another gossip storm? Because I think the servants at Wind House saw my hair, and servants talk. I can dye it black, but word will get out."

"You know I don't care."

He really didn't. Cay closed his eyes against the wonder of it and kissed Adrio's bristly cheek. Pulling back, he looked up at Adrio and added, "I do have one more little secret."

Adrio swallowed with trepidation.

Cay suppressed a smile. "I adopted a cat. The stray who lives on the roof."

"What, the ugly gray ratkiller with the lop tail? You let it inside?"

"Mandru is not ugly. I love him like a son."

Adrio grimaced. "You'll give him a bath and keep him out of our bed."

"Yes, Husband."

He gave Adrio his sweet smile, and Adrio sighed, lowering his head so his forehead rested on Cay's.

"You'll come home? And stay?"

"I will."

"Today? Now? Are you ready to go?"

"Now?"

Adrio turned and nodded up at the balloon, round as a plum against the sky. "The wind is from the north, but not too strong.

We could float on this river straight down Lehoia Pass into Noresposto."

Cay looked at the balloon. Then he looked at Adrio. "The chief said the river had rapids."

"Only down in the canyons."

"She said above the canyons it's a wild man."

"It's a wild man going south. The kites tell us so."

"I see them. Do you see the canyon walls? We'll smash into them."

"We won't. We'll soar."

"You can't be so arrogant to think you can control the wind."

"I can ride it." Adrio paused. "Or we could stay here. Forget I mentioned it, Cay. Never mind."

"What, stay *here* until the snow melts?" Cay laughed. "Don't be ridiculous. Let's go."

Adrio's eyebrows went up. "Are you certain?"

Cay nodded. "We could be in Wind House for supper."

Adrio smiled. And when had Cay ever been able to resist Adrio when he smiled his reckless smile?

He leaned in and gave Adrio a kiss. "Let's fly, Husband."

Dear Reader,

Thank you for reading Jenya Keefe's *The Uncanny Aviator*!

We know your time is precious and you have many, many entertainment options, so it means a lot that you've chosen to spend your time reading. We really hope you enjoyed it.

We'd be honored if you'd consider posting a review—good or bad—on sites like **Amazon, Barnes & Noble, Kobo, Goodreads, Twitter, Facebook, Tumblr,** and your blog or website. We'd also be honored if you told your friends and family about this book. Word of mouth is a book's lifeblood!

For more information on upcoming releases, author interviews, blog tours, contests, giveaways, and more, please sign up for our weekly, spam-free newsletter and visit us around the web:

Newsletter: riptidepublishing.com/newsletter
Twitter: twitter.com/RiptideBooks
Facebook: facebook.com/RiptidePublishing
Goodreads: tinyurl.com/RiptideOnGoodreads
Tumblr: riptidepublishing.tumblr.com

Thank you so much for Reading the Rainbow!

RiptidePublishing.com

Acknowledgments

I gratefully acknowledge the works of Baroness Emma Orczy, which helped see me through the events of 2020, and which inspired the writing of this book.

ALSO BY JENYA KEEFE

The Musician and the Monster
Relationship Material

ABOUT THE AUTHOR

Jenya Keefe was born in the South. She has an advanced degree in European history, and has spent much of her life working the kinds of jobs a history degree qualifies you for: gift shop employee, lumber grader, classifieds clerk, hot glass artist. She currently lives in the Seattle area, where she works at a library. She has always written stories.

Website: jenyakeefe.com
TikTok: @JenyaKeefe
Tumblr: tumblr.com/blog/jenyakeefe

Enjoy more stories like
The Uncanny Aviator
at RiptidePublishing.com!

Guided by the Wind

A path through hell is their
only way toward a future
together.

ISBN: 978-1-62649-979-9

A Taste of Rebellion

He's ready to fight for his
people, but will he fight for
love?

ISBN: 978-1-62649-948-5